How the
Heart Runs

MYSTERY
and the
MINISTER'S
WIFE

How the Heart Runs

ANNE MARIE RODGERS

GUIDEPOSTS
NEW YORK, NEW YORK

Guideposts.com
(800) 932-2145
Guideposts Books & Inspirational Media

Cover design by Dugan Design Group
Cover illustration by Dan Brown
Interior design by Cris Kossow
Typeset by Nancy Tardi
Printed in the United States of America

In memory of our beautiful Maine coon cat Phoebe.
You graced our lives for far too short a time.

"Until one has loved an animal,
a part of one's soul remains unawakened."
—Anatole France (1844–1924)

Chapter One

"Tell me again why we're dining here today?" Kate Hanlon asked as her husband, Paul, parked their Honda Accord in the lot of the Hamilton Springs Hotel, a graceful brick structure in Copper Mill, Tennessee.

Sunday services had concluded at Faith Briar Church, Paul's small charge in the little town. The couple now was headed to the Bristol, a restaurant nestled inside the hotel, where Paul had suggested they have lunch.

"No particular occasion," Paul said as he turned off the car's engine. He came around to open Kate's door, and she stepped out, then tucked her hand into the crook of his arm. "Just a special meal with the most special woman I know."

Kate offered her husband a warm smile as she briefly rested her head against his shoulder. "If you're trying to soften me up for something, it's working."

Paul chuckled. "No ulterior motive, I promise."

Warmth and contentment filled Kate as they walked toward the restaurant on the lovely autumn day. Her husband looked as handsome to her as he had nearly thirty years before when they'd married, though the crow's-feet around his eyes proclaimed the passing of those years.

They entered the stately hotel and made their way to the four-star restaurant off to the left of the foyer.

Kate enjoyed the warm atmosphere of the Bristol, even though she was occasionally unsettled by the large mounted heads of elk and white-tailed deer that adorned the walls. The stone fireplace in the center of the room complemented the room's woodwork and the high, exposed beams of the ceiling. Thick woven rugs lay on the gleaming floors. Large windows overlooked a nearby pond.

Almost immediately, Kate and Paul were directed to a table. As they crossed the room, they saw and greeted Steve Smith, owner of Smith Street Gifts. At the far end of the room, a flash of yellow caught Kate's eye. She returned a wave from Emma Blount, proprietor of Emma's Ice Cream Shop. Emma looked like a perky canary in her yellow outfit with its matching accessories. The beautiful fall weather must have been reason enough for some of the townsfolk to treat themselves to a fine lunch, Kate thought.

Approaching their table, Kate noticed a lone woman occupying the closest table. She wore a pretty teal skirt and jacket, and her short hair was artfully highlighted, with blonde streaks that allowed some gray to show through. Her thin face was pensive. Kate smiled as she passed. The woman's face brightened, and she returned the smile.

Paul held out Kate's chair and tucked it beneath Kate as she sat. Each of them accepted a menu from the hostess.

"Thank you," Kate said.

"Hello, Hanlons," chirped a perky, high-pitched voice.

Kate glanced up to see Violet Fleur, one of their older parishioners, passing the table. When the woman paused, Kate reached for her hand and said, "Hello, Violet. How are you doing?" Violet had been diagnosed with walking pneumonia not long ago, and Kate had visited her at home several times.

"I'm doing much, much better." Violet nodded, beaming. "I wanted to thank you for the coffee cake you brought by last week. It was delicious."

"I'm glad you enjoyed it," Kate said. "It's one of my favorite recipes."

"It's one of mine now too," Violet said, and they all chuckled. "You enjoy your meal now."

"We will," Kate responded. "Have a pleasant day," she added as Violet moved on.

Sensing attention on her, Kate turned her head. The woman next to her quickly glanced away when their gazes met. Then the waitress approached with glasses of water, and Kate turned her attention to the brunch selections.

Their table was covered with a spotless white tablecloth. In the center, a slender amber vase held a trio of bright wildflowers. Kate could see several turtles basking on a log that extended from the bank into the pond at one side.

"Look," she said to Paul, smiling.

"Happy turtles." Paul grinned.

"They had better enjoy it while they can," Kate said. "I imagine they'll soon be hibernating in the mud on the bottom of that pond. It'll be months before they see the sun again."

"Indeed," Paul said. He was quiet for a moment. "Have you thought about when we can take a quick trip up to Philly to visit Andrew and the family?" Their eldest child, his wife, and two children lived in Pennsylvania.

Kate studied her husband's wistful face. "We need to look at our schedules and see if there's some time during the next few weeks when we could get away for a few days. Advent will be here before we know it, and we won't be able to get away then."

Paul nodded. "Sometimes I wish we lived in a simpler era when families lived their whole lives in the same communities. It would be nice to have our children closer."

"I know." Kate sometimes wished the same thing, particularly when one of her grandchildren participated in something special in Philadelphia or Atlanta that she was unable to attend.

"By the way," Paul said, "last night I peeked into your workroom while you were in the kitchen making dinner. That lampshade you've been working on is beautiful."

Since they had moved to Copper Mill, Kate had fostered her hobby of creating stained-glass works of art. The lampshade was for the nursery of a couple who had recently learned they were expecting their first child. Almost as soon as Kate had learned that the nursery was decorated in a theme of pastel-colored alphabet blocks, an idea for a coordinating lampshade had blossomed in her mind's eye. She thought the vision had translated into reality extremely well, and she was glad to have Paul's opinion reinforce hers.

"I am pleased with the way the building-block motif turned out," she said.

"They're going to love it," Paul predicted. He set his menu

aside as the server approached. "What sounds good to you today, Katie?"

"I might—Oh!" Kate's reply was cut short as the woman at the next table lurched to her feet. She clutched her chest, her eyes wide and frightened as they fastened on Kate.

Kate half rose from her chair as the woman staggered two steps to the side. Reflex had Kate moving to catch her, but as the woman fell into Kate's arms, her dead weight was too much for Kate to manage. The most Kate could do was go heavily down on her knees as the woman in her arms fell to the floor.

They jostled against the table as they went down, and Kate felt her hip bang painfully into the sharp edge at the corner. The ice water in Kate's and Paul's glasses spilled across the table, splashing onto the floor and covering Kate in tiny spatters.

She heard her husband shout, "Help!"

The quiet murmur of the other diners' voices fell silent.

The waitress rushed to Kate's side at the same time Paul rushed around the table. The crumpled form of the stranger lay awkwardly across Kate's lap for a moment before Paul and the waitress gently shifted the woman to the floor.

Kate automatically tried to get to her feet, but Paul put his hands on her shoulders. "Just wait," he said. "You may have been hurt when she fell on you. How do you feel?"

"Shaky," Kate responded. "But I think I'm all right."

They both looked at the woman on the floor. She was conscious, although she appeared dazed and disoriented, her hands fluttering feebly up to her chest. She fastened her gaze on Kate. Close-up, the woman looked to be approximately Kate's own age, perhaps in her mid- to late fifties. Her hair was short and stylish, and it appeared she was letting the light brown gradually transform to silver with the help of the highlights Kate had noticed earlier.

She looked so frightened that it tore at Kate's heart.

"Hurts," she gasped.

"I know," Kate soothed. The woman's teal paisley skirt was rumpled around her, and Kate smoothed it modestly down over her knees. "Try to stay calm. We're going to get help for you." She took one of the woman's hands in hers, unobtrusively placing her fingers over the pulse point in the fragile wrist. It was reassuring to feel a strong, steady beat. Kate thought it seemed a bit fast, but she certainly preferred that to the alternative.

The waitress had grabbed several white cloth napkins and spread them over the puddles of water that threatened to soak both women. She knelt on the other side of the woman. "I've called 911," she told Kate in a high, shaky voice.

"Thank you," Kate said, giving the waitress a small smile before the young woman got up and moved away.

A second person, a middle-aged man, knelt beside Kate. "I'm a doctor. What's the trouble?"

With a deep sense of relief and a quick mental *Thank you, Lord*, Kate moved aside to let the physician examine the fallen woman.

"I don't know," Kate told the man. "She just sort of staggered sideways, and when I tried to catch her, we both fell. She was clutching her chest."

"Are you this woman's family?" the doctor asked Kate.

Kate shook her head. "No. I was at the next table when she collapsed. She literally fell into my arms."

Kate looked up at Paul as the doctor began examining the woman. Paul's blue eyes were grave, but he gave her a reassuring smile. She returned her attention to the ill woman on the floor and the doctor beside her. A moment later, when she glanced up again, she saw her husband's lips moving silently. She knew he was offering a prayer for the fallen woman.

The waitress came back with a warm blue blanket, which Kate helped the doctor spread over the woman. Then Kate began to slide away, knowing the doctor was more than capable, but the woman clutched frantically at her hand. "No! Don't leave me. Please," she added, "please stay with me."

Kate patted the trembling hand that gripped hers. "Of course, I'll stay. Now you just lie back and relax and let the doctor look at you."

Wincing, Kate tried to shift her weight from her knees as the doctor bent over his patient.

"What's your name?" he asked the woman gently.

"Emmaline Ash . . . Ashford," she replied. She was still gripping her chest, but she seemed a little calmer than she had a few moments earlier. "Am I having a heart attack?"

"I'm not sure yet. Do you know if anyone in your family has a history of heart disease or heart problems?"

Emmaline shook her head. "I don't think so."

"All right." The doctor patted her hand. "The paramedics are on their way. They'll bring you to the hospital and have you checked out," he said. "Other than chest pain, you don't have the symptoms of cardiac arrest. Your color is good, your pulse is a bit fast but steady, and you aren't sweating."

The woman gave a feeble nod and took a strained deep breath.

Kate heard the sound of sirens rapidly approaching. One good thing about this community, she reflected, was that the nearby hospital in Pine Ridge was first-rate.

The doctor looked at the way Kate was still kneeling uncomfortably on the floor. "Do you hurt anywhere?"

She shook her head. "I don't think so. Just a little bruised here and there." Kate didn't mention the slight pain she felt in her arthritic knee, knowing it would feel fine soon enough and that the doctor's attention should remain on Emmaline.

The doctor looked back down at Emmaline. "Is there someone we can call for you?"

Emmaline bit her lip. Tears filled her eyes, and she whispered, "No. No one."

Minutes later, two men and a woman in blue jumpsuits emblazoned with the medical logo of the Pine Ridge emergency-services division entered the room briskly. They carried a stretcher and a medical kit.

Kate realized she had not even gotten the doctor's name as the man moved back and stood up.

She began to shift back as well, intending to get to her feet and introduce herself, but Emmaline kept a surprisingly strong grip on Kate's hand.

"You said you wouldn't leave me." It was a pitiful statement, delivered as though the woman didn't really believe Kate.

Kate immediately sank back down. "I won't be able to ride in the ambulance with you," she told the woman. "But I promise I'll follow you to the hospital. My name is Kate. Kate Hanlon."

"You'll have to move away, ma'am." One of the EMTs shifted the stretcher to Emmaline's side. "We'll be taking her to the ER in Pine Ridge."

"I'll meet you there," Kate promised.

Emmaline nodded, her wide gray eyes apprehensive as she was carefully lifted onto the stretcher and wheeled away.

Chapter Two

Straightening, Kate took a deep breath and prepared to rise. Both her knees had hit the floor hard when the woman fell on her, and she felt sore. Paul and the doctor both assisted her as she rose gingerly to her feet. She tested both legs.

"I'm fine," she reported. But she didn't feel as steady as she sounded.

Paul put an arm around her waist. "I guess we'll have to take a rain check on our meal," he said as he began to guide her from the restaurant.

"I'm sorry." Kate realized she was trembling a little, and she briskly rubbed her arms. "Is it all right if we go over to the hospital?" she added. "I just feel so bad for her. She was all alone."

Paul smiled a little as he hugged her close to his side. "Of course, it's all right. You wouldn't be the woman I love if you had refused her request."

PAUL STOPPED BY THEIR HOUSE on the way to the hospital to get ice packs for Kate's knees.

He ran into the house while Kate stayed in the car with the passenger-side door open so she could get some air. As he was returning with the ice packs and towels to wrap around them, he heard someone hail him.

"Paul!"

Paul looked up to see Eli Weston pulling into the driveway right behind the Honda. Eli was a member of Faith Briar and the owner of Weston's Antiques in Copper Mill.

Eli got out of his truck, pushing his glasses up on his nose and attempting to smooth his untidy blond hair.

Paul smiled at his friend. "Hey, Eli. What's up?"

"Have you heard about the American Heart Association's 10K Appalachian Ramble? I meant to talk to you about this after church, but I got tied up."

Paul shook his head. "Appalachian Ramble? Sounds more like a hiking expedition than a race."

Eli chuckled, the corners of his brown eyes crinkling as he laughed. "It does, doesn't it? Fortunately, it's just your standard 10K race to raise funds for the Heart Association."

"No up-hill-and-down-dale cross-country running?" Paul chuckled. Paul and Eli were both casual joggers.

Eli grinned. "No. Just a normal, easy paved course. Any chance you'd be interested in running it with me?"

Paul's eyebrows rose as he considered the request. He looked over at the car, where Kate sat watching. She had swung her legs out of the Honda and was ever so gently bending her knees while she listened to the men converse.

Paul ran his fingers through his salt-and-pepper hair and then finally shook his head. "I don't think I'm in shape for that distance," he said regretfully. "I'm really more of a 5K kind of guy."

"Me too, usually," Eli said. "But the race isn't for six weeks. I think we could do it."

Paul grinned. "You're barely over half my age," he pointed out, grinning. "Easy for you to say."

"Oh, you're not that old," Eli said with a chuckle. "And you're in great shape. If we started a training program and stuck to it, I bet you could be ready in time."

Paul felt doubtful. "That's easily twice as far as I usually run. And I don't run every day either."

"We would have to run six days a week to train effectively," Eli admitted. He shrugged his broad shoulders. "But I think you'd enjoy it. Give it some thought," he suggested. "You don't have to tell me right away."

"I'd have to decide soon if we're to have any shot at completing a training program," Paul said, feeling intrigued yet somewhat pressured.

"I think you should do it," Kate chimed in from the car.

Both men turned to look at her.

"You do?" Paul asked.

"Really?" Eli said at the same instant.

Kate laughed at their reaction.

"What's wrong with your legs?" Eli asked. He had moved a step or two closer to the car so he could see Kate better, and Paul realized that Eli didn't know what had just transpired at the restaurant.

"I took a little spill at the Bristol," Kate said cheerfully. "My knees are a bit bruised. No big deal; they should be fine with just a bit of ice."

"Speaking of . . . ," Paul said, handing her the towels and ice packs he still held. He went on to explain to Eli the incident with the woman who fell ill.

"I'm sorry to hear that," Eli said.

"Thanks, Eli. Now, as I was saying . . ." Kate grinned.

"You were saying you thought Paul should run the 10K," Eli reminded her with a smile.

"Indeed I was. It would give you a goal," she told Paul. "Something different to try. Also, you would be raising money for a worthwhile cause. I bet the congregation would be very supportive."

"'Be very supportive,' meaning 'open their pocketbooks,'" translated Eli with a chuckle.

"It would be a good charity to raise money for," Paul said slowly. He didn't know why he was hesitating.

"What's the worst that can happen?" Kate coaxed. "If you tire, you can always walk it."

"When you put it that way, it doesn't sound so daunting." Paul nodded. "All right. You've convinced me."

"Great!" Eli extended his hand, and when Paul took it, the husky younger man gave him a hearty handshake. "I'll put together a training schedule. We can start tomorrow."

"Tomorrow? Ooo-kay." Paul took a deep breath. He was going to be in terrific shape after this race.

THE PINE RIDGE HOSPITAL was just a few miles north of Copper Mill and the drive to Pine Ridge was particularly lovely this time of year. The town of Copper Mill was nestled in a small valley tucked in among verdant hills, and even though the show of autumn colors throughout the oak forests wouldn't peak for a week or so, brilliant displays of red, orange, and yellow were evident. Atop the higher peaks that rolled away into the distance, spruce and fir forests held sway, with dark emeralds that faded into muted shadows of blacks and grays.

Kate took a deep breath. The air rushing through her partially open window was fresh, and the sun was shining. A perfect day, she thought. Unfortunately, Emmaline Ashford probably wouldn't see this view if she was lying flat on her back in the ambulance.

"Thanks, Katie, for the encouragement about the race." Paul turned his gaze toward her, his eyes mirroring the blue of the sky.

"Encouragement I'll give in droves. But don't expect any participation," Kate said with a chuckle, indicating her knees still covered with ice packs.

"It's a deal," Paul said, smiling. He reached over and took her hand. "You were wonderful back there at the restaurant. I was very proud of the way you calmed and helped the lady."

A few minutes later, he parked in the visitor lot outside the one-story brick hospital building.

"I think," he said as he helped Kate out of the car and courteously shut the door after her, "that while you're seeing to your Ms. Ashford, I'll visit Stephanie Miller."

"Oh, that's a good idea," she said as they walked toward the building. "Have you heard anything more about how she's doing?"

Stephanie was a young mother from the Faith Briar congregation. Busy with her three young children, Stephanie had ignored a steadily increasing pain in her abdomen until it became unbearable. Unfortunately, the pain was caused by appendicitis, and her appendix ruptured before it could be removed, complicating her recovery process. Although Paul wasn't on duty as the small hospital's chaplain that afternoon, Kate knew he would never pass up an opportunity to minister to a congregant in need.

"I spoke with Stephanie's husband yesterday," Paul told her. "Frank said the surgery went well. But apparently, peritonitis set in after her appendix burst. He said she'll have to be on intravenous antibiotics for the next eight days."

"Eight days!" Kate's eyes rounded in dismay. "Poor Stephanie."

"And because of the rupture, she wasn't able to have the appendix removed by laparoscopy. She has a much larger incision, which is going to take a while to heal."

"We'll have to get some folks together to help her until she's back on her feet."

"That's a great idea," Paul said, holding open the door that led to the emergency department. "I nominate you to chair the committee."

Kate made a face at her husband. "You buck passer," she said fondly. "I'll be glad to make a few calls. I'm sure there are folks who could help her out. I'll also put the family on the Faith Freezer delivery schedule for at least one meal a day until Stephanie is back on her feet," she said.

Kate increased her pace as they approached the registration desk in the emergency room. "Good afternoon," she said to the woman seated behind the desk. "My name is Kate Hanlon, and I—"

"You're here for Ms. Ashford," the woman said, smiling.

"That's right." Kate was surprised.

"She's been asking for you. Dr. McLaughlin is with her now. I'll call you just as soon as you can go back."

"Thank you." Kate turned to Paul. "I guess I'll see you in a little while."

"I'll come find you when I'm done visiting Stephanie," he told her, squeezing her hand once before heading off into the main section of the hospital.

PAUL CHECKED AT THE MAIN DESK to get Stephanie Miller's room number and then he headed to the surgical wing.

The door of Stephanie's room was ajar, and when a woman's voice called "Come in," Paul entered to find Stephanie lying in a narrow bed in the first of two cubicles in the room. No one was in the second bed, and Paul imagined that Stephanie was grateful for the privacy. A pretty autumn flower arrangement with huge chrysanthemums and cheerful daisies in hues of orange, yellow, and deep red was perched on the bedside table.

"Stephanie," Paul said, crossing to the bed and leaning down to give the young woman a gentle hug. "I was so sorry to hear about your illness."

"Thank you, Pastor." Stephanie smiled wanly. "I kept thinking I must have eaten something that didn't agree with me and that it would pass."

"And it didn't."

She chuckled a little, then sucked in a breath as if the motion hurt. "It sure didn't. I suppose I was in denial."

Now Paul was the one who chuckled. "That's not uncommon. I often see folks who tell me they ignored symptoms because they had too much to do to get sick."

"That's just how I felt. Isn't that silly?" Stephanie shrugged in a helpless gesture. "I don't have time to be laid up like this for weeks."

"I know," Paul said soberly. "Can Frank care for the children while you're unable to get around?"

"Not exactly." The young woman shook her head, and her eyes brimmed with tears. "I've always been a stay-at-home mom. Frank and I made the decision for me to stay home after our first child was born. We both are glad I did, but it has made budgeting for a family of five a challenge. If my husband takes time off, he might lose his job, and we just can't afford that. We can't lose his insurance."

Paul glanced around and found a box of hospital tissues hiding just behind the flowers. As Stephanie took one and wiped her eyes, he said, "I'm sure the folks at Faith Briar would be happy to help out. Kate's going to work on arranging some meals through the Faith Freezer program, as well as folks to babysit."

"Oh, thank you. What a blessing," Stephanie's lips quivered. "Let's see ... my husband works second shift. My mother-in-law lives here in Pine Ridge, and she can help three days a week."

"So you need someone just a couple days a week?" Paul prompted.

Stephanie nodded. "Just in the afternoon. My husband has to be at work at two, and my mother-in-law gets off at four thirty on the two days she works. She's going to stay over on weeknights until I'm back on my feet."

"Two afternoons a week isn't so bad," Paul told her, surprised at the relative modesty of the Millers' need. "Is that all?"

Relief lit Stephanie's red-rimmed eyes. "I think so. Weekends won't be a problem, since my mother plans to drive down from upstate every weekend."

"I'm certain we can find some folks to help you for a while." Paul reached over to squeeze Stephanie's hand.

"Oh, thank you so much."

"You're welcome." Paul smiled down at the young woman. "All right." He tapped the raised bar on the side of the bed. "Now you can stop worrying and concentrate on getting better."

IN THE WAITING ROOM, Kate absently perused the bulletin-board display as she waited to see Emmaline Ashford. Each month, a staff member was featured in one section devoted to hospital personnel. This month, it was Dr. McLaughlin, one of the ER physicians with whom Kate had become acquainted since she and Paul moved to Copper Mill.

When she finished reading every scrap of the bulletin board, she settled down with one of the magazines she found on the sturdy end tables. She was nearly through the last article when the receptionist spoke.

"Mrs. Hanlon?"

Kate rose hastily. "Right here."

The woman motioned for Kate to follow her. "I'll take you

back to see Ms."—the woman made a frustrated face and consulted the chart in her hand—"Ms. Ashford."

Kate walked gingerly on her arthritic knee, now aching from the fall. As she followed the receptionist through a set of heavy double doors into the treatment area, Kate decided she too would probably forget names if she saw as many people as the hospital receptionists did in a shift.

As they reached one of the treatment rooms, Kate's guide stepped aside. "She's right in here."

Kate tentatively stepped into the cubicle, wondering what she might find. All she could see was one side of a blue curtain that hung from a U-shaped track overhead. "Hello?"

"Hello. I'm in here." It was the voice Kate remembered from the Bristol.

Kate slipped around the edge of the curtain and stepped into the small space.

"You came! Oh, Kate, thank you." Looking utterly surprised, the woman in the bed reached out to Kate. Emmaline's eyes lit up as she smiled. Kate had failed to notice earlier that the gray was an unusual, pretty shade, rather like a stormy sky.

Reflexively, Kate took the extended hand.

"Hello, Kate," a voice said behind her. She turned to see Dr. McLaughlin. "Our patient has been asking for you," he said.

Dr. McLaughlin's usual friendly smile was nowhere in evidence as he shook her hand, although his eyes warmed, crinkling slightly as they met hers.

"Hello, Dr. McLaughlin. How is Ms. Ashford?"

"You can see for yourself." His manner was noncommittal, and his face was surprisingly sober. He glanced down at the patient without smiling. "Remember what I said, Ms. Ashford. I'll check in with you later." Had he put special emphasis on "Remember what I said," or was it just Kate's imagination?

"Thank you," Emmaline said stiffly, but she didn't look at the doctor.

Kate glanced back and forth between them, sure now that some odd vibe was going on.

The physician turned and exited through the curtain, and as it flapped shut behind him, Emmaline met Kate's gaze. "I'm so sorry for frightening you, Kate." She blushed and made a face that seemed self-deprecating and charming at the same time. "Not to mention for landing in your lap."

"I'm softer than the floor," Kate said, grinning. She drew closer to the bed. "How are you feeling?"

Emmaline shrugged and rubbed the area high on her chest that Kate had noticed her clutching in the restaurant. "A little better, although not anywhere near one hundred percent. Still, I'm ready to get out of here." She frowned. "Especially after the way that Dr. McLaughlin treated me."

Kate was stunned. "Dr. McLaughlin?"

The woman in the bed nodded her head, short and sharp. "I waited in here a disgracefully long time to be seen. And then when he came in, he barely checked me over."

Kate knew that Dr. McLaughlin had a fine reputation at the hospital and in the community, and she had found him to be kind and compassionate to patients she had known. And the ER appeared especially busy that afternoon, with staff scurrying everywhere and most of the patient cubicles occupied. He probably was just rushed for time. Still, she didn't want to argue with someone she barely knew, so she merely said, "That's too bad." There was a moment of awkward silence before Kate said, "Is there anyone I can contact for you now?"

Emmaline shook her head. "No, thank you."

Kate recalled the sad expression in Emmaline's eyes when the doctor at the restaurant had asked about family. She had told him she had no one on whom she could call. Perhaps she meant no family to whom she was close. She had hoped Emmaline's statement was just an exaggeration in her distress and that there was *someone* she could contact. But it seemed the woman was more alone than Kate had first assumed.

Kate could hardly imagine being so alone. True, she could remember her single days, but even then her home had been filled with family and friends. And now her life was even richer with loved ones. She and Paul had children and grandchildren, Paul's sister and her daughter, and so very many friends. They still treasured relationships from their years in San Antonio, and since moving to Copper Mill, they had formed new friendships that were steadily growing stronger and closer.

Kate tried to think of other ways she could help this lonely woman. "Will you be needing a ride home, then?"

"Not today, thank you. They've decided to admit me for some tests and observation overnight. I'm waiting for someone to take me to my room now."

"I'm glad you're improving. Did you get a diagnosis? Do you know what happened?"

"Chest pain," Emmaline told her. "I just had a little bit of chest pain."

"Will you need to restrict your activities?"

"Sure, but no more than I already do," Emmaline said.

That was hardly an answer, Kate noted. But some people were extremely private about health matters, and she didn't feel it would be appropriate to question a virtual stranger any further.

"Well, it certainly was a scary moment when it was occurring," she said. "My husband is the pastor at Faith Briar Church. We'll be praying for your return to good health."

She rummaged in her handbag, pulling out a pen and a notepad. Scribbling her name and telephone number on a blank page, she tore out the sheet and handed it to Emmaline. "Please call me if you need a ride home after your discharge."

"Thank you." Emmaline accepted the paper. "It's so nice to know someone in the area."

"I take it you're not from here?"

"No." Emmaline shook her head. "I grew up in Philadelphia, although my mother's parents lived in Copper Mill. My mother was born here."

"So what brought you back to the area?"

Emmaline hesitated, and Kate was surprised to see a sweep of red coloring her cheeks. "I just moved into my grandmother's home six weeks ago," she said. "She passed away at the beginning of the year, and the house stood empty for a while."

"I'm sorry for your loss," Kate told her. "What was your grandmother's name?"

"Lena Hemp. Did you know her?"

Kate shook her head. "I don't recall ever meeting her. I'm

sorry." Then she added, "Our son lives in Philadelphia. What a beautiful city. Different from Copper Mill, though. This must be quite a change for you."

"It is." Emmaline didn't look especially thrilled about it, and Kate wondered again what had prompted the move. "Fortunately, my job is portable."

"What do you do?"

"I'm a freelance writer," Emmaline told her. "I work on projects for several national magazines. Do you work? Other than your job as a minister's wife?" She smiled. "I suspect that is a full-time job even if you don't draw a paycheck."

Kate had to laugh. "That's a pretty accurate description. I worked as an executive assistant for an accounting firm when we lived in San Antonio. I miss it sometimes, but I do find that my days are full even without a formal job. One thing I have enjoyed is a hobby I've had for years. I create stained-glass art."

"Heavens! That's exciting," Emmaline said. "I dabble with sketching and painting, but I could never do anything that intricate. What kinds of pieces do you create?"

"A variety," Kate replied. "Window panels, sun catchers, lampshades, night-lights . . . that type of thing."

"I would love to see some of your work."

"When you've recovered, I'll have you over for lunch and give you a tour of my studio. Which should take about five minutes," Kate added with a grin.

"When I've recovered," Emmaline repeated. She sighed heavily, rubbing the area below her left collarbone again. "I can tell I'm going to have to take things very easy for a while."

"I'm sure I can find some folks to help with your house-work if you need it," Kate offered, hoping to reassure her.

"I would appreciate that." Emmaline took a deep breath and smiled. "You were telling me you have your own studio. I'm impressed."

"It's actually just a room in our house," Kate hastened to explain.

"It's still a studio, no matter where it's located." Emmaline sighed. "I have to confess I've been missing the bustle of the city and all the myriad events to be found there. And, of course, I don't know anyone here, so it's been quite lonely."

"I know just how you feel. I missed the cultural amenities San Antonio had to offer when we first moved here. But I've grown to embrace small-town life."

"Perhaps I'll find it pleasant," Emmaline murmured. She suddenly looked tired and dispirited.

Kate was sorry they had talked about their former homes. Emmaline clearly wasn't as enamored of Copper Mill as Kate had become. She suspected it was difficult for Emmaline to reach out and make friends. She seemed friendly one-on-one, but Kate recalled how solitary she had looked at the Bristol. In a crowd, she'd bet Emmaline was rather shy.

"I'm going to have to leave soon," Kate told Emmaline, who pulled a blanket up to her neck. "My husband is visiting with one of our parishioners, and I imagine he'll be waiting for me."

Emmaline nodded with an air of resignation. "I'm sure you have a million things to do. Thank you so much for stopping by."

"I'll see you soon," Kate promised. She shifted her handbag

higher on her shoulder, then she took Emmaline's hand between both of hers and pressed lightly. "Do you have any idea when you'll be released? Will it be as soon as tomorrow?"

Emmaline shook her head. "I assumed tomorrow, but I don't know for sure. They didn't specify a time."

Kate nodded. "All right. Why don't you call me as soon as you find out when you can leave, and I'll just run right over. I don't have a lot on my calendar this week, so it should be no problem at all."

"Thank you," Emmaline said quietly, squeezing Kate's hands before releasing them. "You're a thoughtful person."

Kate smiled. "I'm pleased to have met you, Emmaline, and happy to help. Would you like me to pray with you?"

Emmaline seemed to shrink back in the bed. "Well, I suppose it couldn't hurt ..."

Kate waited.

Finally, the other woman said, "I guess I need all the help I can get."

Kate smiled, then took Emmaline's hand and bowed her head. "Heavenly Father, please be with Emmaline during this difficult time. Fill her with your strength and heal her illness." She felt Emmaline's hand jerk and took a firmer grip. "In your name we pray, amen."

Kate squeezed Emmaline's hand and smiled as she opened her eyes. She was dismayed to see that Emmaline's lower lip was trembling.

But before Kate could attempt to comfort her new friend, Emmaline took a deep breath and said, "Thank you, Kate. I'll call you as soon as I find out when I'll be released."

"Sounds like a plan." After a final farewell, she began to slip out of the enclosed area.

"Kate?"

She turned back. "Yes?"

"Please don't mention anything I said about Dr. McLaughlin. Even though I found his manner quite unfriendly and I felt he was rushing through my concerns, I wouldn't want to be labeled a complainer or troublemaker."

Chapter Three

Emmaline's odd words rang in Kate's head as she pushed aside the curtain and left the treatment cubicle. Dr. McLaughlin unfriendly?

The doctor in question stood in the hallway, chart in hand. A young mother with a toddler in her arms was smiling up at him.

"Thank you again," she said. "I'm so glad the bone wasn't broken."

"Me too," the doctor said. He tousled the young toddler's hair. "You be careful next time you're going down the stairs, champ."

Kate had always been impressed by Dr. McLaughlin's gentle manner and the warmth radiating from him. It was hard to imagine him not being kind or thorough with a patient, despite what Emmaline had said. As for Emmaline's comment that the doctor had kept her waiting, if a patient came in with critical injuries that needed immediate care, it was simply the nature of an ER that those with less urgent problems would wait. Even so, Kate was positive that none of the Pine Ridge staff would allow a patient to be neglected.

As the doctor turned and began to walk away from his young patient, Kate stopped him. "Dr. McLaughlin?"

The physician turned. "Hello, Kate. Done visiting for the day?"

Kate nodded. "Yes. Emmaline told me she needs to have some tests done, but I have a question for you. Will she be okay living alone?"

The handsome doctor's expression became shuttered, and Kate immediately feared the worst. "That depends on the results of the tests she has scheduled." He crossed his arms, looking pointedly at his watch.

"Is Emmaline suffering from heart disease?"

"Kate. You know I can't discuss a patient's medical condition with you without permission from the patient." His face was sober. He glanced over at the desk momentarily as if he was eager to move on.

"I understand." Kate was crestfallen. "But could you perhaps just indicate whether she is going to need additional treatment?"

The doctor hesitated. He looked away, and Kate thought he appeared to be weighing how much he could say to her. Finally he blew out a deep breath and rubbed the back of his neck. Lifting his gaze to Kate's, he said, "I think it's safe to say that unless something completely unexpected shows up on the tests, Ms. Ashford is going to be just fine."

"That's a relief to hear. I'll pray that those test results are all good."

"I suspect your prayers are going to be answered," he said austerely.

Before Kate could respond, Dr. McLaughlin was paged over the speaker system.

"That's for me. I have to go." He turned on his heel and strode away down the hall. The relief in his voice was clear, and Kate felt certain he was glad to be finished with the conversation. She stared after the doctor, wondering what on earth was troubling him.

KATE LEFT THE RESTRICTED AREA of the ER, and walked toward the interior of the hospital. As she turned down the hallway on which the surgical patients stayed, she saw Paul walking toward her.

"How's Ms. Ashford doing?" he asked, taking Kate's hand as they started back down the hallway.

"I'm really not sure. They're keeping her until at least tomorrow to run some tests." Kate shook her head. "The poor woman seems to be alone in the world." She looked up at him. "How's Stephanie?"

Paul sighed. "Can we chat about it over a very, very late lunch? I'm starving!"

"Me too. Do you want to go back to the Bristol?"

Paul shook his head. "Let's save that for another day. I'd settle for the food in the hospital cafeteria at this point."

Kate laughed as they turned toward the main wing of the hospital. "You *are* hungry! The cafeteria it is."

DRIVING HOME AFTER THEIR MEAL in the less-than-fine-dining atmosphere of the hospital cafeteria, Paul said, "This certainly was an unexpected detour in our day, wasn't it?"

"In Emmaline Ashford's day too," Kate said. "I felt so bad for her, Paul."

Thinking back over the incident reminded Kate of her strange encounter with Dr. McLaughlin. She recounted the conversation to Paul. "He wasn't his usual friendly self. In fact, he seemed irritated. And I had the strongest feeling that he would have told me more if he hadn't been bound by doctor-patient privilege."

As Paul pulled the car to a stop in the garage, he chuckled. "You see intrigue everywhere you go, my dear wife. Perhaps he was simply being ethical as the law demands."

"I don't think so," Kate said decisively, recalling the doctor's manner, which contrasted with his normal friendliness. "Something in the way he was acting makes me sure he was hiding something. Something more than just Ms. Ashford's medical condition."

"What exactly did Ms. Ashford say had happened to her?" Paul asked, unlocking the door from the garage into the large living room and stepping aside for Kate to precede him.

"She didn't," Kate said, frowning. "She didn't seem to want to discuss it, and I didn't feel it was appropriate to grill her at that point."

"Meaning you might reserve the grilling for another day?" His blue eyes twinkled with humor.

Kate punched her teasing spouse lightly in the arm. "Very funny."

The telephone rang, interrupting their banter. Kate reached for the phone on the kitchen counter and greeted the caller. "Hello? Oh, hi, Livvy!"

She wandered over to a chair at the oak dining table and sat down, nodding absently when Paul pantomimed that he was going to change clothes and go running. Livvy Jenner was the town's librarian and Kate's closest friend in Copper Mill. She was also the person, besides Paul, whom Kate turned to most for help unraveling a mystery.

"Hey," Livvy said by way of greeting. "How was your meal at the Bristol today? Amazing as always?"

"I don't know," Kate said, "since I didn't get a chance to eat it. I had a sandwich and soup at the hospital cafeteria instead."

"The hospital cafeteria! Are you all right? Did something happen to Paul?"

"Paul and I are both fine, but I had quite an experience." Kate went on to tell her friend about the woman who had landed in her lap and the subsequent chain of events.

"Oh, poor soul," Livvy said. "Did she have a heart attack?"

"I don't know. The EMTs took her to the hospital, and Paul and I followed her over. Then I visited with her in the emergency room for a little while," Kate said, abbreviating a bit.

"How traumatic!" Livvy said sympathetically. "I hope she's okay. I just read an article the other day about women's heart health. Heart disease kills six times as many women as breast cancer does each year," she said. As Kate often did, she marveled at Livvy's ability to retain statistics. "And more women than men die annually of heart disease, despite the fact that it's known as a killer of men. I find that appalling."

"So do I. But I don't know for sure that Emmaline suffered a heart attack. She was very vague about exactly what's

wrong with her. And Livvy, you should have seen
Dr. McLaughlin! I've never known him to act so strangely."

"Strangely, how?"

Kate considered the question. "For starters, the two of
them didn't seem to like each other." Although Kate had promised not to reveal Emmaline's concerns about Dr. McLaughlin,
she didn't believe that was breaking her pledge. "And he was
almost unfriendly, Livvy, when I tried to talk to him. It wasn't
just guarding his patient's privacy. It felt as if he was irritated
or annoyed."

"That's *very* odd."

"It was," Kate agreed. "Emmaline wasn't forthcoming at
all about her illness."

"Maybe she's just a very private person."

"That's what I told myself. But I don't think that's all it
was."

The line was silent for a moment while Livvy considered
Kate's statement. Finally, she said, "I don't discount your sixth
sense."

"Paul does. He says I'm probably imagining a mystery that
doesn't exist."

"He's a man," Livvy said. "They don't operate intuitively
like women do. If you think there's something going on,
I believe you."

"I guess time will tell." Kate chuckled. "Or perhaps I
should say maybe Emmaline will."

"Emmaline is such a pretty, old-fashioned name."

"It is, isn't it? I found out she's from Philadelphia when
I told her Andrew lives there."

"Philadelphia! Small world. Did you ask her if she knew him?"

"Not yet," Kate said. "But Philadelphia's a pretty big city. I'd be surprised if they knew each other. Oh, and guess what? She lives in a home that belonged to her grandmother right here in Copper Mill."

"Oh?" Livvy sounded even more interested. She had grown up in the area, and there was rarely a person in town she didn't know, or at least know of. "What was her grandmother's name?"

"Oh . . . she told me, but I can't recall it. I should be able to tell you where the house is soon. I offered to take her home when she's discharged from the hospital."

"That's kind of you." Livvy paused. "You're going to try to find out more about her, aren't you, Sherlock?"

"Perhaps, Dr. Watson."

"I knew it!"

Both women chuckled at their standing joke.

"I'm glad you called," Kate said. "I was planning to call you, but you beat me to it."

"To tell me about your exciting afternoon?"

"No. Well, not entirely. I was wondering whether you would like to take a meal to Emmaline. As a sort of belated welcome to the community."

"I'd be happy to. Just let me know when she's home from the hospital. I can visit with her for a while too. If she lives alone, she'll probably be happy to see a new friendly face."

"I'm sure she would." Kate had known her friend would come through. Livvy was just that kind of person. "By the way, Paul also saw Stephanie Miller while we were at the hospital. Her appendix ruptured."

"Yes, I heard," Livvy said in a sympathetic tone. "How is she going to manage with three small children? Her kids aren't even in school yet, are they?"

"No, they aren't. Her husband and his mother are going to care for them most of the time, but they need help two afternoons a week. Paul volunteered me for Tuesday afternoon, so that's already covered. I also need to call Millie to add them to the prayer chain and the Faith Freezer roster."

"I bet Marissa Harris would help." Livvy reeled off several more names in succession. "And Abby Pippins. You could ask her to announce it at the Friendship Club."

Kate scribbled down the names. "I'll set up a babysitting schedule."

"I can mention it whenever I see folks at the library," Livvy volunteered. "I feel bad that I can't help with the babysitting." Livvy's full-time job at the library precluded other daytime commitments.

"Oh, Livvy, you're a treasure. Thank you so much!" Kate sent a silent prayer of thanks winging toward God.

After the two friends concluded their conversation, Kate got the Faith Briar Church directory and settled in her rocker in the living room. She decided she might as well start making some calls to line up babysitters for the Miller family.

She called Renee Lambert first. Kate knew Renee would be upset if she wasn't invited to help, mostly because Renee enjoyed knowing the scoop on any happenings in the community.

Renee greeted Kate with enthusiasm the moment Kate identified herself. "You were still at the Bristol when a woman fell ill, weren't you? Tell me exactly what happened."

Kate grinned to herself. Renee and her mother must have left only moments before Emmaline's attack. Clearly, it was killing Renee that she had missed the excitement. Kate was certain Renee was wishing she had still been at the restaurant.

A member of the church board, Renee considered herself exempt from keeping news about her fellow parishioners confidential. Paul sometimes said that he suspected Renee believed she was the only person qualified to make decisions for the church. The same could be said for her view of the entire town.

Kate gave Renee a very brief recap of her lunch experience. She had no desire to pass on gossip, although she recognized that a collapse such as Emmaline's in a public place was bound to elicit some curiosity and concern.

"So she had a heart attack?" Trust Renee to seize on the information Kate *hadn't* volunteered.

"I don't know. I imagine Ms. Ashford will tell us if she wants us to know." She went on to tell Renee about the babysitting for the Miller family and asked Renee if she would like to be included.

"Add me to your list," Renee said. "And since I'll be delivering a meal to the Millers through Faith Freezer, I could take one to the other lady, Ms. Ashford. I could welcome her to Copper Mill."

"You could," Kate affirmed, though she suspected that curiosity motivated the offer as much as kindness. She was a little alarmed at the idea of Renee foisting herself on Emmaline Ashford. But who knew? Perhaps the two women were friends just waiting to find each other.

Setting down the receiver after the conversation concluded, Kate couldn't help but recall Renee's question: *So she had a heart attack?*

Kate certainly hoped if that was the case, Emmaline would take proper care of herself and find someone to confide in. Living alone in a new community with a possible heart condition seemed rather foolhardy.

Chapter Four

The following morning, Kate arose before six. Feeling chilled, she drew on a warm dressing gown and went to the kitchen to start her coffee.

While the coffee was brewing, she stood at the sink and looked out the window. The day was as dreary as any Kate had seen so far that autumn. It had rained during the night, and as the sky began to lighten, no sunshine appeared to banish the gloomy gray.

Paul came into the kitchen a few minutes later, carrying his running shoes and yawning.

"Good morning." Kate walked across the kitchen and kissed him on the cheek. "You're going running this early?"

Caught in midyawn, he nodded as he rolled his eyes. "Eli wants to get started right away."

"You might want to take your waterproof jacket. It isn't raining anymore, but it looks as if it could start again."

"Thanks, mother hen. I will." Paul poured himself a glass of orange juice and washed down his vitamin supplements as well as the antihistamine he took for his seasonal allergies. "Miss me while I'm gone," he ordered.

"I'm on it." Kate blew him a kiss as he vanished out the front door. "Say good morning to Eli for me."

Returning to the kitchen, she grabbed a mug of coffee and settled herself in her rocking chair. She had begun a new devotional series recently, and she opened the devotional book, her Bible, and a journal she occasionally used to record her faith journey. This was her favorite time of day, these quiet early mornings spent in prayer and studying God's Word.

But today, it was difficult to feel cheerful. The plop of raindrops against the window alerted her that the rain had begun again. Kate felt her mood sinking into a dullness that matched the color of the sky. Still, she was determined to slog through her devotional time.

She turned to the suggested reading for the day, a selection from the fifth chapter of First Thessalonians. Paul's letter exhorted the believers of Thessalonica to be joyful and thankful no matter what the circumstances. As she read, Kate began to smile. God always had a way of meeting her needs. Even when she was too caught up in the mood of the moment to heed his counsel, he reminded her of his love and of the wonderful world around her. She thought of her newest friend, Emmaline Ashford. Even though Kate didn't know what kind of healing to pray for, she knew that God would offer Emmaline comfort and care.

She was anxious to see Emmaline again. Not only did Kate want to help her through her illness, but she also thought she would love to talk with Emmaline about their mutual interest in art.

Kate finished her devotional time after praying for the

Lord to heal Stephanie and care for her family during this difficult time and asking the Lord to surround Emmaline with his love and give the doctors wisdom in treating her. Paul hadn't returned from his run yet, and she knew he would be out a while longer. She figured she had time for a shower before Paul returned for breakfast. Just as she finished dressing, she heard Paul come through the door.

Returning to the kitchen, she asked, "How did it go?"

Paul took a moment to answer, chugging down a large glass of water first. When he set down the glass, he frowned. "Not so well, if you want the truth. I'm not in nearly as good a shape as I thought I was."

"Oh dear."

"Oh dear is right. I usually run two to three miles. Eli's training plan is supposed to bring me up to six and a half miles, which is just a shade over 10K." His shoulders slumped. "And he intends to accomplish this feat in just six weeks! I'm not sure I'm up for it, honey."

"Six weeks is a long time," Kate agreed, rubbing his back with one hand. "What exactly does Eli have planned?"

Paul rolled his shoulders. "We will be running every day except Sunday. *Every day*. We're starting with three miles this week, and we'll progress to four miles. Then he wants to increase the start distance by a half mile per week. By the end of the sixth week, we'll be at seven miles. In theory, that should make running the 10K very manageable."

"It seems to be a sound plan," Kate said. "I believe you can do it."

But Paul looked doubtful.

"What about it is bothering you?" she asked.

"I'm just worried about the intense training." Paul grimaced. "It's not the plan, I guess. It's me. I'm no spring chicken anymore, and this is an ambitious training regimen."

"You're in good shape," Kate assured him. "I have faith in you."

Paul gave her a hug. "Thank you."

"Now," Kate said, "could I interest you in an omelet for breakfast?"

"You could." Paul rubbed his palms together in anticipation. "I'll start the toast."

The two of them worked side by side in the tiny kitchen and then took their seats at the dining table. Paul offered grace before they began to eat.

"So, what's on your agenda for the day?" he asked.

"Well, I need to do some baking and cooking," Kate told him. "I want to make some cookies and some kind of main dish—perhaps a casserole—for Emmaline. I can freeze it if she isn't released today or tomorrow. And then I'm going to work in my studio. Emmaline said she'd call to let me know when she would be discharged, so if she's released today, I'll go get her."

"Oh, I forgot you offered to drive her home from the hospital." Paul gave her a fond smile. "That sounds like something you would do. I wonder if we should add her to the Faith Freezer delivery program."

"Already taken care of." Kate made a large check mark in the air with one finger. "Renee and Livvy each are participating in that. I believe Renee intends to make it a social occasion."

Paul's eyes widened and he grinned. "Perhaps I should say a prayer for Emmaline now."

EMMALINE CALLED KATE shortly before eleven to tell her that the doctor had just approved her discharge. Kate wondered if it had been Dr. McLaughlin, but she suspected that the cardiac-care physician on call took Emmaline's case once she was admitted, if indeed she was a cardiac patient.

Kate tore herself away from her stained-glass artwork. She took a quick moment to tidy her studio, then brushed her hair and picked up her handbag.

As she drove the short distance to the hospital in Pine Ridge, she wondered if she might run into Dr. McLaughlin again. What would she say if she did? He had made it clear that discussing Emmaline's health would be a breach of confidentiality.

Kate sighed as she got out of her car and walked into the hospital. Recalling the ER doctor's unusual demeanor the day before, she was certain something was odd, or off, or . . . or something! And it was going to bother her until she figured out what it was.

Emmaline was waiting for her in the lobby, sitting with a paper bag in her lap. She wore the same clothes she'd been dressed in the previous afternoon, but she looked neat and well kept.

"Hello, Kate," she called the moment Kate entered the lobby. "Thank you so much for driving me. I can't wait to get home. It's impossible to sleep well in a hospital."

"I'm glad I could help." Kate walked behind Emmaline while an attendant wheeled her out to the covered driveway in front of the building. Emmaline looked perfectly healthy, but Kate knew it was standard hospital policy for discharged patients to be taken right to their vehicles in wheelchairs.

Kate took Emmaline's paper bag and placed it in the backseat while the attendant helped Emmaline transfer herself from the wheelchair into the front seat. The attendant didn't appear to be extremely concerned about Emmaline's mobility. She settled herself in the passenger seat and then reached for her seat belt as the attendant closed the car door.

"So," Kate said casually once she was seat-belted behind the wheel, "shall I take you to get your car at the Bristol?"

Emmaline put a hand to her mouth. "Oh! I had forgotten my car. No, if you don't mind, I'd rather go straight home. I'll get the car later."

"Paul and I could pick it up this evening," Kate offered.

"That would be wonderful. Then I won't have to try to drive today." She dug into her handbag and came up with a set of keys. "Just let me take the house key off, and you can have these."

"I bet you were glad Dr. McLaughlin decided to discharge you," Kate said as she pocketed the key ring. She was hoping to find out which doctor had been assigned to Emmaline's care after she was admitted.

"Oh, it was a different doctor, but yes, I was awfully happy to get out of there."

"We have some excellent doctors here. Which doctor was it?" Kate asked, hoping to learn which unit Emmaline had been admitted to for her tests.

"I'd have to look at the discharge papers," Emmaline said. "I'm terrible with names. But I did appreciate the care."

Stymied, Kate drove silently for a short while. She couldn't think of any other clever way to elicit the name of Emmaline's doctor. Was she being overly suspicious, or was Emmaline giving evasive answers? Kate's instincts told her the latter was the case. But why?

By now they were driving along Pine Ridge Road, heading back toward Copper Mill. "What's that wonderful smell?" Emmaline asked.

Kate smiled. "I made you a chicken-and-broccoli casserole and some cookies. I thought you might not feel like cooking this evening." She didn't mention the meals that Livvy and Renee were planning; they could be a nice surprise.

"Oh, I have such a sweet tooth. What kind of cookies?"

"The original no-bake," Kate said, "with chocolate, peanut butter, and oatmeal. I haven't made them in a long time. When my children were small, I made them often. My daughters loved to help."

"It's one of my favorite kinds of cookie. My si—uh, friend —used to make them."

For a moment, Kate thought Emmaline was going to say "sister." But maybe Kate was mistaken. Emmaline had said there was no one to call when she became ill. Or maybe there wasn't . . . *now*. Perhaps Emmaline had a sister who was no longer living, and she was unable to talk about her. How sad that would be.

The trip back to Copper Mill didn't take long. The women filled the remainder of the drive with talk of the town, Kate sharing her meager supply of knowledge with Emmaline, who knew even less about the little community.

When they arrived at a neat little white two-story home to

which Emmaline directed Kate, Kate pulled into a short driveway at one side of the house.

"Could I offer you some tea?" Emmaline asked.

"I'd enjoy that." Kate took a moment to drop her keys into her handbag. She unbuckled her seat belt and got out. Before she even turned to shut her door, she heard the passenger door close.

Kate watched, slightly surprised, as Emmaline walked to the back passenger door and pulled it open. She leaned in and retrieved the bag of hospital things, then straightened and shut that door too. Then she set off across the drive toward the sidewalk with long, steady strides.

Kate followed, amazed at Emmaline's progress. "It's nice to see you looking so well today."

Emmaline immediately slowed and turned to wait for Kate. "Thank you. It's hard to remember to restrict my activities when I feel well."

Indicating that she had been through this before? It was the opening Kate had been waiting for. "What did the doctor say about your attack yesterday?"

"Oh, he fussed around and finally did some tests," Emmaline said, flapping a hand as if to dismiss the topic. "I shouldn't be lifting anything heavy, exerting myself too hard . . . typical restrictions.

"That Dr. McLaughlin kept coming in and discussing me with the doctor who took my case." She wrinkled her nose. "And I didn't like him any better today than I did yesterday." Then she laughed in a self-deprecating manner. "Of course, the poor man probably feels the same way about me."

Kate just smiled.

As Emmaline unlocked her door and ushered Kate into the house, Kate caught a glimpse of her discharge papers peeking out of the paper bag. At least, she assumed they were discharge instructions.

"Oh, it's good to be home," Emmaline said, sighing with pleasure.

Kate could see the contentment in Emmaline's face as she led Kate into a small but pretty kitchen. It was dated, with cherry red gingham curtains and matching seats for the chairs around the little walnut dining table, and the appliances were older. But the kitchen was clean and neat, and a little oak washstand that looked like an antique displayed several pieces of what Kate thought looked like milky white Depression glass. On one wall hung a framed oil painting of Copper Mill's old train depot back in its glory days, when locomotives routinely made stops in town. Currently, the depot was used as a banquet space for community events.

"This is cozy." Kate gestured to the room. "All these things were your grandmother's?"

Emmaline nodded, some of the happiness fading from her eyes as she busied herself preparing tea. "Yes. She and my grandfather moved here right after they were married. They raised their family in this house, and she continued to live here after his death until she passed away."

Kate stood at the window and looked out at the mountains visible beyond the town while she waited. She was beginning to feel a bit frustrated. The previous afternoon at the Bristol, Kate had assumed that the woman was having a heart attack. But Emmaline's evasiveness when Kate had asked straightforward questions about her health and diagnosis was starting to appear deliberate. Also, Kate reminded herself, the doctor who had been on the scene had said that Emmaline was not showing signs of cardiac arrest. Kate wondered what she was hiding.

"I didn't even ask if you would prefer coffee," Emmaline said. "I'm sorry. All I drink is tea."

"Tea will be fine." Kate smiled and took a seat at the table as Emmaline bustled around the little kitchen.

"So you told me you like to sketch and paint," Kate said. "Have you ever had any training?"

"Only basic drawing lessons," Emmaline said. She set two mugs of tea on the table, placed a creamer and sugar within reach, and took a seat. "I'm mostly self-taught. My favorite medium is watercolor."

"That's difficult to do well," Kate said, truly impressed. "I've tried it before, and I never can get the vision in my head to translate well to paper."

Emmaline laughed. "I know that feeling. That's how I am with oils. I used to belong to a studio club in Philadelphia, and my oil works were so bad I never even showed them."

"But you did show your other pieces?"

Emmaline nodded. "Pencil sketches and watercolors."

"I'd love to see your work sometime," Kate said.

"I haven't unpacked any of my drawing supplies yet," Emmaline said. "I just couldn't get enthusiastic about it for some reason." She smiled at Kate. "But now that I've met a fellow artist, perhaps that will change. Oh! I just remembered something."

She set down her mug of tea and left the room.

As Kate waited for Emmaline to return, she realized that the sheaf of papers Emmaline had been carrying lay fanned across the kitchen table. The top one, she could see, was a sheet of discharge instructions. Unfortunately, the physician's name across the bottom was written in such a ridiculous scribble that she couldn't even make out the first letter.

Then the second page caught her eye. Kate leaned forward, sure she had misread something. The second sheet was an invoice. It showed a cash payment, but what really had Kate gasping was the size of the remaining balance due. Surely that was before insurance, she told herself. Emmaline was self-employed, but Kate felt certain she must have some type of insurance. At their ages, to forego insurance coverage would be foolhardy.

Then she saw a large red stamp across the bottom: NO INSURANCE. Her heart plummeted to her stomach at the thought of Emmaline paying off such a sizable bill with no insurance to absorb any of it.

A moment later, Emmaline returned, carrying a small framed picture no more than eight inches by ten. Handing it to Kate, she took her seat and blew on her tea to cool it. "I did this for my grandmother years ago," she said. "She loved irises and had a stunning iris garden out back. I thought she might like to have it with her even in the middle of winter."

Kate turned the frame around and looked at the picture. It was a watercolor, far more sophisticated than anything Kate ever expected. The artist had been looking along a row of irises in full bloom as they stood edging a garden path. There were lavenders and deep purples, shades of yellow, pink, and orange, and the sky blue shade that was one of Kate's favorites.

Kate gaped. "Emmaline, this is extraordinary! What a lovely piece of work. You're extremely talented."

The level of skill in the little painting Kate held plainly indicated that Emmaline knew her way around an easel. Kate thought she probably had shown her work and was familiar with other highly skilled artists.

Emmaline smiled modestly. "Thank you. It's my personal favorite of anything I've ever done in watercolor."

"I can see why," Kate said with feeling. "More! I must see more!" Kate said with a laugh.

Emmaline chuckled. "I wish I could oblige, but I left everything else I've finished at home in Philadelphia."

"Oh, so this isn't a permanent move?" Kate wasn't sure why, but she had assumed that Emmaline was going to stay in Copper Mill.

Emmaline shook her head. "I don't think so. At least, I hope not. I miss Philadelphia." Her voice was melancholy and her shoulders slumped.

Hoping to regain the happier mood, Kate smiled at Emmaline. "I'm so glad we met. We'll have to plan some regular get-togethers once you're feeling more energetic. You'll be a wonderful inspiration for me." Then Kate noticed the tiny signature in the bottom right corner of the painting. "E.N.? Is N your middle initial?"

There was a sudden taut silence in the room. Kate regretted her impulsive question when she saw unmistakable sorrow cloud Emmaline's gray eyes. But before she could form some subject change to bridge the awkward moment, Emmaline spoke.

"No," she said. "My...ah...my maiden name began with an *N*." She let the bald statement hang in the air with no further explanation.

You were married? Kate was certain she hadn't hidden her surprise very well. Since Emmaline had said she had no one to contact, Kate had assumed she wasn't married.

Emmaline awkwardly stood and left the room to return the painting to its spot. Kate let out a deep breath and digested the revelation. What, she wondered, had happened to Emmaline's husband? Divorce, statistically speaking, was the most likely answer. But somehow Kate didn't think a divorce, painful as it could be, had put that desolate look in Emmaline's eyes.

Chapter Five

Tuesday afternoon, Kate made her promised appearance at the home of Stephanie Miller.

Stephanie and her husband, Frank, lived just outside the center of Copper Mill on Sweetwater Street, right after it split off to the right. The home was a pleasant-looking little brick ranch that still had masses of summer flowers blooming around it.

When Kate stepped onto the stoop in front of the door, she hesitated. Should she ring the bell? It was either that or knock, and both options would make noise if there was a sleeping baby in the home. Then she heard the sound of a child crying and realized waking the baby would not be a problem. She pushed the doorbell.

A series of deep tones chimed. Kate waited. Finally she lifted her hand to ring the bell again. But before she could do so, the door opened.

Frank Miller stood on the other side of the screen, juggling a crying baby in one arm and a toddler in the other. The toddler, Anna, stared at Kate with solemn eyes before hiding her face in her father's neck.

"Hi, Mrs. Hanlon," he said with a harried smile. "Please come in."

Kate opened the screen door and stepped inside, making sure the door latched behind her. She smiled at the frazzled-looking young man.

"May I?" she asked, indicating the infant girl, Alaina.

"Please," he said with such undisguised relief that Kate had to chuckle.

Kate slid her hands beneath the baby, supporting her little head, and cradled her in the crook of her arm. "There, now," she said, automatically beginning to rock from side to side. "What's the matter, sweetheart?"

If anything, Alaina screamed louder. She had a powerful set of lungs for such a tiny person. Kate shifted the baby up to her shoulder, rubbing her little back, and gradually the child quieted.

"'Laina quit cryin'," observed a little voice from somewhere beneath her. Peeking down, Kate saw Adam, the four-year-old. Adam was always easy to spot at church. The little boy had brilliant red curls all over his head. He was looking up at her with interest.

"Adam, say hello to Mrs. Hanlon," encouraged his father. "She's going to babysit for a little while until Nana can get here."

"Okay." Adam didn't seem perturbed in the least. "Hello."

Anna, the little girl in Frank Miller's arms, took the news far less well.

"*Nooo*," she shrieked. "Want Mommy!"

Kate looked down at the little face sleeping on her shoulder and was happy to see that Anna's protest hadn't awakened the infant.

"I know, sweet pea, I know." Frank's face fell. "Me too. But Mommy is sick, and she can't come home just yet. Mrs. Hanlon is going to play with you for a little while."

As the toddler continued to protest loudly, Frank looked at Kate. "She just woke up from her nap. You could give both of them an s-n-a-c-k if you like."

He took Kate on a whirlwind tour of the pertinent parts of the house, including the children's bedrooms and baths, the kitchen, and the all-important TV and DVD remote operations.

As they reached the baby's room, Kate asked, "Do you think I should lay Alaina down?"

"Probably," Frank said. "She just finished a bottle, so she shouldn't be hungry again until after my mother arrives. She should sleep for at least two hours now."

"All right." Carefully, Kate lay the sleeping infant on her back in the crib. Afterward, she followed Frank to the front door.

"Stephanie and I cannot thank you enough," Frank said, grabbing his keys from a hook by the door. "I'm sorry I have to run. Good-bye, Adam," he said to the little boy playing in the adjoining living room.

"Bye, Daddy." Adam didn't even look up.

Just as Frank was walking out, Anna began to scream.

Frank looked apologetic.

"Go," Kate told him. "We'll be fine."

Frank managed a wan smile. "Thanks again," he said as he departed.

Kate picked up Anna and smoothed her hair, which calmed the little girl down a bit. Then Kate looked down at Adam. "Would you two like some milk and a banana?" she asked. Frank had clued her in to the children's typical afternoon snack—milk and some type of fruit—and had said bananas were Anna's favorite.

"Yeah!" Adam said. The little boy scrambled to his feet and went running to the kitchen table. "Fanks!"

Kate moved to the counter. Still holding Anna, she awkwardly poured two nonspill cups full of milk and put the lids on tightly. Then she peeled a banana and split it in half, placing the two pieces on two plates Frank had set out for her.

She set the snack on the table, then sat Anna in a chair beside her.

The little girl shook her head. "Lap," she said.

"All right." Kate lifted Anna onto her lap, pulling the plate close. "Here you go."

As Anna ate, she smashed banana all over her face. While Kate kept a steady vigil with a damp washcloth, her thoughts returned to Emmaline. The woman's talent was staggering, in Kate's opinion. But as talented as she was, she clearly wasn't a happy person. And perhaps not a well one.

Emmaline seemed so reluctant to discuss her health that it made Kate fear she was hiding something serious. Something like a terminal illness, at the very worst. The things she *didn't* say would fill a book.

The rest of the afternoon passed swiftly. Kate read stories to Adam and Anna after their snack. When baby Alaina awoke, Kate changed her and dressed all three children for a walk down the block and back. Before she knew it, Frank Miller's mother was walking through the door.

Kate said her farewells and left, plodding back to her car with far less spring in her step than she had going in. Her arthritic knee was still sore from the fall and she had forgotten how taxing young children could be, but the reminder was good. She was determined to ensure Stephanie had help for as long as she needed it.

Sliding behind the wheel of the Honda, Kate wondered if anyone would mind if she just took a teeny nap right then and there.

ON WEDNESDAY MORNING, Kate awoke with a vision. Her discussion with Emmaline two days before must have been working in her subconscious during the night, because all she could think about were irises. She began planning a large stained-glass panel of irises in soft shades of pink and lavender. In her mind, it was an extraordinarily stunning piece. She could already imagine it hanging prominently in the window of Smith Street Gifts.

The iris panel remained in the back of her mind during her morning prayer time and throughout breakfast. It clamored for attention while she was bolstering Paul's uncharacteristic lack of confidence about his 10K training. She showered and dressed in a trance as she thought about the detail in the piece. Finally, she rushed off to her studio.

She hummed "Jesus, I My Cross Have Taken" to herself as she set out her tools. The old standard had been a mainstay of her childhood church, and for some reason, it had popped up in her mind that morning.

She sat down at her drafting table, picked up a soft lead pencil, and took out a large pad of drawing paper. Carefully, she began to sketch the bottom of the iris stalks. The vision translated surprisingly easily onto her sketch pad.

She responded with a distracted side hug when Paul came in to tell her he was off to the office. He chuckled and walked away as she kept working.

An hour later, she added the main stalk and decided to wait to complete the leaf detail until she was finished with the flowers.

She stretched, then laid down her pencil and rose. Her fingers needed a break. She would call Emmaline and tell her about her idea, she decided, picking up the telephone. Emmaline's number was right beside it on a piece of scrap paper she had given Kate.

"Hello?"

"Emmaline?"

There was a dead silence. Then Emmaline said, "Yes?" in a wary tone. It was clear that she didn't recognize Kate's voice.

"It's Kate Hanlon. I wanted to tell you how much you inspired me."

"Oh! Kate. Hello." Her voice instantly sounded livelier. "I inspired you?"

"Yes. Ever since you showed me your gorgeous iris piece, I've had visions of irises dancing in my head. This morning I went right to work sketching out a large panel I'm going to attempt. I hope you don't mind if I played off your idea."

"Oh, I don't mind at all," Emmaline said. "Isn't it wonderful when inspiration strikes like that?"

"It is," Kate agreed. "Except that the finished piece rarely matches the image in my head," she added with a laugh. "I suspect most artists feel like that."

"Frustrated by our limitations."

"Exactly!"

"I would love to see what you're working on when you have time," Emmaline told her.

"I'll have you over to see it once I've got the glasswork under way. Right now I'm still refining my sketch and choosing colors and materials." Kate paused, thinking ahead. "Actually, I was going to run some errands this afternoon. I could stop by and show you the sketch if you like."

"That would be great," Emmaline said with enthusiasm.

After another moment of conversation, Kate said good-bye and set down the handset. She felt inspired by her conversation with someone who understood what it was like to create.

Eager to complete more of the design, she took her seat again. She began to sketch quickly and decisively as the picture of the irises in bloom continued to flow from her head onto the paper.

When she finished the sketch, she clipped it to an easel and stood back to study it. The trick now would be to make each piece of stained glass an unobtrusive part of the whole panel, so that the beholder saw irises rather than individual pieces of glass.

As she worked, she thought about the new friend she had made. Emmaline sounded quite well, although Kate still worried about her health. That afternoon, Kate promised herself, she would ask Emmaline more specifically about her condition.

PAUL WAS LUNCHING at the Country Diner today, so Kate made herself a tuna-salad sandwich and sliced an apple. Afterward, she packed a basket to take to Emmaline's, including two jars of vegetable stew wrapped in cold packs, brownies, and a small jelly jar full of zinnias that had resisted the cooling weather. She slipped on a corduroy jacket and tossed a creamy woven-cotton scarf around her neck, then she placed the food and flowers in her car and drove into town to the library.

Kate loved the library. It looked, to her, exactly like a small-town library should look. The old red bricks from which it was constructed glowed in the afternoon sun. A young mother sat on a bench on the edge of the lawn while her toddler cavorted in the soft grass.

Entering the library, Kate passed the U-shaped counter and went directly to the office on the other side. The nameplate on the door read: Olivia Jenner, Head Librarian. The door was ajar, and inside, Kate could see Livvy, a pair of reading glasses perched on her nose, absorbed in some sort of large publication that looked like a reference volume.

"Hey, you," Kate said, poking her head into the room.

Livvy glanced up, smiling when she saw her visitor. "Hey, yourself," she replied. "What are you up to?"

"Errands and a visit to Emmaline Ashford," Kate said. "But first I'd like to do a little online research."

Livvy's hazel eyes sharpened. "Anything I might find interesting?"

"I don't know," Kate said honestly. "I want to find out the symptoms of heart disease."

"You're still concerned about Emmaline?" Livvy joined her as she walked toward the stairs. "But didn't you tell me the doctor who helped at the Bristol didn't think she was having a heart attack?"

"Yes," Kate said. "So I asked Emmaline what Dr. McLaughlin said, but she was very vague and brushed off my concern. When I asked him myself, he wouldn't give me much information, but he did tell me very pointedly that Emmaline would be just fine." Kate gave the words the same emphasis the doctor had. "She may not have had a heart attack, but I wonder if she has a heart condition."

She frowned as she reached the top of the steps and headed for one of the computers on the second floor. "Even if it's a chronic disease, it's as you said: heart trouble is nothing to mess with. If I know what type of illness she has, perhaps I can help the next time—heaven forbid—she has a problem. Plus, it might help me broach the topic with her better if I know specifics about the disease."

"Well, there are many kinds of heart disease," Livvy said. "Do you have anything narrowed down?"

"No, that's just it. When she collapsed, she was clutching at her chest as if she was experiencing pain. But the doctor said her color was good, her pulse was a little fast but steady, and she wasn't sweating."

"All right. Call me if you need a sounding board or research help," Livvy told her. "Oh, also, a library patron asked

about the babysitting arrangements for Stephanie Miller this
morning. She had heard that you were looking for volunteers.
She lives down the street and wanted to offer her services."
She withdrew a piece of paper from her pocket. "Here's her
name and number."

"Terrific!" Kate exclaimed. "We have people lined up to help
for nearly six weeks. I'm sure Stephanie won't be able to lift
anything until her incision heals, so she won't be able to be
alone with the children for at least that long."

"Six weeks. That's amazing. People are so generous when
they learn about a need, aren't they?"

"They often are," she agreed. "Thanks for passing that on,
Liv. You're the best."

"That's not what Justin said this morning when I made
him clean out the pockets of his jeans before I washed them."
Justin was the younger of Livvy's two teenage sons. "I think
he was growing a science experiment in there."

"Ick." Kate shuddered, recalling the days of seemingly end-
less rounds of laundry when she had children at home. Laundry
was one of the things she didn't miss as an empty nester.

Livvy went back downstairs, and Kate went to a Web site
called WebMD, which offered definitive information on all
kinds of health issues. She typed "kinds of heart disease" into
WebMD's search engine and sighed when a list of well over a
dozen heart conditions popped up. Although she found several that detailed symptoms of the most commonly known
heart ailments, as she read about arrhythmias, attacks, and
abnormalities, she realized that she didn't know enough about
Emmaline's health to decide which, if any, of the illnesses
might apply. All she knew about were the merest hints of a

few symptoms and Dr. McLaughlin's assurance that Emmaline's illness was something she could recover from.

She tried "causes of chest pain" and came up with one thousand seven hundred and twenty-nine possibilities that included such diverse causes as panic attacks, muscle spasms, broken ribs and angina.

Angina. She had known people with angina. Many of them kept medication with them that would give them quick relief if they began to experience symptoms. She did a search for "angina." *Hmm.* It was the most common symptom of coronary artery disease. Unfortunately, most of the symptoms described were ones that only a patient would be able to identify: discomfort, heaviness, pressure, aching, burning, fullness, squeezing or a painful feeling in the chest area. It often was mistaken for indigestion. None of which Kate was able to say for certain were problems Emmaline suffered. Still, angina and coronary artery disease sounded like serious illnesses, not something that Dr. McLaughlin would have made light of.

With a sigh, Kate closed the browser program and rose from her chair.

As she descended the stairs, she saw Livvy helping a patron at the desk. Livvy glanced up and their gazes met. Livvy's face softened. "Any luck?" she asked as the man she had been serving departed.

"No." Kate sighed. "I think I was indulging in a little wishful thinking, expecting to learn something from the research when I don't have enough basic information about Emmaline's health."

Livvy nodded. "You can't make a diagnosis without adequate knowledge."

"Yes. Am I just being nosy?"

"Concern for another person isn't necessarily being nosy," Livvy reminded her.

"True." Kate made a face. "I suppose the best thing to do is simply to ask Emmaline again." She glanced at her watch. "And I promised her I would stop by this afternoon, so I'd better get going."

Bidding farewell to her friend, Kate left the library and hopped into her black Honda for the short drive to Emmaline's home. The address was only a couple of blocks north of the library.

Emmaline must have been watching for her. The moment Kate's feet touched the weathered boards of the wooden porch, the front door opened, and Emmaline said, "Come in. Come in."

"Thank you." Kate lugged the food basket past her hostess, and then she stopped in her tracks. "Heavens, what beautiful flowers!" Kate said.

On a long, narrow sofa table against one wall stood a handsomely sized vase containing an enormous flower arrangement in shades of pinks and purples. Kate saw roses, stock, carnations, yucca blooms, baby's breath, Dutch irises, and more.

"Aren't they, though?" Emmaline asked with delight. "Someone from the Bristol called yesterday to see how I was, and they sent these today. Wasn't that sweet?"

"It certainly was." *And smart*, Kate thought. Even though the restaurant staff had done nothing wrong, in this lawsuit-happy age, they were probably holding their breath, hoping Emmaline didn't try to bilk them out of something.

"They also sent a very generous gift certificate for my next meal there and a German-chocolate cake that was just made this morning."

"Goodness," Kate said. "Not only sweet but extremely generous." She lifted the basket slightly. "My goodies aren't as sophisticated as the things the Bristol sent, but I can guarantee they taste good. Could I take this to the kitchen?"

"Of course. Follow me." Emmaline laughed, almost a giggle, as she led the way into the small kitchen. She was dressed in a trim navy sweater and matching slacks, and blonde highlights and silvering strands gleamed in her short, stylish hair.

Kate set the basket on the table, then slipped off her jacket and scarf, laying them over the back of a chair before she turned to give Emmaline a warm hug. "Still feeling better?"

"I am. I've overdone it a couple times," she said, smiling, "but I'm fine as long as I'm careful."

"What might happen if you overexert yourself? Is there any risk of a relapse or another attack?"

"I'm not really sure," Emmaline said. "The doctor said to be careful, so I'm being careful." She lifted the edge of the towel Kate had draped over the basket and peeked inside. "So what's all this?"

Kate drew out her offerings, thinking, *Oh well, I tried.* Emmaline clearly did not want to talk about her health anymore. Kate hoped the woman was being careful, although she couldn't help feeling that Emmaline wasn't taking her health seriously enough. Although, Kate reasoned, perhaps Emmaline was just tired of all the attention—Kate knew she would be—and wanted to move on with her life. Understandable, but still, Kate hoped that Emmaline wasn't moving on at the expense of sharing her burden with others.

Out loud, Kate said, "Vegetable stew, brownies, and a few late flowers of the plain and simple garden variety."

"Zinnias," the other woman said as she drew out the jelly jar full of blooms. "My grandmother used to grow these and snapdragons all along the sides of the front walk. They bring back very sweet memories." She set down the flowers and picked up a jar of stew, examining its contents. "You made this?"

Kate nodded. "Do you like vegetable stew?"

"I love it," Emmaline said fervently. "My grandmother used to make the most wonderful vegetable stew. It'll seem almost as if I was a child again, sitting in this kitchen eating stew."

Kate held up a sketch pad she had tucked beneath one arm. "I also brought my idea for the iris panel to show you."

"Wonderful," Emmaline said, enthusiasm coloring her voice. "I'm dying to see the beginning of your project. In fact, our conversation inspired me as well. I have something to show you too."

"Now you've got me curious," Kate said.

"And I wanted to thank you again for the ride home, as well as for the delicious meals."

"You're welcome," Kate said warmly. "If you don't want to eat all of the stew right away, you easily can freeze some."

"Good idea. I also wanted to thank you for sending Renee Lambert over. She stopped in earlier today."

Kate blinked. Emmaline wanted to *thank* her? "Ah, you're welcome," she said cautiously. "I didn't send her over. Renee came as part of our church's Faith Freezer program."

"Yes, she explained that to me. Very thoughtful. She brought me several jars of her special spaghetti sauce, with a loaf of homemade bread. I'm going to have some of that for dinner tonight. Between the two of you, you've saved me the exertion of shopping for groceries for several days." Emmaline continued to chatter. "Renee brought me a whole stack of books that she has already read. Did you know she belongs to a book discussion group? They meet at the library, and she asked me if I would be interested in attending. Isn't that kind of her?"

"Very." Kate was somewhat amused that Emmaline seemed to regard Renee as a beneficent fairy godmother, but then she realized that probably was exactly how Renee imagined herself. Almost as soon as Kate had the uncharitable thought, she was sorry. *Lord, forgive me*, she thought. *Help me appreciate Renee's thoughtful gestures.*

"Would you be interested in attending with me?" Emmaline asked. "It might be a fun thing to do together."

Kate made a moue of regret. "I'm sure it would, but I have to decline. Since we moved here, I've said yes to almost everything coming down the pike. I've promised myself I won't get involved with one more group, organization, or activity for a while. Being a pastor's wife often feels like about three volunteer jobs rolled into one." She grinned.

Disappointment flashed across Emmaline's face, then she shrugged. "Too bad. But I can certainly understand that."

"You should still do it," Kate encouraged. "You might enjoy it, and it would be a great way to meet some new people."

"Perhaps . . ." Emmaline appeared unwilling to commit,

although she had seemed excited about the book club only moments before. Her gaze lit on Kate's sketch pad. "Let's have a look at your work."

Kate pulled out the sketch pad and perched on the edge of the couch in Emmaline's compact living room. She flipped past a couple of pages. "Here it is."

Emmaline sat down beside her and perused the sketch Kate showed her. "Gracious! It's stunning, Kate. I don't know much about stained glass, but this looks ambitious."

Kate grinned. "It may be. I'm determined to try it, although the finished product may not live up to the perfect piece in my imagination."

Emmaline snorted in amusement. "Every artist on the planet feels that way, I think." She tapped the paper. "What's this?"

"A list of the colors I'm trying to find for all the parts of the pattern. I may have some in my own stash of glass, but I might have to order some."

"Did you design the pattern?"

"Yes." Kate went on to tell Emmaline the specifics of pattern drafting.

Emmaline asked dozens of questions, which Kate answered in detail. Kate was flattered by Emmaline's apparent interest. It was fun to talk about her craft with someone so enthusiastic.

Kate had an idea during a short silence that fell after their long discussion. "If you'd like to try your hand at stained glass, you could come work with me someday."

"Really? I might just take you up on that." Emmaline smiled. Then her eyes rounded. "Oh! I almost forgot." Leaping to her feet, she dashed from the room.

Kate stared after her, surprised by the spring in Emmaline's step.

In a moment, Emmaline returned.

"You certainly appear to be feeling better," Kate said, smiling.

"I do feel quite well for short periods. If only it lasted." Emmaline was carrying a huge sheet of paper torn from a drawing pad. It was rolled up, and as she began to unroll it over the coffee table, Kate saw that the image on it was covered with a piece of tissue paper, presumably to keep the drawing from smudging or being erased.

Kate hoped Emmaline would elaborate on her health, but she only grabbed a ruby pedestal candy dish and anchored one corner of the paper. She used a *TV Guide* on the other corner. Then she pulled away the tissue paper and held the remaining corners in place with her hands.

"What do you think?"

Kate was speechless as she took in the sketch. Emmaline had used soft pencils or charcoal to draw a portrait of Kate.

Chapter Six

For a moment, Kate puzzled over the setting for the portrait Emmaline had just unveiled. Then she realized Emmaline had drawn her as she must have looked the day they first met in the Bristol. She recognized the cut of the brown suit she had worn, and the pattern in her scarf, even though it was all sketched in black and white. It was a three-quarter profile view of her upper body in which she was laughing at something, probably some silly observation Paul had made. The only jarring note was her expression. Kate could not recall having any reason to laugh during that frightening episode when Emmaline collapsed. Still, it was an excellent likeness.

"You've really captured me, Emmaline." *Right down to the exact shape of my teardrop earrings*, she thought.

As badly as Emmaline must have been feeling that day, it was surprising that she could have paid such close attention to Kate. She could understand Emmaline being able to get a good likeness of her face—they had spent enough time together that week—but even the details of her clothes?

"You must have a photographic memory," she added.

"Oh no, although I've often wished for one." The other woman beamed. "So you like it?"

"Like it? I love it."

"You may have it if you like." She hesitated. "But you don't have to—"

"Of course, I'd like to have it," Kate said. The odd sense of unease she had been feeling subsided as she sought to reassure her friend. "Wait until I show this to Paul! He's going to love it. Thank you very much."

Emmaline's smile appeared to falter for a moment as if she was upset, but then she recovered. "You're welcome. Can you stay for a bit, Kate? I haven't even offered you a drink, have I? How about some tea?"

"Yes, please," Kate said.

What had Emmaline been thinking of just then? In her head, Kate replayed the conversation, but nothing came to mind that should have been upsetting.

Kate looked around the living room with interest as Emmaline returned to the kitchen. Pie-crust side tables, lacy doilies, and stern upright chairs all shouted of an era past. In a concession to modernity, a modest entertainment center with a large television positioned in the middle compartment sat along one wall. A recliner sat across the room, and by the slight impression on the cushion, Kate could see it was Emmaline's seat of choice. Beside it on a table lay a manila folder with a sheaf of papers inside. It partially covered a laptop computer.

"I don't want to interrupt your work," Kate called through the doorway. "Are you writing magazine articles?"

"Yes." Emmaline, too, raised her voice to carry. "The pay isn't terrific, but I do enjoy working with words."

"I would love to read your articles," Kate returned.

There was a momentary silence. "Sorry," Emmaline said finally, "but I'm in exactly the same boat with my writing as I am with my artwork. I didn't bring along anything complete. If you like, I'll e-mail you my current assignment when I'm done, and you can read it before it's published."

"Oh, that's okay. I can find some of your work on the Internet," Kate said.

Emmaline didn't respond.

Kate noticed that a basket of what looked like needlework had been set beside the chair. A piece of Aida cloth used in cross-stitching lay over one arm of the recliner.

Kate walked over to the piece. It wasn't finished yet, but enough of the pattern had been completed that Kate was able to see what it was: an elaborate bouquet of flowers in a basket adorned with the pink ribbon symbolic of the breast-cancer awareness campaign.

A frisson of worry traveled up her back. Breast cancer! Was that what was wrong with Emmaline? Kate wasn't sure how that would have occasioned Emmaline's collapse in the restaurant, but she wasn't a doctor. Maybe Emmaline was on some treatment regime that tripped up her system. Maybe she had had a mastectomy . . .

Just then, Emmaline entered the room carrying a small tray with two steaming cups and a plate of brownies on it. She set it down on a small table in front of a love seat, then sat down and gestured toward a chair at a right angle to her.

"Come sit down, Kate. I've made us some herbal tea, and I couldn't resist your brownies."

Kate smiled as she crossed the room and took the seat her hostess had indicated. "That was the idea. So you've tasted them?"

Emmaline smiled. "I must confess I had one while I was waiting for the water to get hot. Did you make these from scratch? They're excellent. And they have walnuts in them. I adore walnuts."

"I do too and yes, I made them from scratch. I enjoy experimenting with different recipes." Kate pointed at the unfinished piece on the arm of the recliner. "I was looking at your cross-stitch. It's going to be beautiful."

"I designed the pattern myself," Emmaline said.

"Really? You're multitalented," Kate told her. "If there was an *America's Most Talented* show, I'd nominate you."

Emmaline laughed. "Yes, I'm just so talented," she said, pretending to bow to an invisible audience.

"Has breast cancer touched your life?" There. That wasn't too intrusive, was it? Kate felt as if she and Emmaline were forging a good friendship. Still, she hoped the way she formed her question was sensitive enough that Emmaline wouldn't feel that Kate was invading her privacy.

Emmaline dropped her gaze and looked away, out the window. "I believe most people in Pennsylvania could say that they know someone who's been touched by the disease. It's a state with a particularly high incidence of breast cancer." Her fingers plucked at the fringe on a throw pillow.

Oh, forget tact. "I've known several friends who have

survived and done quite well. Do you have breast cancer, Emmaline?" Kate said softly.

"What would give you that impression?" Emmaline sounded genuinely startled. She indicated the unfinished piece of needlework. "This is for an eBay auction I read about."

Kate realized that once again Emmaline had deflected the question without giving a straight answer. She started to pose a more frank question when she noticed Emmaline putting her hand against her chest, then rapidly patting it.

"Are you all right?"

Emmaline was breathing heavily. "I'm having a little chest pain," she said. "Just give me a minute."

"Is there something you can take?" Kate glanced around the room in concern. When Emmaline didn't answer, Kate said sharply, "Emmaline?"

"Yes," her friend gasped. "On the window ledge above the sink."

Kate rushed to the kitchen. Above the sink, as Emmaline had said, were several loose oval blue tablets. There were no markings on them, although they looked a lot like a common pain medication Kate sometimes took. But, of course, Kate knew that with the huge variety of medications in the world, there were a certain percentage of pills that were going to look similar. Kate filled a glass of water and hurried back to the living room.

"How many of these do you take?" she asked.

"One," Emmaline murmured, accepting the glass and the medication from Kate. She took several sips of water after the pill. "Thank you," she murmured.

"You're welcome." Kate had heard Dr. McLaughlin's words herself, indicating that Emmaline would be just fine, and yet she had just witnessed her friend in pain and distress. Could he have been mistaken? It seemed to Kate that Emmaline's distress might have been related to the conversation they had been having. She remembered that panic attacks had been listed as a cause of chest pain on WebMD. But would a panic attack be averted so quickly by taking a pill?

THURSDAY MORNING, Kate had a dentist's appointment in Pine Ridge. Afterward, she intended to visit Stephanie Miller and several other people whom she knew were hospitalized at the present.

The moment her dental checkup ended, she drove over to the hospital and parked in the visitor lot outside the single-story brick building. Entering, she began to walk toward the surgical wing where Stephanie's room was, but she was stopped by a voice calling her name.

"Mrs. Hanlon?"

Kate turned.

"Hi there, I'm Sue Velden. Good to see you. I bought one of your stained-glass panels, remember?"

Kate did remember. Sue Velden was an oncologist and had paid what Kate considered an extraordinary sum of money for the piece. Admittedly, it had been one of Kate's best, but she never would have dared to assign it the value Steve Smith of Smith Street Gifts had, where her work was on display.

She took the hand Sue extended. "It's nice to see you. I hope you're enjoying your piece."

"I adore it!" Sue bubbled with enthusiasm. "In fact, I've

been considering asking if you would create a companion piece. I checked at Smith Street Gifts to see if you had done something similar, but I didn't see anything."

Kate shook her head. "No, that was the only piece of that type. What do you have in mind for a second piece?"

"I'd leave the design up to you, but the color combination is striking and works so well in my home that I'd like more of it."

Kate grinned. "And I'd like to sell you more of it."

Both women chuckled.

"Terrific." The doctor wrote a number on the back of a prescription form. "Here's my home number. Why don't you give me a call later, and we can discuss particulars."

"All right." Kate took the paper and placed it in her hand-bag, then shook Sue Velden's hand before the doctor hurried off. Kate hadn't begun to walk again when her name was called a second time.

"Hello, Kate." Lucy Sullivan waved as she walked toward Kate. Lucy was a widow in Renee's bridge club. They had met socially on several occasions and exchanged pleasantries, and Kate had felt a warm connection with the tiny, silver-haired woman, although they never had a chance to get to know one another better.

"Hello. It's nice to see you. How are you?" Kate asked.

"I'm fine. How are you?" Lucy glanced down the hall at the oncologist walking away and then back at Kate.

Kate smiled. "Quite well, thanks. Are you visiting someone?"

Lucy shook her head. "I volunteer in the gift shop." She glanced at her watch. "And I must run. I have to work there until four."

After saying farewell, Kate, too, went on her way. First, she visited Stephanie Miller, who was glad to see her and asked a million questions about Kate's time babysitting her children. The doctor was still being cautious about an exact date for her release from the hospital, but he had told her the very earliest would be the following Monday. More than a week in the hospital sounded like a lot to Kate. That much inactivity would drive her absolutely mad.

After leaving Stephanie's room, Kate moved on to another room, where an elderly parishioner from one of the nursing homes was recovering from a bout of pneumonia. And finally, she visited with a woman she had met some months ago at the diner. The woman had broken a leg in a fall off a ladder while putting up curtains. She had had surgery the previous day and was already walking. She told Kate she expected to be released the following day.

Modern medicine was miraculous, Kate thought. She could remember when a broken leg meant a great deal of time in the hospital.

She was so wrapped up in thought that Dr. McLaughlin nearly walked right past her before she realized it.

"Dr. McLaughlin!" Kate spun as his face registered.

The doctor slowed his steps and turned. When he saw who had called his name, he gave her a friendly nod. "Hello, Kate. How are you?"

"Just fine, thank you," Kate responded. "I was hoping to run into you, actually."

"Oh?" Instantly, a wary look came into the physician's eyes.

"I don't mean to pry, truly," Kate said. "And I know you

said she would be fine, but Ms. Ashford had another episode of her illness yesterday, and—"

"She what?" The words practically exploded from the doctor. Kate was so startled, she actually took a step back.

For the first time since Emmaline had made her claims about Dr. McLaughlin, Kate wondered if there was some truth to them. For as long as Kate had known the doctor, she had never seen him so volatile. She rushed on. "It's just that Ms. Ashford is completely alone in Copper Mill, and I feel responsible for her. I'm afraid she may not ask for help if she needs it. Isn't there *anything* you can tell me about how I might assist her?"

Dr. McLaughlin exhaled heavily and shook his head. "Mrs. Hanlon, you know that HIPAA laws don't permit me to discuss anything about my patients with anyone other than the patient's authorized representative. Which"—he held up a finger before Kate could speak, giving her a knowing, almost impatient stare—"you are not. I'm not even supposed to acknowledge that I know the patient in question. Okay?"

Kate felt properly chastised. "Okay," she said. "I'm sorry I bothered you. I'm just concerned for her."

His handsome face hardened. "Kate, I know you're concerned, but you have to let medical professionals handle this." He grimaced, then let out a frustrated growl. "Am I making myself clear?"

Puzzled, Kate stared at the doctor. *Handle what?* She wondered. "Yes, but if she doesn't have heart trouble, does she—"

He made an exasperated sound. "You should stop worrying about this."

Kate nodded. She was sure her face gave away her confusion.

Dr. McLaughlin was watching her expectantly, eyebrows raised. His curt, almost angry tone perplexed Kate. She got the impression that she had done something to upset him, other than merely inquire about a patient. Or perhaps it was Emmaline with whom he was upset. Another thought flickered in her mind. Was he trying to tell her something he couldn't say outright?

"I trust we won't be having this conversation again," the doctor stated.

"No," Kate said, eyeing him carefully. "I promise I won't ask you another single thing about, er, the person I mentioned."

"Good." It was nearly a snarl. "And you can tell the person you're not mentioning anymore that I *will* be in touch with her."

Kate was flabbergasted as the doctor turned away without another word. Was this the man Emmaline had seen? Heavens, he *was* terrifying! Kate watched the physician's retreating figure in consternation. What had just occurred?

She sat down on the edge of an unyielding chair in a nearby waiting area, burying her head in her hands. Okay, so if she were to believe Dr. McLaughlin, she should stop worrying about Emmaline's health. But wasn't telling her not to worry just as much of a breach of HIPAA laws as suggesting otherwise?

And anyway, what did the doctor mean when he said "Stop worrying"? Did he mean, simply, that Emmaline's health wasn't Kate's business? But just five days ago, he had said she was going to be "just fine." Did he mean that whatever was wrong with Emmaline was treatable, that her ailment wasn't life-threatening? That would be good news if it was what he had been trying to tell her. Or did he mean something else entirely? And why on earth had he gotten so angry when he'd learned that Emmaline had another attack?

Kate rose and began to walk absently toward the main hospital entrance. Then she stopped. Something had been tugging at the edges of her consciousness all afternoon, and now she remembered what it was. Spinning on her heel, she hurried back down the hallway to the emergency department. In the waiting room, she had seen something . . . Ah, there it was!

The current staff feature on the bulletin board was about Dr. McLaughlin. She had seen it on Sunday, but she had been far too distracted to absorb it. Now she paused, rapidly reading through the paragraph of information posted below the picture of the smiling doctor.

McLaughlin . . . graduated from—oh my!—Harvard Medical School. He did his internship and fellowship at Boston . . . residency at Emory, in Georgia . . . held a certificate in internal medicine, cardiovascular disease . . . the list went on. His special interests included heart-failure management, noninvasive specialties, as well as emergency medicine. How fortuitous that Emmaline would have been treated by someone who had studied heart disease so extensively.

That made Kate feel much better about what he had said. Whatever the problem was, Emmaline didn't seem to have a serious heart condition. Dr. McLaughlin's frustration must have been directed toward Kate. She must have stepped over the line in asking questions that created an ethical dilemma for him. With that realization, Kate decided she would obey the doctor's instructions, not only to stop asking him questions about Emmaline, but also to stop worrying about her.

She wasn't going to stop *thinking* about Emmaline, though, or praying for her. Especially since she had witnessed the doctor's out-of-character explosion for herself. Ever since Kate had visited Emmaline in the ER, her mystery radar had been working overtime. She may have promised she wouldn't bother Dr. McLaughlin again, but there were plenty of other ways to seek information. Something funny was going on, and she remained determined to find out what was making her intuition jump up and down and scream for attention.

Chapter Seven

Late on Thursday afternoon, Kate still was thinking about Dr. McLaughlin's cryptic comments and his impressive résumé as she walked into the kitchen to contemplate dinner. They had lots of leftovers, and she had intended to clean out the refrigerator. But she wasn't really in the mood for leftovers. So what could she make instead? It was only four o'clock, but that didn't leave a lot of time for a creative gourmet effort.

The ringing of the telephone interrupted her musings, and she closed the refrigerator door before reaching for the receiver. "Hello?"

"Hey, there, Sherlock."

"Watson! What's up?" Kate grinned. There were few people in Copper Mill with whom Kate would rather speak than with her friend Livvy.

"I have a favor to ask."

"Ask away."

"On Saturday evening, Danny and I are going to a charity auction to support the humane society in Pine Ridge. I found a darling little black dress, but it needs something at the neck. Could I borrow that pretty woven black scarf you have with the red glittery threads running through it? I think it's just what the dress needs."

"Of course." Kate was delighted that Livvy felt comfortable enough to ask. "I could drop it by the library sometime tomorrow."

"That would be great," Livvy said. "I'm swamped here this week."

"I'll be glad to drop it off," Kate said. "See you then."

Just as she hung up the phone, a peremptory knock at the front door startled her. "Who could that be?" she murmured as she walked through the large living room to the door.

The moment she opened the door, a whirlwind of pink and perfume came sweeping past her.

"Hello, Renee! Would you like to come in?" It was a joke, of course, since Renee hadn't waited for the invitation. But the woman didn't appear to notice Kate's delivery.

"Hello, Kate." Renee was wearing deep pink wool slacks paired with a paler pink twinset. Black patent leather pumps with at least three-inch heels and enough gold jewelry to outfit three other women completed the outfit. Without the leopard-print coat, which often dwarfed her slight frame, Renee looked almost elegant. Until one noticed the huge pink plaid handbag over one shoulder or the tiny Chihuahua she cuddled beneath the other arm. The dog, Kisses, was attached to a jeweled leash that dangled down to Renee's knee. Kisses wore a pink sweater as well, with a tiny collar studded with pink gems.

As soon as Kate shut the door, Renee bent down and set Kisses on the floor, unsnapping the jeweled leash.

"There, my Little Umpkins," she cooed. "Look where we are. Grandma's house!"

Kisses immediately began running circles around Renee, clearly delighted to be unfettered.

"Would you like some tea?" Although it was a bit late for tea, Kate knew Renee would expect it. Mentally, she resigned herself to serving leftovers for dinner, since she fully expected this visit to consume any preparatory time she might have had for making something else.

She knelt, and when Kisses came rushing over to put his paws on her knee, she stroked his tiny head. "Hello, little man. Welcome to Grandma's." It had become a source of amusement to both her and Paul that they had gained a "grand-dog."

"Tea would be acceptable. You know how I like it." Kate knew all too well. "And a bowl of water for my Sweet Umpkins, of course." Renee inclined her head, and Kate grinned, suspecting that Renee thought the effort looked regal. It might have worked if she'd been to Betty's Beauty Parlor anytime recently. But her dark roots showed, marring the look created by Renee's blonde hair and carefully applied makeup.

Kate went into the kitchen after Renee seated herself on the love seat, Kisses' diminutive nails making tiny clacking noises as he followed Kate from the carpeted living room to the vinyl on the kitchen floor. First, she set down a small bowl of water for the little dog. Kisses attacked it as if he had been in the desert for a week. He drained nearly three-quarters of the bowl, and Kate eyed him with trepidation.

"I know what goes in must come out," she said to the dog, "but I would appreciate it if you would wait until you get outside again to get rid of all that water."

Then she rose and put a kettle of water on the stove. Working with practiced motions refined by many years of hostessing, she placed a pretty doily on a silver tray and set out Renee's tea just the way the older woman liked it, pouring some warmed half-and-half into a small milk pitcher. She added the loose-leaf Earl Grey tea Renee insisted upon and the bowl of natural sugar cubes Kate had purchased after learning of Renee's often and loudly stated preferences. She included a flowered china plate with several peanut-butter cookies from a batch she had made a few days ago.

Kate chose a teapot from among those she had collected over the years and filled it with hot water, then completed the tray with two pretty china cups.

Carrying the tray into the living room, she set it on the coffee table and took a seat in one of the overstuffed chairs at a right angle to Renee.

"So, what's the occasion for today's visit?" Kate asked as she handed Renee her tea and set about making some for herself. She watched as Kisses trotted across the moss green shag carpet and settled himself beneath the coffee table.

"Tell me everything you know about Emmaline Ashford," Renee demanded.

Kate raised her eyebrows. "You know I don't just give away details of other people's lives, Renee." Kate gave her an admonishing smile. "I *can* tell you she's from Philadelphia."

Renee fixed an unblinking stare on Kate.

Finally, Kate said, "What I know about Emmaline would fit on the head of a pin. She works from home writing for magazines, and she's a very skilled artist. Why do you want to know?"

"She's not very friendly," Renee said, huffy annoyance in her tone.

Kate knew the older woman well enough to suspect there was hurt buried beneath her irritation.

Surprised, Kate echoed, "Not very friendly?"

"Not at all." Renee nodded her head in one short, sharp motion. "I have called her several times to invite her out, but she always has an excuse. If I hadn't promised you I would take care of her, I'd forget it altogether!"

Kate remembered Emmaline gushing over Renee's thoughtfulness, so she found Renee's statement puzzling. Then again, given Renee's propensity for sticking her nose into other people's business, it was surprising that she wasn't rebuffed more often. Perhaps Emmaline had been put off by Renee after they had spent a little time together.

"She seems to be a very private person," Kate said diplomatically. "Perhaps she's simply busy." Although in the five short days Kate had known her, Emmaline certainly hadn't been too busy to spend time with her.

"I heard you were at the hospital this morning," Renee said in a lightning shift of topic.

Kate shook her head, chuckling. "I swear, news travels faster in this town than rumors on the Internet." She picked up her tea and took a sip. "So, tell me how your mother is getting along."

Paul came through the door a short while later. Renee

finally was getting ready to leave, and Kate walked her to the door. The moment Renee was gone, Kate went in search of her husband.

She found him in the office, thumbing through a thick text, mumbling to himself. "Uh-oh," she said, smiling as she wiggled her way between Paul and the book and slipped her arms around his waist. "You're hot on the trail of a reference for a sermon, aren't you? I recognize the signs."

"Caught in the act." Paul laughed as he set the book aside and returned her hug. "How was your day?"

"Well," Kate said, "other than Renee derailing my plans for supper, my day was fine. I did have a slightly weird moment yesterday, but I didn't get a chance to tell you about it last night because of choir practice." She grabbed the sketch Emmaline had given her. "Look at this."

Paul unrolled the paper and immediately whistled in appreciation. "Wow! This is excellent, Katie. Who did this?"

"Emmaline did it."

"I didn't know you were sitting for her." Paul studied the sketch.

"I didn't."

That got his attention. "Really?" he asked, lifting his head. "This is from *memory*?"

Kate nodded. "Paul, that's the outfit I wore to the Bristol last Sunday. She has reproduced it exactly, right down to the scarf and jewelry."

"She's really good," Paul murmured.

"She is," Kate agreed. "But I have to tell you, I feel a little . . . unsettled, thinking that someone I really don't know very well at all has been studying me so closely. She insists that she doesn't have a photographic memory. And she can't even seem to remember the name of the doctor who took her case at the hospital. So it seems odd that she'd be able to draw such an amazing likeness of me from memory."

Paul stroked his chin. "I can understand why this would make you feel a little odd."

"Then it's not just me?" she asked.

"Not just you," her husband confirmed. "It's weird. Period."

THAT EVENING, Kate went into their home office and logged on to the computer to do a little Internet sleuthing. Their dial-up access at home was so slow and frustrating that she rarely got online. But the library was closed, and Kate was curious. She Googled "Emmaline Ashford," hoping some of Emmaline's articles could be downloaded free.

The search engine ground on and on, showing the little hourglass icon for what seemed like hours to Kate, though it was only minutes in reality. Finally, the results popped up: "0 results for 'Emmaline Ashford.'"

"What?" Kate blew out a frustrated breath. Must be the computer. She double-checked her spelling, then tried again with a different search engine.

A few minutes later, she was staring in perplexity at the same result.

"No Emmaline Ashford? How can that be?" Then a thought occurred to her. Emmaline had signed some of her paintings with her maiden name; perhaps she wrote under that nom de plume also.

Quickly, she typed in "Emmaline N." Even though she didn't know the last name, Emmaline was unusual enough that a search should pull up something pertaining to the Emmaline Kate wanted. After the usual lengthy search process, the results came up: "0 results for 'Emmaline N.'"

"You have got to be kidding me," Kate muttered. "Where are you?" She deleted the "N" and Googled just "Emmaline." This time, the computer yielded results. But they weren't the ones Kate was seeking.

First on the list were several sites dealing with baby names and the meaning of the name *Emmaline*. Wikipedia, the free online encyclopedia, had a biography of Emmaline Henry, a twentieth-century actress of modest acclaim. Flickr, a photo-sharing site, had some pictures posted by a girl named Emmaline.

But nowhere did Kate read anything about *her* Emmaline.

"I don't get it," she said as Paul came in to see what she was up to. "Emmaline says she writes for several magazines, and yet I can't find any mention of her anywhere on the Internet."

"On our dial-up connection," Paul said with a grin.

"I thought the same thing. But it does the same thing the library computers do," Kate told him. "It just takes four times as long."

She got off-line and shut down the computer for the evening. As she got ready for bed, Kate couldn't help but wonder why she hadn't been able to find any articles written by Emmaline.

PAUL HAD BARELY LEFT for the office on Friday morning when the Hanlons' telephone rang.

Kate, lugging a basket of laundry toward the washing

machine in the garage, blew her hair out of her face and hurried to grab the cordless handset in the living room. "Hello?"

"Good morning, Kate, it's Emmaline." The voice was cheery and enthusiastic.

"Good morning," Kate said. Her thoughts immediately flashed back to the previous night. She was anxious to ask her new friend about her puzzling nonappearance on the Internet, but she could wait until she saw Emmaline. "Are you having another flash of inspiration?" she asked.

Emmaline chuckled. "Not of the artistic kind. But I had another great idea. How about if I treat you to lunch somewhere today?"

Kate thought through her day. Nothing urgent was on her calendar. The only thing she had to do was to drop off the scarf for Livvy at the library. "All right. Shall I drive?"

"I'd appreciate that. I'm still not feeling very confident about getting behind the wheel. I'll be ready right around noon, if that suits."

"Sounds good. I'll see you then." Kate couldn't help wondering why Emmaline didn't want to drive. Was she afraid she'd have another attack like the one she had at the Bristol? But Dr. McLaughlin had reassured Kate that Emmaline was fine, and she seemed healthy to Kate, for the most part. So what was going on?

A few hours later, Kate changed into a casual pair of khaki pants and a light blue blouse for lunch. Although it was a warm autumn day, she slung a navy V-neck sweater around her shoulders and knotted the sleeves in front of her. Restaurants were often chilly, and Emmaline hadn't specified where she wanted to eat.

Picking up her handbag and the scarf for Livvy that she had laid beside it, Kate went out to her car and drove off.

EMMALINE CAME OUT her front door the moment Kate pulled into the driveway. Wearing navy slacks with an ivory twinset, she came down the walkway with a spring in her step, looking as healthy as anyone Kate had ever met.

Kate couldn't ignore the obvious inconsistencies in Emmaline's behavior. How could a person with a chronic illness look so healthy and energetic most of the time and not seem to suffer any lasting effects from her recent attacks? And perhaps even more important, why would Emmaline lead Kate to believe she had some type of heart trouble when the doctor had said she would be fine? What kind of sickness could make her so determined to protect her privacy that she would deliberately mislead Kate? The more Kate grew to like Emmaline, the more she cared about the woman's well-being and felt afraid that Emmaline was hiding a painful secret.

"Hello, hello," Emmaline sang out as she climbed into the passenger seat.

Kate laughed, setting aside the puzzle for later. "Hello. Someone's in a good mood."

"Someone is." Emmaline smiled. "It's a beautiful day, I feel absolutely fantastic, and I'm going out to lunch with one of my new favorite people. Why wouldn't I be in a good mood?"

"You're right. Why wouldn't you?" Kate smiled as she backed out of the drive and started down the street. "Do you mind if we stop at the library before going to lunch? I have to drop off something."

"I don't mind at all."

"By the way, Emmaline," Kate began casually, "I tried to look you up online last night to read one of your articles—I mentioned it the other day, remember?—but I couldn't find anything in the search results. Do you publish under a pen name?"

Emmaline was silent for a moment. "No," she said, "I use my own name."

"That's weird," Kate said, "because not a single thing came up."

"I guess I'm just not that famous," Emmaline said, apparently unconcerned.

Kate decided to let the matter drop but filed it away in her memory for another time. Authors of even the smallest works could be found on the Internet in today's world. It seemed implausible that Emmaline wouldn't be among them. Maybe, Kate thought with a touch of humor, she was a wildly successful famous author living incognito in Copper Mill.

The two women talked a bit about their recent art endeavors as Kate drove south on Sweetwater and parked in the lot behind the library. When she opened her door, she said, "I'll just be a moment."

But Emmaline had already opened her own door. "I've never been into the library," she said. "Do you mind if I tag along?"

The two women made their way up the steps and through the double-glass doors. "I believe you met my friend Livvy when she dropped off a meal for you this week," Kate said to Emmaline. "She's the head librarian."

"Actually, we didn't meet," Emmaline said. "I was napping

and didn't hear the doorbell, so she left the casserole on the porch and called me. I'll have to thank her. It was delicious."

They entered the library. Livvy was behind the circulation desk, checking out a patron. She winked at them and held up one finger, and Kate grinned back. A moment later, the customer took his books and walked out, and Livvy came out from behind the counter.

"Hey," she said.

Kate indicated the woman who accompanied her. "Livvy, this is Emmaline Ashford. Emmaline, Livvy Jenner."

Her two friends shook hands.

"It's a pleasure to finally meet you," Emmaline said. "I wanted to thank you for the casserole. It was delicious."

"I'm glad you enjoyed it," Livvy said. "It's one of my favorites."

Kate held out the scarf. "Here you go, Livvy. You're going to look fabulous. Are you thinking of buying anything at the auction?"

"An auction?" Emmaline interjected.

Livvy explained the Humane Society's fund-raising event to Emmaline. "So my husband and I are going, and I bought this black dress, but I realized it needed something. I remembered Kate had this scarf—"

"So she called and begged," Kate broke in.

"I hope you weren't planning to wear it," Livvy said.

Kate shook her head. "The only place Paul and I are planning to go anytime soon is back to the Bristol for brunch on Sunday. And I certainly won't have any trouble finding something in my wardrobe that will work for church and brunch."

Both women laughed; Kate's sophisticated "citified" wardrobe had been the object of discussion in town from time to time.

"So," Kate said, "back to the auction. Are you hoping to find anything special?"

"I would love to have a print in some sort of soft pastels for the downstairs bathroom," Livvy said. "You know how boring that tan and brown theme is, and I want to redo it. I figure if I buy a print, I can talk Danny into painting the walls and maybe even get a new floor."

"Good idea," Kate said. "The current color scheme could use a little spicing up, I must admit."

Livvy snorted. "Oh, stop being so tactful, Kate. It's horrendous and you know it!" Both women laughed again.

Emmaline said, "Kate and I are working on projects together."

It was an awkward segue, at best, and Kate stopped chuckling. "We are?"

"Well, not working on the same one together," Emmaline amended, "but we've been inspiring each other. Kate's starting an iris panel in her stained glass after seeing a sketch I did of irises."

"Well, aren't you feeling creative," Livvy said to Kate. "What are you going to do with it?"

"Oh, I'll probably let Steve Smith put it up for sale." She caught the gleam in Livvy's eye. "Uh-oh. I recognize that look. What do you want me to do with it?"

"Well," said Livvy in her best sugary-sweet tone, "I would say donate it for the auction tomorrow night, but since it's not finished, that's a bit of a problem. So if you really wanted to be beneficent, you could donate it to the Friends of the Library for the raffle next spring at Sidewalk Sale Days. Something beautiful like that would really bump up ticket sales, I imagine."

"You," said Kate, "are a con artist."

"You already knew that," Livvy said, grinning.

"You could donate something too," Kate said to Emmaline. Her friend was turned toward the window, watching a group of teenagers cavort in the grassy courtyard.

Emmaline hesitated. "Possibly," she said in a distant tone. "If I'm still here."

There was an uncomfortable pause.

"It's a good idea," Kate said hurriedly to Livvy, "and I'll be happy to donate something. Do you want to mention it to the president of the group for me?"

"Sure. I'll let you know what she says next time we walk."

Livvy had to have noticed Emmaline's fit of pique, or whatever it was, but she was taking her cue from Kate and ignoring it.

"Speaking of which, when do you want to walk again? You're the one with the busy schedule right now."

Livvy considered. "We could go after the library closes. Do you want me to come over after I get off?"

"That would be great," Kate said. "I haven't walked in a couple of days, and I don't want to let myself get out of the habit."

"See you later, then," Livvy said. She smiled at Emmaline. "It was nice to meet you."

Emmaline had already begun to move away and must not have heard Livvy, because she didn't answer.

Kate sent a confused look Emmaline's way, then said to Livvy, "We're off to lunch. I'll see you later. Enjoy the auction tomorrow."

KATE WALKED AFTER EMMALINE, who seemed in a hurry to return to the car. She was already seated on the passenger side with her seat belt fastened by the time Kate reached the driver's side.

As she slid behind the wheel, Kate said, "Let's eat!"

There was a silence. Then Emmaline said, "If you still want to go." Her tone was sulky.

Kate was so taken aback that all she could think was that Emmaline sounded like her daughters, Melissa and Rebecca, during their early adolescence.

Finally, Kate said, "Excuse me?"

"I didn't know if you still wanted to go," Emmaline said. "It seemed like you would rather have just stayed at the library with your friend."

Nothing to do but ignore it, Kate decided, although Emmaline's apparent jealousy—was there another word for her attitude?—felt more than a little unsettling. Trying to mask her discomfort, Kate said, "Lunch will be fun. Did you have a place in mind?"

Emmaline seemed to shake off some of her strange mood at the question. After weighing the options, they decided to drive over to Pine Ridge to a restaurant called Le Peau's.

Lunch was pleasant. Under a steady stream of questions, Kate spent much of the meal telling Emmaline about her life in San Antonio and Paul's desire to make a drastic change in his ministry that led them to Copper Mill. Emmaline talked a little about her grandmother and what she remembered of the town from her childhood visits, but Kate noticed she seemed much more interested in asking the questions than in answering them.

Afterward, Kate drove back to Emmaline's house.

"Would you like to come in?" Emmaline asked when Kate pulled into the driveway.

Kate smiled. "Thank you, but I had better pass. There are a few things I want to get done around the house this afternoon."

"But you have time to go walking with Livvy," Emmaline said. The words had an almost accusatory ring. They verged on being outright sarcastic.

"Well, yes," Kate said, taking a deep breath. "I try to build some exercise into my schedule several days a week."

"Okay. Well, don't have too much fun without me," Emmaline said with a wink as she climbed out of the car.

She may have meant the comment as a joke, completely innocent banter. If Livvy had uttered the words, Kate never would have given it a second thought. But in light of Emmaline's earlier behavior and the seeming accusation a moment before, Emmaline's words sounded more like a warning than a jest.

As Kate waved and drove off, she shook her head. Emmaline appeared to have made Kate her new best friend, although Kate hadn't realized it until that afternoon. Gracious, they hadn't even known each other a full week! Perhaps it would be good to back off a little, let Emmaline develop friendships with some other people rather than becoming so attached to Kate so quickly.

Chapter Eight

"Hello, Pastor." A quiet voice behind Paul caught his attention, and he turned to see Frank Miller standing nearby. Paul and Kate were in the Faith Briar foyer mingling with parishioners before the Sunday service began.

Frank held little Anna in one arm, and with his other hand, he held his son Adam's hand firmly. Stephanie's mother trailed behind him, carrying the baby. The group was dressed nicely, and it seemed half the congregation was cooing over the infant's tiny dress.

"Hello, Frank. How are you?" Paul asked.

"Fine, thanks."

"And Stephanie?"

"Still in the hospital," Frank said, twisting the corner of his mouth in obvious disappointment. "But she's doing better. The doctor is talking about releasing her in a few more days, as long as we can promise that she won't overdo it once she gets home." He smiled, although there were two vertical grooves of worry lining his forehead. "Easier said than done with these three."

Kate stepped forward and waved two fingers at the little girl Frank was holding.

"Hi, Kate," Frank said, smiling. "Thanks for being willing to come over again this Tuesday. I guess these little hooligans weren't too terrible then?"

"They weren't terrible at all," Kate told him. "We had a wonderful time." She smiled down at Adam, and then blew a kiss to Anna. To Paul's surprise, the tot lunged toward Kate, nearly falling from her perch on her father's arm.

Kate reached out reflexively as Paul leaped forward, doing the same. Little Anna landed squarely in Kate's embrace, and Paul looked at Kate, chuckling.

"Well, hello," Kate said, looking down to smile at the child. "Shall I come and play with you this week?"

Anna said "Yesh" and snuggled against her.

Paul felt a surge of tenderness for his wife. Kate had always possessed some quality that babies and children found appealing. She could calm a cranky infant when no one else had any luck. Seeing her with a child snuggled against her made him remember fondly the years they had spent raising their own children.

Frank said to Kate, "Stephanie and I both want to thank you so very much for everything you've done: the babysitting arrangements, the meals—"

"All I did was make a few phone calls," Kate said. "Other people stepped in and took care of the details. Faith Briar is such a supportive church family."

"It is, indeed," Frank said, nodding. He reached out his arms and took Anna back from Kate. "We'll see you on Tuesday."

"I'll be there," Paul heard Kate promise before she went to join the choir. As she walked away, he noticed that she paused to greet several people, leaving a trail of smiling faces in her wake.

DURING THE SERMON, Paul offered the first in a five-part series on "The Five G's of Discipleship." The first sermon was titled "Grace," and it was preceded by a brief overview of the series.

"No one," said Paul, "can be a perfect disciple. But every new day brings an opportunity, presents a chance for you to decide to follow Christ's teachings and embrace his way of living."

As Kate listened, a thought suddenly struck her, and she felt terribly remiss. She hadn't invited Emmaline to church. What had she been thinking? Perhaps it was more that she *hadn't* been thinking. Even if Emmaline was a bit clingy, Kate should have shared her faith with her.

Kate resolved to extend an invitation to worship at Faith Briar the very next time she visited Emmaline. In addition to offering her an opportunity to experience comfort and peace in the presence of the Lord, it would be an opportunity for Emmaline to make some new friends, a move Kate whole-heartedly supported.

As the more vigorous strains of a lively postlude began, Kate made her way to Paul's side at the entrance of the little church. Together, they exchanged greetings and thoughts with the members of the congregation as they filed out.

When the parade of parishioners had ended, Paul placed

an arm around Kate and squeezed her shoulders. "Shall we go to the Bristol again and have our meal?"

"That would be wonderful," Kate said.

As they made the short drive to the hotel, Kate was struck by how different the landscape looked from the way it had one short week ago. It had been windy off and on throughout the previous week, and many of the brilliantly colored leaves had fallen from the trees. Leaves were ankle-deep in some places, and as Paul and Kate leisurely made their way toward the restaurant, their feet made a pleasant rustling sound amid the leaves.

Kate thought of Emmaline as they walked. How could she not? The previous week, they had come to the Bristol, only to find themselves supporting players in a medical drama within minutes of their arrival. She fervently hoped this week would not be as exciting. She was starving!

They entered the hotel and walked over to the restaurant off the foyer. The hostess took them to a table in the Bristol's main dining room, very close to where they had been seated the previous week. Both of them decided to have the brunch buffet, and as soon as their server left to bring their drinks, they rose and made their way to the buffet line.

Sunday brunch buffets at the Bristol were extravagant affairs. The first station contained a variety of fruit, while a salad bar, with items such as Waldorf salad with apples and walnuts and spinach salad with a warm egg-and-bacon dressing, lay just beyond it. There was an entire section of side dishes, such as home-baked macaroni and cheese, succotash, and yams drizzled in a brown sugar glaze. Among the selections of main dishes were seafood pasta, herb-stuffed chicken breasts, vegetable-stuffed portobello mushrooms, and a mouthwatering prime-rib roast served au jus in thin slices. An entire table laden with desserts, including red velvet cake, key lime pie, peach cobbler, and several additional confections, many with chocolate, lay just beyond the main entrée area.

Kate groaned as she carried her plate back to the table. "I'm going to try my best to save room for dessert, but everything looked so good!"

"I know." Paul set down his loaded plate ruefully. "Eli's been after me to eat a balanced diet to get my body in top shape for this race. If he saw this, he'd have a fit."

Kate couldn't quite imagine soft-spoken, gentle Eli having a fit. She chuckled. "Tomorrow we'll make an effort to get back to healthy meals, I promise."

The couple plunged into their extravagant meal with gusto. Kate particularly enjoyed the seafood pasta, while Paul went back for a second helping of the tender prime rib.

Before Paul returned to their table, Kate was surprised to see Emmaline Ashford appear in the doorway of the dining room. She took a look around, then her face lit up when she saw Kate. She said something to the hostess and made a beeline across the dining room.

"Hello, hello!" she called to Kate as she drew near. Kate recognized the enthusiastic trill as Emmaline's stock greeting.

"Hello," Kate said, taking a deep breath.

"May I join you?" Emmaline didn't wait for an answer, but simply slipped the strap of her handbag over the back of the chair to Kate's left and plopped into the seat. A waitress appeared instantly.

"I'd like a glass of ice water, and also hot tea with lemon, please," she told the server. "And I'll have the buffet."

"Thank you, ma'am." The girl nodded and hurried off.

As the waitress moved away, Kate saw Paul returning. Puzzlement registered on his face.

"Paul," Kate said as he set down his plate, "you remember Emmaline Ashford, the lady I visited in the hospital last week. Emmaline, this is my husband, Paul Hanlon."

"Hello," said Paul. He offered Emmaline a hand.

She took it gingerly. Kate could almost swear there was an expression of dismay on her features for a moment.

"Hello." Quickly, she rose. "I'm going to get my meal."

Paul sent Kate a quizzical look. "Was it something I said?"

Kate laughed. Then she sobered. "I'm sorry about this," she offered. "I didn't invite her. Perhaps she wanted to replace the memory of last week's incident with a better one."

But after witnessing Emmaline's direct route to Kate's table, Kate couldn't help but wonder whether Emmaline had come to the Bristol looking for her specifically. Then she recalled a snippet of her recent conversation with Livvy at the library—a conversation to which Emmaline had been privy. She realized that Emmaline very well may have planned to meet them there, even though she had to know that Kate hadn't invited her to join them.

"Perhaps," Paul said, a hint of disappointment in his smile.

Emmaline returned a few moments later with a loaded plate. As she set it down, Kate noticed that she appeared to have taken some of every dish at the buffet, including a large slice of the rare prime rib a chef had been carving.

Dr. McLaughlin had suggested that Emmaline didn't have heart trouble, and from the look of her plate, she certainly didn't have any digestive issues either.

"Those stuffed portobellos look delicious," Kate said, eyeing Emmaline's selections. "I didn't get any because I didn't have any more room on my plate, but I may have to make a second trip."

Emmaline smiled. "They do look good. A second trip is definitely in my future." Then she silently shook out her napkin and picked up her cutlery.

Kate saw that the conversational ball wasn't going to begin rolling until she tossed it. "I thought of you this morning," she told Emmaline.

Emmaline's head came up quickly, and she smiled at Kate. "You did?"

Kate nodded. "We went to church," she said, gesturing at Paul, "and it occurred to me that I've never invited you to visit Faith Briar. I apologize for that. Our congregation is full of friendly, welcoming people. It might be a good way for you to make some new friends in the area."

Emmaline shook her head. "I don't think so. I'm not really much of a churchy-type person. Thank you anyway."

There was another awkward silence at the table. Kate wondered why Emmaline had seemed so delighted to join them. She certainly didn't seem very thrilled about it at the moment.

Paul cleared his throat. "Did Kate tell you that I'm training to run in a 10K race next month?"

Emmaline shook her head politely. "I don't believe she has."

Paul smiled. "My friend Eli suggested it. He knew I was a runner. Although, as I told him, I rarely run more than three miles at a time, if that."

"I think three miles is a lot. How far is a 10K in miles?"

"A bit more than six miles," Paul told her.

Emmaline's eyes widened. "That's twice as far. Do you really think you can do that?"

Kate nearly laughed out loud at the expressions that flitted across Paul's face. Her husband wasn't vain in any sense of the word, but he strove to keep himself in good shape. He wasn't affronted . . . exactly. He definitely wasn't annoyed. But there was no denying he was taken aback.

"Er . . . that's a good question. I hope I can. Eli and I plan to train together six days a week." His lips twitched as his sense of humor asserted itself. "If I can't complete the race, I made Eli promise to give me a ride to the finish line on his back."

Emmaline didn't respond. Kate didn't think she was enjoying Paul's humor. Why on earth would her friend be standoffish with Paul, who was one of the kindest, most easygoing people Kate knew? Even if he hadn't been her husband, she was certain she would appreciate those qualities in him.

Finally, Emmaline spoke again. "Well, good luck," she said with a grimace. "I suspect you're going to need it."

Kate couldn't believe her ears. What a slam Emmaline had just directed at Paul!

Kate opened her mouth to bring Emmaline to task for her rudeness, but she was interrupted by someone calling her name.

"Yoo-hoo! Kate. Pastor Paul. How are you doing?" The

speaker was Dot Bagley, a plump, kindly woman whom Kate often ran into at Betty's Beauty Parlor. Dot was an incorrigible gossip, a bad habit which Kate tried to avoid. But because Dot didn't have a malicious bone in her body, her busybody ways didn't seem to offend most people.

Kate smiled as Dot paused beside their table, a laden plate in each hand.

"We're fine, thanks," Kate said.

Dot's gaze sharpened. "That's good. Let me know if you need anything."

"Need what?" Kate was mystified.

Dot blushed. "Oh, you know. Just . . . anything." She gestured with the two plates she was carrying. "I'd better set these down before I drop them." And she scurried off.

Kate stared after her. "How odd. I wonder if she's referring to helping the Miller family. Perhaps we should ask her to babysit the children, although I'm not sure how well Dot would handle a screaming toddler."

Emmaline looked doubtful. "I'm not sure how well *I* would handle a screaming two-year-old. I might just run screaming myself."

"They're not that bad," Kate said. "I babysat the children last week and enjoyed them. Anna, the middle child, is a very sweet little girl, once she gets to know you."

"That's good," Emmaline said. "Did I tell you about the new watercolor I've started?"

As a segue, it was abrupt and jarring. But Kate had come to expect less-than-stellar social skills from Emmaline, so she smiled and said, "No, you didn't. What's the subject?"

For the rest of the meal, Emmaline talked art. Her own

work, Kate's current project, pieces at a museum she'd recently visited . . . Kate could see Paul's eyes glazing over. Emmaline didn't appear to notice.

Kate enjoyed talking art with Emmaline and continued to be inspired by the woman's creativity, but she felt that Emmaline was excluding Paul rather thoughtlessly. At one point, Kate attempted to draw Paul in by telling Emmaline about Paul's cooking abilities, particularly his specialty, chili.

Emmaline said vaguely, "I'm not much for cooking. You know, Kate, I was reading online the other day about a new technique for blending watercolor pencils." She proceeded to speak at length on the subject.

They finished the meal over coffee and samples of several of the delectable dessert confections.

"You're going to need a wheelbarrow to get me out of here," Kate predicted.

Paul grinned. "I'll run right home and get one."

As they left the restaurant, Emmaline said, "Would today be a good day for me to visit and see your studio, Kate?"

"We're busy today," Kate told her as she slipped her hand into Paul's, deliberately including him. "Perhaps another time. It was good seeing you."

"All right." Emmaline turned away with barely a backward glance. "I'll see you in a day or so, Kate." She acknowledged Paul with little more than a halfhearted wave.

"Well!" Kate said indignantly as she and Paul got into the car. "Emmaline certainly wasn't displaying her friendly side today, was she?"

"She was to you," Paul said with a wry smile. "She just wasn't thrilled with the competition."

Kate nodded in chagrin.

"There's something very sad about her, isn't there?" Paul said.

Kate continued to nod. "Well, she's lonely down here with no family around," Kate began, but her husband shook his head.

"I think there's more to it than just loneliness. It's almost as if there's something broken inside her. She's trying to heal it by clinging to your friendship, but it's not working."

Kate stared wide-eyed at her husband, then realized she shouldn't be surprised at his insight. "You're exactly right, honey." She sighed. "So how do I help her without letting her take over my life?"

Chapter Nine

Kate arose early on Monday morning, well before Paul's alarm. She had laid her robe and slippers near the end of the bed so she could easily retrieve them, and she slipped out of the bedroom without waking Paul.

Coffee. She needed coffee. Yawning, she started the pot and then sank into a chair, staring blankly at the coffeemaker until it was finished brewing.

Retrieving a mug from the cabinet, she filled it and carried it to the small table beside her rocking chair. Then she fetched her Bible and her devotional guide and journal. Shaking her head vigorously like a dog just coming out of water, she said bracingly, "Time to wake up, Kate Hanlon!"

Sitting down in the familiar old chair she loved, she spread open her materials in her lap and drew her mug close. First, she stilled herself, sitting quietly and preparing to listen to God. Then she opened with prayer.

In addition to scriptural references, her devotional selection that morning was based on a quote by Pablo Casals, the great Spanish cellist: "Of course the gift to be cherished most of all is that of life itself. One's work should be a salute to life."

She pondered the wisdom of Casals' words, praying that everything she did would be worthy of "a salute to life." Not just the stained-glass creations she made, although certainly she hoped that her faith was reflected in her pieces, but also in her ministry with Paul at Faith Briar and in the relationships she had with the citizens of Copper Mill.

Finally, she concluded her devotional time with specific prayer concerns for various friends and parishioners, particularly lifting up her concerns about how to help Emmaline.

AFTER HER TIME in prayer and reflection, Kate got out her silver polish and soft cloths to polish her silver service. She had noticed the other day it was showing signs of tarnish, and she had tentatively planned to clean it that morning. She had just started inspecting the silver to see where tarnish might be lurking when the telephone rang. She veered toward the phone on the counter.

"Hello?"

"Hi, Mom."

"Andrew! Hi, honey. What's up?" Kate was surprised to hear from her son. She talked to each of her children once a week, and she had just spoken with Andrew a few days prior.

"Hi, Mom. Are you and Dad going to be home next Sunday?"

"Of course. No Caribbean vacations on the horizon. Why? What's up?"

"How would you like houseguests?"

"We'd love them!" Kate was nearly hopping up and down in delight. "All four of you?"

"Yep! We'd fly down on Sunday. The kids have three days off school for autumn break, so we decided a trip to Copper Mill would be in order. We'll fly home on Wednesday."

"Oh, Andrew, this is great. It'll be wonderful to see all of you. Your father will be ecstatic."

Her eldest child laughed. "I'll see you Sunday, then. We'll take a rental car from Chattanooga up to Copper Mill, so you don't have to worry about meeting us. I'll let you know an approximate time when we make flight reservations."

"I can't wait to see you!"

"Same here. Love you, Mom. I'll see you next Sunday."

"I love you too, honey. See you soon."

Just as she set down the phone, Paul came in from his training run.

"Guess who called while you were gone?" Kate said.

Paul arched an eyebrow in question.

"Andrew! He's bringing the whole family to visit. They'll be arriving next Sunday. Andrew said he'll let us know an approximate time after he makes their flight reservations."

"That's terrific news."

"I thought so," Kate said. "You look beat." She went to the cupboard and took down a large plastic cup, which she filled with ice water.

Paul limped a bit as he hobbled to the kitchen table, then sank down into a chair with a sigh of relief. "I am ... it did not go well."

"Define 'not well,'" Kate requested, patting his shoulder. She handed him the water before going back to her silverware.

"Thanks." Paul sighed again. "Eli can run rings around me. This week we're running 5K distances. Today we trained on a hill, running a 5K time up the same hill twice."

"A 5K time is a faster pace than a 10K would be on the same hill?" asked Kate, trying to grasp his meaning.

"Right." Paul bent over and massaged his calves. "I used to *enjoy* running," he said in an aggrieved tone. "Running used to be *fun*. I may never run again."

Kate laughed. "Oh, come on now, surely it wasn't that bad."

"No." Paul gave her a lop-sided smile, then the twinkle faded from his blue eyes as he said, "But seriously, Katie, I'm not sure I can do this."

He sounded so discouraged that Kate had a moment's sudden worry that he might be feeling worse than she thought. Was this training too much for him? She nearly mentioned it but forced herself to be positive and encourage him.

"Well, I believe you can. Think of the good you'll do with the funds you raise to support heart-disease research."

"Thanks for the pep talk, coach." He turned his attention to the breakfast Kate had made as she slid into her own seat. After they had eaten, he smiled as he rose from the chair, then groaned and grabbed both thighs. "I think I'll go shower and then pray for myself."

"I think that's a grand idea," Kate said, trying not to laugh as she watched him hobble off. "I'll include you in my prayers as well."

"Thanks." Paul's voice faded as he closed the door of the bathroom.

As soon as the silver was cleaned and put away, Kate pulled out her new *Southern Living Cookbook*. She thought it would be nice to welcome Andrew and Rachel and the kids with some genuine Southern cuisine.

The telephone rang. Sighing at the interruption, Kate reached for the receiver. "Hello?"

"Hello? Kate?" It was a woman's less-than-robust voice. "This is Emmaline."

Kate said, "You don't sound so great. Are you feeling ill?"

"Well . . ." Emmaline's voice was breathy. "I'm sure I'll be fine."

"What can I do for you?"

"Pardon?"

Kate frowned. Emmaline sounded odd—distracted or disoriented. Kate couldn't decide which. "You called me. Is there something I can help you with?"

"Yes, I was wondering if you would have time to come by for a little bit."

Kate hesitated. After Emmaline's recent rude behavior, Kate had intended to be a bit less available to her new friend. But Emmaline sounded unwell, and Kate's ministering heart wouldn't allow her to ignore her friend's distress.

Finally, she said, "I guess I could. Is there a time that works best?"

"How about right now?"

Kate's eyebrows rose. She wasn't exactly busy, she reasoned, but she had been looking forward to going through the cookbook. "Let me finish a few things, and then I'll see you in a little while."

"Thank you." The short sentence apparently exhausted Emmaline. She breathed heavily, and Kate heard a soft noise like a stifled groan. Was Emmaline having another episode like she'd had the other day in her living room?

Kate's level of concern rose significantly. "I'll be right over," she said, hanging up the receiver. The cookbook would have to wait.

She hunted for her handbag and keys. Moments later, she climbed into her little black Honda and quickly backed out of the garage for the short journey to Emmaline's home.

As she drove, she took deep breaths. If Emmaline had experienced another attack, surely she would have mentioned it. What could have happened? It seemed like a good idea to pray for Emmaline as she drove.

Lord, please be with Emmaline as she struggles with her health and the emotional burdens that seem to afflict her. Please make her strong and well. Help me to show her your way and to be an example of your grace. Give me the wisdom to discern how to help her. Amen.

Peace flooded her. God would take care of Emmaline, Kate felt certain. And Kate felt compelled to offer herself as an instrument to assist him with that task.

She pulled into the driveway beside Emmaline's little white two-story home and parked the Honda. Arriving on the small porch, she rang the bell.

It seemed a long time before she saw Emmaline's shadow as her friend approached the door. Kate heard her fumbling with the lock, and finally the door swung open.

Emmaline was wearing a faded soft blue sweat suit and lamb's-wool-lined moccasins. Still, she was wearing light makeup, and her hair was neatly done.

"Come in," she said, gesturing halfheartedly toward the living room.

Kate entered and removed her coat. "Would you like me to make some tea first?"

Emmaline shook her head. "Thank you, but I was resting when you arrived, and I'm still feeling very weak."

Emmaline certainly didn't seem herself, although Kate didn't hear the stentorian breathing that had concerned her during the phone call. "Have you eaten anything today?"

Again, Emmaline shook her head. "No. Breakfast just seemed like so much effort . . ."

"Could I make you something?" Kate asked.

The other woman's eyes brightened a bit. "Would you mind? I would appreciate that so much."

"One fine breakfast coming right up!" Kate sang out.

Her prayer had given her a new surge of optimism and energy, and she was gratified to see Emmaline smile in response. But as she opened the refrigerator to see what she might offer her friend for breakfast, she became aware of a growing concern. She was afraid Emmaline was laboring beneath a burden that went far beyond her health, a burden that Kate felt certain was at the root of much of her trouble.

Kate filled Emmaline's pretty copper teakettle with water, which she set on to boil. While she waited, she found eggs, grated cheese and some luncheon ham, perfect for a ham-and-cheese omelet. Then she hunted through cupboards and drawers for tea bags, sweetener, utensils, a plate, and a mug. In a lower cupboard, she found a pretty place mat embroidered with violets, which she placed on the kitchen table.

Then she arranged the place setting in an attractive manner before beginning the omelet.

When the meal was ready, she went to the living room. Seated in her recliner, Emmaline smiled wanly when she saw Kate. "This is so kind of you."

"Emmaline," said Kate gently, "I'm your friend. This is what friends do."

The smile Kate received in return was worth every second of the time she had spent helping the other woman.

"I guess it is, isn't it?" Emmaline said. She stood carefully and began to walk toward the kitchen. Kate hovered behind her, wondering if she should offer support.

"There's tea on the table. I didn't know how much sweetener you used, so I didn't add any," Kate warned her when she made it to the chair Kate had pulled out. Kate sat across from her at the table.

Emmaline took a long sip of her tea. She gave Kate a weak smile, then put her hand on her heart.

"You seem exhausted, Emmaline," Kate said. "Why don't I leave you to rest?"

"No, I . . ." Emmaline lowered her head, then lifted her eyes to Kate. "It's just . . . it's really nice that you're here."

Emmaline's loneliness felt more palpable to Kate than ever in that moment. "Okay," Kate said gently. "I'll stay." She didn't have the heart to leave abruptly, despite her vow to limit her time with Emmaline.

"I'm sorry to be such a wet blanket," Emmaline said. "I just don't seem to have any energy. Nothing is getting done."

"Well, I can take care of that," Kate said briskly. "Are

there any chores I can do for you? Vacuum, dust, clean bathrooms?"

Emmaline looked up, astounded. "You would do that for me?"

"Of course, I would. Now, how can I help?"

Emmaline hesitated. "Well, my bedroom and the living room really need to be vacuumed. Are you sure you don't mind?"

"Not at all." Kate stood. "Where do you keep your vacuum?" She felt relieved to have a task that would keep her busy. "I'll start in your bedroom," she said. "By the time I'm done, you'll be finished with your meal."

Kate climbed the stairs. When she entered the bedroom, she saw that the bed was unmade; a pretty blue Dresden Plate quilt was rumpled, the pale blue sheets askew. Kate surveyed the room. There was a handbag on a chair and pieces of jewelry on the dresser. On a night table lay a folder with a thick pile of papers and a red pen—perhaps something Emmaline had been working on? But Kate felt a ripple of shock when she saw a chestnut wig setting on a stand atop a chest of drawers.

A knot of dread congealed in Kate's stomach. A wig! Who kept wigs around other than cancer patients who were suffering through the loss of their hair? True, Emmaline had denied having breast cancer . . . but had the question been too specific? Could she have been diagnosed with some other type of the disease?

Kate tried to think positively. There were all kinds of reasons why someone might choose to wear a wig. Perhaps

Emmaline suffered from some form of natural hair loss. Or maybe she simply wanted to change the style and color of her hair without messing with her color and cut.

Kate shrugged off the thoughts and plugged in the vacuum. She vacuumed the hardwood floors and the powder blue rug beside the bed. But the wig drew her like a lodestone, inviting her to take a closer look. She vacuumed over to the high dresser and took a quick, close look at the wig.

It was soft and silky and appeared to be real hair; if Emmaline were wearing it, Kate would bet a stranger would have no idea it was a wig. The color was an extremely close match to Emmaline's hair, light chestnut with blonde highlights. The difference was that this wig had little gray in it, as Emmaline's natural color did. Another difference was the style. While Emmaline wore her hair in a short, attractive pixie cut, the wig was a full head of chin-length hair cut in a bob, with feathered bangs that would probably fall over one eye.

While Kate continued vacuuming, her mind was racing. Was Emmaline having chemotherapy or radiation, some type of treatment that would cause her to lose her hair? That would make sense if she truly did have cancer. But why, when Kate had clearly asked if Emmaline had cancer, did Emmaline simply evade giving her a straight answer? It *did* seem to indicate some level of deceit, didn't it?

Kate switched off the machine and wound up the cord. After securing the plug that clipped onto the cord, she called down the steps, "Would you like me to put fresh sheets on your bed?"

There was a momentary silence, and then Emmaline said, "I would *love* it, Kate. Thank you."

After Emmaline's answer floated up the stairs, Kate retrieved a clean set of sheets from the linen closet and carried them into Emmaline's room. She made short work of stripping the bed, then took the dirty sheets into the bathroom, where she had seen a large laundry hamper against one wall.

Returning to Emmaline's room, Kate wondered if the wig on the dresser was the only one Emmaline owned. On the spot, she decided to take a quick look in the closet.

Pulling open the closet door, she saw that it was a very small space, a common characteristic of an older home. There were no wigs in sight, no wig boxes stored on the single shelf above the hanging bar.

But what Kate did see that had her mouth falling open were three pairs of sneakers. All three looked used, one far more broken in than the other two, but all three also looked like serious cross-trainers, not simple walking shoes. Kate herself owned no sneakers so . . . so *serious looking*.

The sneakers were well worn. Mud—the consistency of clay—was stuck to the sides of one pair. How long ago had Emmaline worn these? Kate couldn't tell exactly, but it must have been recent—the mud hadn't yet dried. Just like the mud lingering outside from the rain two days ago.

Had Emmaline been exercising since her episode at the Bristol? And more important, was grueling exercise like jogging appropriate for a woman with serious health concerns? According to Emmaline, the doctor had ordered her not to exert herself. Had she ignored the orders?

Maybe Emmaline had just gone for a leisurely walk, she

reasoned. But if that was the case, why would she have three pairs of shoes clearly meant for serious exercise? There seemed to be no simple answer, but she suspected if she asked Emmaline, she would hear yet another story that didn't fit the facts.

When Kate finished cleaning, she rejoined Emmaline in the kitchen. "There. Vacuuming done, bed made."

"Kate Hanlon, you are an angel," Emmaline said. "You're going to spoil me."

"That's the idea," Kate said, chuckling. "The only other person I have to spoil these days is my husband."

There was a silence that didn't feel entirely natural or comfortable to Kate. When she looked at Emmaline, she saw that the other woman had tears in her eyes.

"You're very lucky to have a husband to spoil," she said in a hushed voice.

Kate recalled the painting signed with the initial of Emmaline's maiden name. What had happened to her husband? Yet another question about Emmaline's secretive behavior, Kate thought.

Before Kate could decide how to respond, Emmaline said, "I was hungrier than I realized. Thank you so much for suggesting I eat. Without you, I probably wouldn't have bothered."

It was a clear signal that Emmaline didn't wish to continue the thread of the conversation. So Kate let the moment pass, even though her instincts told her that she was on the verge of learning something more about Emmaline's mysterious illness and her equally mysterious past. After all, what had Kate actually learned about Emmaline? Her mother was from Copper Mill, and her grandmother had left her house to

Emmaline, who seemed to have no close friends or family in the area. She was a freelance writer, and she lived in Philadelphia before moving to Copper Mill. She owned a wig and exercise sneakers, and she did counted cross-stitch. She was also a very talented artist. A pretty sparse accounting of fifty-some years of a life, in Kate's opinion.

In an effort to get Emmaline to talk about the sneakers in her upstairs closet, Kate said, "Paul didn't have such a great run today. He's a little concerned that he won't be in good enough shape by the race."

"*Hmm*," said Emmaline, only mildly interested. "I see."

"I've never jogged," Kate said, trying a different tactic. "It never held any appeal. Are you a jogger?"

"No," Emmaline said. That was it. The woman fell silent.

Since Kate couldn't bring up the sneakers specifically without appearing to have been snooping, she finally changed the subject. "That's a beautiful wig on your dresser upstairs. It's nearly an exact match for your own hair."

"It is a good match, isn't it?" Emmaline said tranquilly. She made no effort to explain its presence.

Abandoning any plan to pose further questions, Kate rose. Squeezing information out of Emmaline Ashford was proving more difficult than getting fruit juice from a potato.

"I must get going. I hope you begin to feel better soon. Are you going back for a checkup in the near future?"

Emmaline watched her mug as she twirled it around and around between her fingers. "I'm not exactly sure when my next appointment will be." She made a face. "I'm really not very fond of that Dr. McLaughlin, but since he is an ER physician, I doubt I'll have to see him again."

Kate didn't know what to say to that. Apparently, the lack of dissatisfaction Emmaline had expressed regarding the doctor had not abated. The question Kate wished she knew was this: what was the diagnosis *he* had rendered?

Before Kate could respond, Emmaline said, "Have you ever had a manicure? I've heard there's a wonderful spa at the hotel."

Kate grinned. "Yes. I can vouch for that from personal experience."

"Why don't we go together?" Emmaline suggested.

It would be better, Kate thought, to have another companion join them. "Sure. If we go on the weekend or in the evening, Livvy could join us."

Emmaline shook her head. "No, the weekdays are much better for me. How about Friday? We could do lunch afterward."

"Oh, I already have lunch plans for Friday," Kate said. "How about Saturday?"

"I suppose that would work," Emmaline said reluctantly. "Who are you having lunch with?"

"With Livvy." Since Emmaline clearly hadn't wanted to include Livvy in their manicure plans, Kate had no intention of inviting Emmaline to lunch.

Emmaline said, "You two seem to be very close."

Kate smiled. "She was one of the first people I met in Copper Mill, and we've become good friends." Best friends, actually, but Kate kept that to herself.

Emmaline frowned. "You know, Friday really would suit me better than Saturday. Could you change your plans with Livvy?"

Kate's eyebrows rose in surprise. "Oh, Emmaline. I'm sorry, I don't think so."

"But you could check, right? Or maybe I could come along with you, and all three of us could have lunch." She brightened. "That would work, wouldn't it?"

Kate remembered the way Emmaline had practically pushed Paul right out of the conversation at the Bristol on Sunday.

"I'm sorry," Kate said firmly. "That wouldn't work. Livvy and I have some church business to discuss, and also, I don't have time for the spa on Friday. But if Saturday can work for you, I'd love to see you then."

Emmaline hesitated, her face sullen.

Just then, the telephone on the kitchen wall rang. Both women jumped, and Emmaline said, "Goodness. That hardly ever rings. I wonder who it could be."

She rose and went over to answer the call. The phone wasn't cordless, but it did have a long cord so that whoever was using it could still move around the kitchen. "Hello?"

Kate didn't know who the caller was, but Emmaline's sudden stillness alerted her that it was an important call. Welcome or not, Kate couldn't tell.

Kate stood and began clearing away the remains of Emmaline's meal. There was no dishwasher, so she washed each item and placed it in the drying rack. As she worked, Emmaline was speaking in a low tone with her back to Kate, making it impossible to hear anything intelligible.

As Kate dried the last of the dishes, then hung the dishtowel neatly over the handle of the oven, Emmaline hung up the phone and joined her by the sink. Her face looked dazed, and when her gaze met Kate's, Kate was shocked to see that Emmaline's eyes were brimming with tears.

She said, "My sister is coming to visit."

Sister? Hadn't Emmaline said she had no one she wanted to contact? Yes, but Kate recalled Emmaline's near slip when they had discussed it in the ER. Now Kate realized she almost *had* said "sister."

Kate replied, "That's not a good thing?"

Emmaline covered her face with her hands and began to sob, her thin shoulders shaking.

Afraid the woman might make herself sicker, if indeed she was sick at all, Kate hastened to draw her to the couch. She wrapped her arms around the slighter woman's shoulders and slowly rocked her, much as she had when her children needed comfort.

When Emmaline's tears had subsided to occasional hiccupping sobs, Kate drew back and reached for the box of tissues on the end table behind Emmaline.

"Emmaline, what's wrong? I can't help you unless you tell me the truth."

Emmaline sighed, her breath hitching. "I was afraid I might never see my sister again," she said haltingly. "You can't know how much this means to me."

"You're right," Kate said. "Explain it to me."

Emmaline sighed again. "It's not easy . . . We had a falling out."

"You weren't speaking to each other?"

"*She* wasn't speaking to *me*," Emmaline said.

Ah. So the falling out was a part of the anguish and pain Kate sensed that Emmaline was hiding. For the first time, Kate felt that she was hearing something truthful.

Chapter Ten

Tuesday was sunny and milder than normal for autumn. Paul and Eli went out for a training run before the sun had risen fully. The two men stretched and began an easy pace. Eli had decreed that they would run a little farther again today, upping their total training distance. Paul had a feeling he was going to be challenged to his limit. Again.

They set off from the church parking lot and ran into town. Their plan was to veer northwest toward Pine Ridge and catch a small connecting road about halfway between the two towns and circle back to Copper Mill on Sweetwater Street.

"How are you feeling?" Eli asked after the first mile.

"Decent," Paul responded. And it was true. After the initial stages of the run, he settled into a rhythm and breathing pattern that lasted for quite a while.

As they jogged through town and out the other side, he allowed himself to feel hopeful. Maybe—just maybe—he really could be in shape to run in this race in a few weeks. On Pine Ridge Road, they passed a gym, where the morning crowd was coming and going in their sweats and sneakers. Some carried dress clothes so that they could go straight to the office after their workout. Paul waved at a fellow who called his name, recognizing him from the diner.

Then his eye caught a familiar pixie hairstyle on an older woman. She walked with a spring in her step as she entered the gym. If it hadn't been for that walk, he would have sworn the woman was Kate's new friend, Emmaline Ashford.

But that made no sense. He had seen Emmaline collapse at the Bristol with his own eyes, and he'd witnessed Kate's concern as the woman's condition seemed to fluctuate throughout the past week. Emmaline Ashford couldn't—or shouldn't—be working out.

As Paul and Eli pounded on past the gym and turned east to head back in the direction of Copper Mill, Paul couldn't get the woman out of his mind. Emmaline had a very distinctive hairstyle, a sophisticated short do.

After a lengthy cooldown, Paul parted company with Eli and headed home. Kate was breading chicken when he walked in.

"Dinner?" he asked hopefully, even though he hadn't even had breakfast yet.

Kate nodded, smiling. "Yes. How was the run today?"

He spread his hands. "Not too bad. Not too bad at all."

"Starting to feel a little more confident?"

"A little," he admitted. "Hey, I saw something kind of weird today."

"Your youth?" Kate joked.

He grinned. "No, it wasn't quite that thrilling. But strange, definitely strange."

"What did you see?"

"It's more what I think I saw," he told her thoughtfully. "While Eli and I were running along Pine Ridge Road, I saw a woman in exercise clothing going into that gym just past the little Appalachian craft shop. Kate, I would almost swear it was Emmaline Ashford."

Kate was quiet for a long moment. "Could you have been mistaken?"

Paul shook his head. "Kate, this woman was the same height as Emmaline. She had that same skinny build, and she had the same hair color and style as Emmaline."

A troubled expression crossed Kate's face. "You know, when I vacuumed for her the other day, I found several pairs of sneakers in her closet that looked like expensive cross-trainers. There was fresh mud on one of the pairs . . ." She trailed off, her gaze far away. "Just yesterday morning, she had trouble breathing and seemed very weak. And a few days before that, she had what looked like a very real episode of chest pain. She never did really say what was wrong. Why would she be exercising the very next morning?"

Paul shook his head. "Sorry, but I don't have any brilliant insights. I'm not the detective in this family."

"You don't suppose she could be making herself ill, do you?"

"On purpose?" Paul shook his head. "What makes you say that?"

Kate shrugged. "It's probably way off base. But sometimes she seems so miserably unhappy . . ."

"I don't know, Kate. Is it even possible to make yourself ill? Short of taking something that would make you sick, of course?"

Kate nodded. "I read a story in the paper a few weeks ago about a woman who actually did become ill after spending several years acting as if she was."

"That could have been a fluke." Paul wasn't sure he could buy into a story like that.

"Or maybe she isn't doing it on purpose. You said yourself she seemed sad. And the way she reacted to a phone call she got the other day makes me positive she's struggling with some big emotional issue. Could stress or anxiety be making her physically ill?"

Paul's eyebrows rose. "Now *that* I've heard stories about. If you research it, I bet you'd find lots of documentation. I'd have to say it's possible. Unlikely, but definitely possible."

KATE HEADED BACK to the Miller home to watch the three children again. Stephanie's release from the hospital was scheduled for the next day, and in any case, she was going to need help for several weeks at least, given the magnitude of the abdominal surgery she had endured.

Alaina, the baby, was sleeping when Kate arrived, and Adam was singing along with gusto to a children's program on television. Anna, who had greeted Kate so happily at church, was having none of her today. As she had the previous week, she screamed when her father left. The chief difference was that this time it took less than a minute before she stopped screaming and demanded, "Down."

Kate read Anna stories and helped her with a wooden puzzle. Her own children had loved puzzles, she recalled. So did her grandchildren. That thought reminded her that in five more days, she'd be seeing her son and his family. She smiled as she tapped a puzzle piece that Anna had missed.

When Adam finished his program, the three of them took sidewalk chalk out into the Millers' driveway and created a complicated roadway on which the children "drove." Adam was on a sturdy blue tricycle-looking thing, and Anna was chugging along in a tiny orange-and-yellow car when Kate's cell phone rang.

She fumbled in the pocket of the snug fleece vest she wore and pulled out her cell phone.

Flipping open the little phone, she said, "Hello?"

"Kate?"

"Yes, this is Kate."

"Oh, hello. This is Emmaline . . . Ashford," she added, as if Kate might know half a dozen ladies named Emmaline.

"Good afternoon, Emmaline. How are you?"

"I'm doing well." There was a lilt in Emmaline's voice; she sounded as if she was feeling well. It was a huge contrast from her last phone call and from the sad, depressed woman Kate had left the previous day. "Kate, I have a huge favor to ask of you."

"Ask away. If I can manage it, I'll be happy to help."

"My sister called again. Her schedule changed, and she's coming tomorrow. First thing in the morning!"

Kate realized why the other woman sounded so happy even as she detected a note of agitation in Emmaline's voice.

"I don't have anything to eat in the house, and I was hoping that perhaps you could take me to the grocery store."

"Take you to the store?" Kate repeated. "Why can't you drive?"

There was a momentary silence. "I can drive," Emmaline said. "But walking through the store, pushing a cart, picking up grocery bags—I'm afraid all those activities would be too much for me."

Kate was beginning to have her doubts about that. "Oh, Emmaline, I'm sorry. But I can't," Kate responded. "This is my afternoon to babysit for Stephanie Miller's children. Do you remember I told you about her? The young mother who had an emergency appendectomy the day before you had your attack?"

"Oh, I remember. They're quite young, aren't they?"

"Quite," Kate answered with a laugh. "The baby girl is eight months, the middle girl just turned two, and the boy is nearly five."

"I don't know very much about children. They make me nervous," Emmaline said. "But I would enjoy meeting them someday."

"That certainly can be arranged," Kate told her. "But not today. And I can't help tonight either, because I have a meeting for the children's Christmas play."

"All right," Emmaline said, disappointment heavy in her tone. "I guess I'll just have to wait and ask Francie to take me. I hate it, because she's flying down and then driving out here from Chattanooga, but there's no help for it."

"Why don't you call Renee? Or perhaps I could find another lady from the church to take you."

"Oh, no." Emmaline sounded horrified. "You're my friend. I feel bad enough about asking you. I could never impose on a stranger."

An arrow of guilt shot through Kate, though she knew her

refusal was legitimate. Emmaline knew so few people in town. Frank Miller *had* left Kate the keys to the family van, in case she needed to go somewhere, although, as he said, "Taking all three of them out in public is a gamble. You just never know what might happen."

"Well," Kate said hesitantly, "I suppose I could bring the children along."

If she had intended to deter Emmaline with that warning, it had the opposite effect. "That would be wonderful!" she cried. "I can be ready anytime."

Just then, Kate heard rustling and cooing on the baby monitor she had clipped to her waistband. "The baby is just waking up," she reported, "so we can start getting ready. It will probably take me the better part of an hour to get all three of them dressed and in their car seats."

"That's all right," Emmaline said. "Oh, Kate, I appreciate this so much. I promise we'll make it a quick trip."

Kate doubted there was such a thing as a quick trip when one had three young children in tow. Checking the time, she decided she'd better leave a note for Frank's mother explaining where they had gone.

AFTER WHAT FELT like an enormous effort to get the children ready to leave, Kate was finally behind the wheel with the children safely buckled into their car seats. She had discovered, with Adam's direction, that the CD player held a variety of children's music, so they were singing along to a bouncy rendition of "If You're Happy and You Know It, Clap Your Hands" as she backed out of the driveway.

She directed a brief prayer heavenward for safety as she began the short drive to Emmaline's home.

Emmaline was as good as her word. She must have been sitting at a front window with her jacket on, because mere moments after Kate pulled the van into her driveway, she saw Emmaline locking her door and walking across the driveway. The van was higher off the ground than a car, and the two women giggled as Emmaline heaved herself into the front passenger seat.

"Gracious!" Emmaline said. "Any mom who drives one of these and wrestles all three of those"—she indicated the children in the backseat—"must be in terrific shape."

"It does take a lot of energy," Kate agreed. She turned down the volume of the CD player. "I hope you don't mind listening to children's music." She rolled her eyes as the theme song for *Sesame Street* came on for at least the third time.

"I'm going to be singing that in my sleep tonight," Kate predicted.

Emmaline laughed. "It's delightful." She peeked over her shoulder at Anna, who was clapping and bobbing her head. "They're adorable." She cleared her throat. "Thanks for picking me up, Kate. I made a short list of the things I need. It shouldn't take long."

Getting into the Mercantile with all three children was no small feat. Kate took a moment to fit a baby carrier over her torso like a forward-facing backpack. She placed Alaina in it, and then took a firm grip on Anna's hand. Emmaline held Adam's hand.

To Kate's surprise, Emmaline was wonderful with the little boy, gently teasing him as he relaxed and chattered to her
about everything under the sun. Kate hadn't expected that
after the way Emmaline had spoken about children the previous Sunday during brunch.

Kate commandeered a shopping cart, and Anna rode in
the seat. Adam, thankfully, didn't want to ride and was content to walk along with them, still talking madly to Emmaline,
who needed to do little more than smile and nod.

"Why, hello, Kate. Aren't those the Miller children?" The
voice belonged to Phoebe West, a member of Faith Briar
Church and a friend of Kate's.

"Good afternoon, Phoebe. They certainly are. Stephanie
comes home from the hospital tomorrow."

"My mommy!" piped up Anna, and they all laughed.

Kate introduced Phoebe to Emmaline. Then Phoebe
looked at Kate with a gentle smile and said, "Is there any way
I can help, Kate?"

For a moment, Kate didn't know what Phoebe meant. Her
question sounded almost personal. But then Kate realized
what she was asking. She had a full complement of volunteers lined up to help the Millers already. "I don't think so,
Phoebe, but thank you for the offer. If anything changes, I'll
call you."

"I'll be there in a New York minute if you need me,"
Phoebe promised. They all laughed, and after a few more
pleasantries, Phoebe moved off down the aisle.

Emmaline's speed was more of a shuffle than a stride,
which suited Adam's short legs well. Compared with the

speed at which Kate had seen her move around the house when she was excited about something, today's pace was slower than a slug.

As they moseyed along, Kate picked up eggs, milk, bread, and several other items Emmaline needed. She also grabbed a few things for the upcoming visit with Andrew and his family. While she shopped, she realized just how much bending, lifting, and reaching was required in grocery shopping. It wasn't grueling work, but it did demand a physical ability that Kate hadn't considered before.

Emmaline followed a few steps behind the cart with Adam. Several times, Kate found that she had to stop and wait for the pair, but Adam was chattering a mile a minute, and Emmaline was smiling and nodding, and Kate didn't have the heart to rush them along.

A few moments later, Kate pushed the cart past a towering stack of boxes waiting to be unpacked just outside the storeroom in the back. As she passed, Anna reached out without warning and caught a corner of a box. "Bosk!"

The next few seconds happened in slow motion. The stack began to topple, falling backward rather than sideways onto the cart. With sudden horror, Kate realized that Adam had lagged a few steps behind her and was now in the direct path of the falling boxes. She rushed toward him, but she was too far away to get there in time.

Just then, Emmaline lunged forward. She whipped an arm around Adam's waist and yanked him backward as the boxes rained down on the very spot where he had been standing.

Relief made Kate weak in the knees.

Emmaline and Adam had landed on the floor, and the little boy began to cry. Emmaline rose to her knees and pulled him into her arms, then got to her feet while still holding him. She rubbed Adam's back, rocking from side to side, bouncing him, and talking in his ear as his sobs subsided.

Kate was astonished; she couldn't help staring. Emmaline looked fine, as if she felt as well as Kate herself. The strength and agility with which she had responded to the crisis showed no sign of a woman who couldn't do her own grocery shopping! It certainly was a marked contrast to the woman who had been making her way so slowly through the store a few moments before.

As the noise of the boxes crashing down attracted other people, Emmaline looked up. Her gaze met Kate's, and a deep red flush crawled from her chin to her hairline. She set Adam down and began to pat her chest, taking ostentatious deep breaths.

Sam Gorman rushed up in time to circle an arm around Emmaline's shoulders as she seemed to waver. "Get a chair," he called to Arlene Jacobs, a young employee on the fringe of the gathering crowd.

Arlene dashed away through a set of double doors and returned moments later with a folding chair, which she opened and set behind Emmaline.

"That was quick thinking," exclaimed Arlene with admiration. "I saw what happened. That little kid could have been hurt badly by those boxes."

Sam eased her into the chair. "Are you all right, ma'am?"

"I'm fine," she said in a weak voice. "Just a little bit of chest pain."

"Chest pain!" Sam blanched, perhaps envisioning a lawsuit. "We'd better call 911," he said to Arlene.

"No, wait," Emmaline said weakly as the young cashier began to flip open her cell phone. "I'll be fine."

She fumbled her handbag onto her lap and searched through it, finally coming up with a small brown bottle. She shook a little white pill from the bottle into her palm, then in one quick motion popped the pill into her mouth and dry-swallowed it.

"I'll be fine," she reiterated. "Just give me a moment or two."

Kate watched in silence. White pill? The magic cure the other day had been blue.

"You take all the time you need," Sam soothed, hovering close by.

Kate was still incredulous. "How did you react so quickly?" she asked.

"Just adrenaline, I suppose," Emmaline said. She avoided Kate's gaze. "If I had stopped to think, I might never have done it. But I acted before I ever considered the health consequences."

"Which are?" Kate asked pointedly.

Emmaline ignored her as Sam said, "Do you think you should get Kate to take you to the doctor?"

"Heavens, no." Emmaline shook her head. "I should be right as rain in a day or two."

"Your groceries will be compliments of the store today," Sam told her. "You prevented what could have been a serious accident."

Kate looked at Adam, who was turning in circles with his arms out, making airplane sounds. She shuddered. *He's safe, uninjured. Thank you, Lord.*

Chapter Eleven

Kate took Emmaline home and then brought her groceries into the house before unbuckling all the children and bringing them in as well. In the kitchen, Emmaline sat in a chair at the table and cuddled baby Alaina while Kate quickly put away the groceries and prepared two cups of tea. The other two children were sitting on the floor in the living room, occupied with the contents of a bag of toys Kate had set out for them.

Before she sat down, Kate opened an odds-and-ends drawer to put away a roll of Scotch tape that Emmaline had gotten at the Mercantile. There, on top of a haphazard pile of other items, lay three hospital bracelets.

At the exact moment Kate opened the drawer, Emmaline said, "Oh, wait, I'll—"

Silence fell in the kitchen as Kate closed the drawer with a soft snick. Three hospital bracelets? Three admissions with overnight stays of at least one night? All Kate could envision was the hospital bill that she had seen laying on this very table the previous week. The one that indicated that Emmaline had no insurance.

Emmaline cleared her throat. "Those aren't mine," she said. But she wouldn't meet Kate's eyes. She was still holding the baby on her lap, nervously bouncing Alaina lightly, her gaze on the infant.

"Not yours."

"No. They are, uh, my sister's. From when she had each of her children. Little mementos, you see."

"Your sister has three children?"

Emmaline nodded, then turned her attention to the baby and started speaking to her in an animated tone.

Kate took a sip of her tea as her brain hummed along at high speed. She suspected that the bracelets were really Emmaline's. Her unease for the woman's health increased, as well as her concern for Emmaline's lack of insurance.

Kate considered Emmaline's recent symptoms in a new light. Could the chest pain be from panic attacks? Financial stress could be a terrible burden. Was Emmaline not only sick but also broke? Was she living in her grandmother's house—even though she obviously preferred to be in Philadelphia—because she didn't have to pay rent or a mortgage?

It didn't really fit, Kate thought, reviewing what she knew about panic attacks. Emmaline's heart rate hadn't been sky-high, she hadn't been terribly short of breath, sweating or dizzy. She had seemed to have an overall weakness, but her symptoms certainly didn't fit neatly into a diagnosis of panic attacks.

Still, if she'd been having panic attacks, Kate could understand why Dr. McLaughlin had so firmly told Kate not to worry. This didn't explain why her activities would be limited, though. Or why she would ignore the doctor's instructions,

Kate thought, recalling Emmaline's muddied gym shoes and Paul's sighting of her at the gym. No, panic attacks probably weren't the most likely explanation.

She decided she'd have to confirm her suspicions if she'd ever be able to help Emmaline.

"By the way," she broached carefully, "Paul thought he saw you going into the gym on Pine Ridge Road this morning. He was positive it was you."

The silence that fell after she spoke seemed suddenly electrified to Kate. Emmaline was perfectly still for a long moment.

Finally, Emmaline picked up her spoon with her free hand and placed it in her tea, beginning to stir methodically. Fixing her eyes on the motion of her spoon in the cup, she said, "Of course, it couldn't have been me, could it?"

"I suppose that's what I'm asking you," Kate began. She was becoming more and more aware of how cleverly Emmaline played with vocabulary. The question Emmaline had just posed was such a subtle evasion that Kate knew most people would say she had told them it wasn't her. When in fact—

Suddenly she realized that Anna was nowhere in sight. The tot had been playing happily with a set of stacking cups a moment earlier, and Adam was still sitting on the living room floor.

"Where did your sister go?" she asked him, abandoning her questioning.

Adam pointed toward the front of the house without even looking up.

Kate sprinted, ignoring the twinges in her arthritic knee. Anna wasn't in the living room, and the doors to the dining room on the other side were both closed. Quickly, she hurried up the steps, cringing to think of the tot climbing the entire steep flight of steps alone.

As she neared the top, she heard splashing sounds. She skidded around the first door on the left, and there was Anna. She was smiling. "Wawa!" she said when she saw Kate.

Kate groaned. "Oh, Anna, no."

The little girl could just reach the top of the sink when standing on her tiptoes. Her tiny fingers clearly had grasped at anything she could reach and, with unerring accuracy, had tossed the item into the toilet.

Kate rushed across the bathroom floor and tugged Anna away from the sink. Anna, predictably, began to scream. Kate set her down on her bottom in the far corner near the cabinet and said, "You are in time-out. Do. Not. Move."

Returning to the sink, she saw with relief that Anna hadn't been able to reach Emmaline's toothbrush holder or toothpaste. Kate peered into the toilet. Anna had, however, gotten hold of a number of other items. In the toilet bowl, the things Kate could see included a bar of white soap, a plastic dental-floss dispenser, and a bottle of some kind of over-the-counter medication. Floating merrily on top of the water were three tiny paper cups of the type people kept in bathrooms.

Kate glanced at Anna. She was still sitting in the corner, but the howling already had diminished, and she was watching to see what would happen next. Kate sighed and rolled up her shirt sleeve.

Just then, Adam entered the bathroom, followed a moment later by Emmaline. "Alaina's asleep," she said quickly.

"I buckled her in her carrier." Then she glanced around, taking in the scene. "Oh!" she said.

"I'm so sorry," Kate said. "There are several things in here. I'm going to take them out."

Emmaline chuckled. "At least I just cleaned the toilet bowl this morning."

"Thank heavens she isn't strong enough to flush yet," Kate said with a small laugh.

"I'll take them downstairs and give them a snack, if you like," Emmaline said.

"That would be great." Kate knelt and began fishing things out of the toilet as the threesome disappeared. As she brought up the dripping items, she tossed the replaceable ones into the trash. The bottle of medication, thankfully, looked empty. But as Kate glanced at it, she noticed a warning pasted vertically on the bottle, although the print had been partially erased by the water. The warning mentioned something about chest pain and shortness of breath, which Kate assumed were side effects of the medication.

Kate peered at the bottle. Could it be Emmaline's? She turned the bottle right side up again and tried to read the label. Unfortunately, it had gotten a little too wet, and the name of the medication was incomplete. All Kate could see was "P-l-a-g-r-i." And the patient's first name was completely washed away, as was the last, except for three letters: A-s and what looked like the remnants of an *h*.

Kate wondered if it was anxiety medication. While she still wasn't convinced that Emmaline was having panic attacks, she hadn't come up with a more likely explanation. The day of the incident at the store, Emmaline had popped a small white pill, which seemed to act very quickly. Had it been for angina rather than some kind of panic disorder? She felt as if she was growing more confused by the minute.

KATE DROPPED OFF the Miller children and chatted with Frank's mother for a few moments, telling her about Adam's near miss with the boxes in the store. Then Kate headed for the library.

"Hey, Livvy," she greeted her friend as she breezed past the front desk.

"Hey, yourself," Livvy said. "You look . . . purposeful. Hot on the trail of an idea? And, hey, I have your scarf in the car. Remind me to get it before you leave."

Kate stopped for a moment. "Okay. Don't forget to get my scarf before I leave." She snickered when Livvy gave her a narrow-eyed stare. "I need to look up information on a med-ication," she said. "Try to, anyway. Do you have an up-to-date medicine index?"

"Prescription or over-the-counter?" Livvy asked.

"Prescription, I think."

Livvy pointed a finger toward the ceiling. "I think your best bet, in that case, is to use the comprehensive indices upstairs."

"Thanks." Kate made a beeline for the stairs. At the top, she headed for the reference section and located the huge tomes of medical information.

Quickly, she looked up "plagri" and found that Plagridyll was the only one that fit. It appeared to be one of the brand names for a common allergy medication. There was absolutely nothing for any other medications with a similar spelling.

Kate looked up "panic attacks" in a different book of diseases and perused the information. There were several extensive lists of medications that were used to treat panic disorder. But nothing with "plagri" anywhere.

She returned to the book in which she had found the drug. The warnings for Plagridyll included instructions to call a doctor if the patient experienced any myriad of symptoms, including chest pain and shortness of breath. the description in the book said not one word about anxiety.

She snapped her fingers in chagrin and said, "Rats."

Three other people around her lifted their heads and glared at her. One girl said, "Shhh!"

Kate mouthed "Sorry." She closed the book and wandered back down the steps much more slowly than she had come up them.

Livvy saw her coming. She said something to Morty Robertson, and he nodded, then slid into the seat at the circulation desk as Livvy beckoned Kate to her office.

Kate followed Livvy, closing the office door behind her.

"No luck?" Livvy asked sympathetically. She handed Kate her scarf, which she apparently had retrieved from her car.

"Thanks." Kate shook her head in answer to the question. "I thought I might really have a clue, but I was shot down in flames." She grinned. "And then several people fussed at me for making noise."

Livvy laughed out loud. "Problem child." Then her amusement faded as she gave Kate a serious look. "So, what's the latest on your investigation of the perplexing Emmaline Ashford?"

Kate sighed. "She wasn't very pleasant to you, was she? If it's any comfort, she treats Paul the same way."

Livvy's eyebrows shot up. "Really? So we're the dogs, and you're the bone."

Kate blinked. "That's one way to put it."

She told Livvy about the hospital bracelets and the earlier finding of the enormous hospital bill.

"And, oh, I forgot to tell you I went fishing in Emmaline's toilet this afternoon." She described Anna's adventure, and Livvy laughed.

Kate went on to describe finding the medication bottle and seeing the warnings about chest pain and shortness of breath.

"But as I researched it, I found out that this medication treats common allergy symptoms. Some of its side effects include chest pain and shortness of breath."

Livvy's eyebrows rose. "Yikes. If I were taking a medication and it gave me chest pain or shortness of breath, I'd quit taking it and go back to the doctor."

"Me too." Kate rubbed her temples. "I need to think about what to do next."

Livvy patted her arm. "Hang in there. There will be an answer at the end of this adventure."

After leaving the library, Kate went home, exhausted from her long day but anxious to tell Paul about everything that happened. But when she got there, she remembered that he had a dinner meeting in Pine Ridge with all the other area pastors. He wouldn't be home until late, if the meeting followed its usual course. And by then, she was quite likely to be sound asleep.

LATE THE NEXT AFTERNOON, Kate returned home from an almost full day of running Faith Freezer meals to shut-ins and the elderly in town. When she walked in to find that Paul had made chili for dinner, she smiled.

"Oh, bless you," she said. "I was looking forward to cooking about as much as I would having a cavity filled." She hurried off to the bedroom to change into more casual clothes and wash her hands.

Paul had just called her to the table when the telephone rang. Kate reached for the receiver. "Hello?"

"Kate, the strangest thing just happened."

It was Renee. Half the time she didn't even bother to identify herself when she phoned. She didn't seem to think it was necessary. Kate suspected it never occurred to Renee that Kate might receive other calls.

"Hello, Renee," Kate said mildly.

The unspoken rebuke went right over Renee's head. She took a deep, dramatic breath that was audible over the phone in preparation for her story. "This afternoon I took Mother to an audiologist in Pine Ridge. She's certain her hearing aid isn't working properly, although I told her she's just getting older and therefore more deaf."

And Kate just bet the older woman had loved hearing *that* blunt assessment. Which, doubtless, was exactly the way Renee had said it to her mother. Kate couldn't help grinning. Renee definitely was an original.

To steer Renee back to the topic of interest, she prompted, "So you were driving . . . ?"

"We were coming home when I saw Emmaline. I was near that gym on Pine Ridge Road when I saw her pulling into the parking lot. I would have stopped, but Mother was in a mood after the doctor told her she needed to turn up her hearing aid."

Kate's attention had sharpened the moment Renee mentioned the gym. "Are you sure it was her?" Although in her heart, she was sure Renee was right.

"I never forget a face," Renee said grandly. "Or that hairstyle. It's rather modern for Copper Mill, don't you think? There was someone else in the car with her, but I couldn't see who it was."

Her sister had been scheduled to arrive that morning, Kate thought instantly. Most gyms offered guest passes, so Emmaline could have taken her sister with her.

Before Kate could respond, Renee said, "Besides, Kisses saw her too."

Kate had to cough to disguise the laughter that nearly burst out. Renee wouldn't have been at all amused. Kate simply had to ask. "How do you know?"

"He was sitting on Mother's lap. He puts his paws on the windowsill, you know, and then he's just tall enough to see out. He started to bark when we passed the gym, and I'm certain he saw Emmaline too. Why else would he have barked?"

Why else, indeed? Kate was afraid to wonder what it meant that she actually understood Renee's logic. "Thanks for telling me, Renee," she said. "I must go. We're about to eat."

"Wait," Renee said. "How have you been doing?"

Kate frowned. "Fine. Why?"

"No reason," Renee said hastily. "I was just checking."

As conversations went, that one couldn't have gotten much more bizarre, Kate thought.

Thinking back to the primary reason for Renee's call, she wondered why Emmaline had denied visiting the gym the previous morning. Well, strictly speaking, she *hadn't* denied it. But she had very carefully avoided answering when Kate had asked her about it flat out.

"As you surely heard, that was Renee," she said to Paul as she returned to the table. "She saw Emmaline at the gym today."

"Huh. So I'm not crazy."

"I never thought you were." She went on to tell him how Emmaline had danced around the question the previous day and about her suspicions regarding panic attacks.

"That's very plausible," Paul told her. "Good work. Are you ready to eat?"

"Sorry," she said, "I've delayed dinner."

"That's all right. My chili only gets better the longer it cooks."

Kate laughed. "Is that so?"

Paul had already set the table and added salad and warm bread. She took her seat and gratefully allowed him to serve her and offer the prayer.

Since they hadn't had a chance to have any extended conversation during the day or the night before, Kate recounted the events of the previous afternoon from start to finish as they ate. By the end of her monologue about the incident with the toilet, Paul was laughing out loud.

"Oh, Katie," he said, wiping tears from his eyes, "You always get yourself into the wildest adventures."

Kate was laughing too, but then she sobered as she told him about finding the allergy medication and being disappointed that it had nothing to do with treating anxiety or panic attacks. "In fact," she told Paul, "some of the major side effects of this medication include chest pain and shortness of breath. So now I'm wondering if that could be the cause of her problems. It might explain why Dr. McLaughlin told me she would be fine."

"It might. At least now you have another clue to work with in trying to find out what's wrong with Emmaline," he said, clearly attempting to be encouraging.

"At this point, *what* is less important than *why*," she responded. "Listen to all these facts and tell me if they fit any health problem you've ever heard of. Dr. McLaughlin says she's just fine, but her in-patient doctor tells her to limit physical activity. She has episodes of chest pain and short-ness of breath, she has hospital-admission bracelets, though she claims they belong to her sister, *and* she takes different kinds of medication. Yet she exercises and looks healthier than I do. She's temperamental. And she stonewalls me every time I attempt to find out what's really going on. I just know, Paul, that Emmaline is wrestling with some kind of major problem that goes beyond health struggles. I guess I need to do some research into anxiety."

"Panic disorder is sounding less and less likely," Paul told her. "Exercise is a recommended treatment for that, so it doesn't make sense for her doctor to tell her to limit her physical activity." He frowned. "Although after Renee and I both saw her at the gym, you're pretty sure she is indeed exer-cising. That's contradictory to the doctor's instructions."

"She has told me several stories that contradict each other, but when I try to ask her about them, she always man-ages to wriggle out of telling me the truth. It's clear that she values and desires my friendship—maybe too much," she added wryly. "But on the other hand, she won't be vulnerable with me. My intuition tells me she's definitely hiding something—several somethings, perhaps—that have to do not only with her physical health but also with her well-being in general."

"Well, Katie, far be it from me to argue with your intuition," Paul said. "I'm convinced that your intuition has a direct pipeline to heaven." He smiled to lighten the atmosphere. "Don't give up. Continue to befriend Emmaline, and don't give up getting to know her. Of course, keep maintaining healthy boundaries too. There may be a reason Emmaline has been such a tough nut to crack." Kate smiled as he continued. "I think God is testing your GSR."

"My GSR . . . gunshot residue?" Kate asked in bewilderment. She was familiar with the term only because it was so widely used in both fictional television.

Paul chuckled. "No. Your Good Samaritan Rating."

Chapter Twelve

The following morning, Kate was out and about early. She had made several apple pies earlier in the week, and she decided to take one to Joshua Parsons. Livvy had told her that the old man had come down with a bad cold. Since he was ninety-three years old, Kate was concerned and wanted to check on him herself.

To her relief, Mr. Parsons—referred to around town as Old Man Parsons—answered the door himself. He was coughing, but his color was good, and his delight when Kate handed him the pie made her glad she'd brought it.

"Well, isn't this fine," he said over and over again. "You know I love your pies, Kate Hanlon."

"I know you do," Kate said in a teasing tone. "You try to weasel them out of me often enough."

Parsons' eyes brightened. "Come on in."

Kate entered the house. It was stifling hot, as Kate had often noticed was the case in older folks' homes. But as she glanced around, she saw the home was neat as a pin, an afghan folded carefully over the back of the sagging couch, and books and newspapers stacked in precise piles all over the living room.

The sheer quantity of newspapers that Parsons kept around was always a bit astounding to Kate. There were at least four sizable stacks on the coffee table alone, from big-city papers in Chicago, New York, Atlanta, and Memphis.

"Have you read all these newspapers?" Kate asked with an incredulous chuckle.

"Yup." He beamed proudly. "Need a magnifying glass, but I manage. Don't read 'em cover to cover anymore, 'course, but I still get all the headlines."

"I bet you do."

"Think I could try a bit of this pie right now, if you don't mind," the old man said. He shuffled toward the kitchen. Kate followed, holding her breath as his ancient arms trembled beneath the slight weight of the pie.

She breathed a sigh of relief when he reached the small counter in his kitchen and set down the pie. "Would you like me to cut it?" she asked.

"That would be nice," he responded.

He moved to the tiny card table in the corner of the room and sat down slowly on one of the folding chairs while Kate found a plate and a knife and cut him a slice of pie. She set it before him with a fork. "There you go."

"Thank you kindly." He grinned as he dug into the dessert.

There were more stacks of newspapers in the kitchen, neatly separated by publication. These, she saw, included Los Angeles and Philadelphia.

"Joshua," Kate said, taking the visit with Old Man Parsons

as an opportunity to do some sleuthing, "I'd like to pick your brain about someone who once lived in the area. Do you remember a pair of little girls who visited their grandmother on Barnhill Street? The grandmother's last name was Hemp."

Mr. Parsons snorted. "Remember her? How could anybody forget her? That old woman could complain louder and longer than anybody in the whole town. Lena Hemp was her name. She inherited that house from her folks. Her husband was killed in the war and left her a widow with one little girl. She never married again."

"The war?" Kate asked.

Joshua scratched his chin. "Well, lemme think. Musta been World War Two. Yes, yes, that's right. I recollect her husband volunteered right off. He died at Guadalcanal."

Kate nodded, making a mental note in case the story warranted research. "So she had the one little girl?"

"Yup, just the one. Lena weren't too bad back then. My wife, Alma, was on some Independence Day committee with her for a coupla years, and I recollect she was a hard worker. It wasn't till after her girl grew up and moved away real young that Lena got testy."

Testy. Kate tried the word in her head and found it surprisingly useful. Funny that it occasionally described Lena Hemp's granddaughter to a T.

"You say the daughter moved away when she was young?"

He nodded. "Took up with some fella from Pine Ridge before she was even outta high school. Lena threw her out, and she and her young man moved away."

"Do you remember Lena's granddaughters?" she asked him.

Parsons shoveled in another bite of apple pie and raised one finger, indicating that she should wait. He chewed laboriously and swallowed. "Just a bit," he said. "They were city kids. Come all the way from Philadelphy, where her daughter lived. Can't recall their names, but they were cute little things."

"Francie and Emmaline."

Joshua frowned. Slowly, he said, "No, that don't sound right. Familiar, but just not quite right, y'know?"

Kate figured after ninety-plus years, a little memory lapse wasn't such a terrible thing. "What do you remember about them?"

He shrugged. "Not too much. One was a lot older 'n t'other. Used to come round for the county fair every year and stay for a coupla weeks." He smiled. "Lena was prouder 'n a rooster with shiny tail feathers when those girls got married. One of 'em had children. Don't think t' other ever did, though."

So Emmaline might really *have* children. It wasn't implausible, since Kate knew now that Emmaline had misled her about having a sister. On the other hand, the children could be the sister's. The story about her sister's hospital bracelets could have some element of the truth to it. But how much?

Kate already knew that Emmaline had once been married, but she still didn't have a clue about what had happened to her husband.

Kate had already glimpsed flashes of sorrow in Emmaline's eyes from time to time. Was the grief from the loss of a loved one? Otherwise, what had precipitated it?

She visited with Old Man Parsons for a while longer,

letting him ramble about years past in Copper Mill. As he talked, she idly glanced at the headlines of the Philadelphia newspaper on top of the stack closest to her. The Eagles had lost in their play-off bid for the Super Bowl. A notoriously savvy congressman from the Pennsylvania House of Representatives had secured yet another major highway contract. A man was accused of insurance fraud. And an eighty-year-old man was training for a marathon.

Chuckling at the marathon headline, she asked Joshua if she might borrow the paper. Paul would enjoy that article.

THE FOLLOWING MORNING, Kate baked several loaves of bread for the Faith Freezer Program.

She had just removed the last pumpkin pie from the ancient oven and changed the temperature to better bake her apple pies when the telephone rang. "Hello?"

"Hello, Kate." It was Emmaline. "Are you free any time this afternoon?"

Recalling Paul's warning about maintaining boundaries, she said, "I'm sorry, Emmaline. I have a busy afternoon. I believe I mentioned that before. Are you feeling all right?"

"I'm fine. But my sister, Francie, wants to meet you. I told her how kind you've been during my time here."

Kate considered. She was having lunch with Livvy, after which she had a number of errands to run, but she was curious to meet Emmaline's sister. "I could stop by around three thirty if you like. But I can't stay long," she warned.

Kate had barely set down the handset when the telephone rang again. "Hello?"

"Hey, Sherlock."

Kate chuckled at Livvy's greeting. "Hey, yourself! Are we still on for lunch?"

"Actually, that's why I'm calling. I am swamped here. Could we possibly make it tomorrow instead?"

"Of course." Kate thought fleetingly of changing the time of her visit with Emmaline. But after a moment's consideration, she decided to keep it as they had left it. She had some cleaning to do, so she still wanted to keep the visit brief.

AFTER LUNCH AT HOME, Kate delivered her cooled loaves of bread to the Bixby house next door where the Faith Freezer Program was located, keeping one aside for Emmaline and Francie. She also ran to the bank and the pharmacy before she turned her car in the direction of Emmaline's little white house. When she arrived, there was an SUV parked in the driveway, so she parked along the street.

She retrieved the bread from the seat next to her, then headed for the house. She wasn't even halfway up the walk when the front door flew open.

"Kate!" cried Emmaline. "Hello, hello."

Emmaline was neatly dressed in a pair of light blue trousers and a pretty matching sweater with a bluebird embroidered on the front. Her hair was styled and shining, and she had on a bit more makeup than Kate had seen her wear, but her eyes looked slightly panicked as Kate drew closer.

Before Kate could enter the house, Emmaline stepped outside, pulling the door closed behind her.

Kate offered her the loaf of bread. "I just made this earlier today. I thought you would enjoy some. It's cracked wheat bread."

"Thank you." Emmaline accepted the loaf. Then she leaned close and said, "Kate, I have to ask you a favor. Could you please not mention what happened at the Bristol to my sister?"

The request was startling. Kate had assumed that part of the reason the sister was coming was to lend support to Emmaline during a difficult time. Surely her sister would be the one person with whom Emmaline would be willing to share her troubles. But apparently, Emmaline was secretive even with her own kin.

On second thought, if Emmaline was indeed having psychological problems, she might have good reasons for not wanting her sister to know it.

"Are you sure you don't want to talk to your sister about what's been happening?" Kate gently placed her hands over Emmaline's as the woman gripped the loaf of bread Kate had handed her.

Emmaline's eyes filled with tears. She nodded. "Please, Kate, don't say anything." She turned away and placed her hand on the doorknob as she said, "She would be so upset with me."

At least, that's what Kate thought she said. She had already turned away, and Kate still was standing behind her on the porch. Kate could imagine that Francie *would* be upset. She couldn't imagine a sibling failing to share news of a serious illness with another, particularly one serious enough to land her in the hospital.

As Kate followed Emmaline into the house, another woman stepped forward. She was slightly taller than Emmaline, but with features and hair color similar enough that it was easy to tell that the two were sisters. She looked somewhat younger, although Kate couldn't have guessed at an exact age.

"Hello," the woman said. "I'm Francie Morlen."

"It's nice to meet you, Francie," Kate said.

"You too. Em has told me how much you've done for her since she moved here. Thank you. I know it's hard to settle into a new community, but I felt certain that once she met a few people, she would be fine."

"Um, yes, that's certainly true." Kate was afraid of saying something that might let Emmaline's secret slip out. The safest thing was to talk about herself, she decided, though normally that wouldn't be her choice of topic. "We moved here not long ago when my husband, Paul, came to lead a church in Copper Mill, so we went through the whole new-kid-on-the-block syndrome too."

"So your husband is a pastor?" Francie led the way to the living room while Emmaline went to the kitchen.

"Yes. He was with a large church in San Antonio for years, so this has been quite a change for us."

Discreetly she studied Francie Morlen, wondering why on earth Emmaline wouldn't want to confide in her sister. Francie wore an oatmeal-colored twinset that looked like cashmere to Kate, paired with fine wool trousers and trendy leather shoes that probably cost more than the contents of Faith Briar's weekly offering plate.

"Is this sort of a retirement?" Francie asked.

"Not exactly," Kate said. "Paul felt called in a different direction."

Francie smiled. "I bet Copper Mill was a bit more 'different' than you had expected. It's practically the polar opposite of San Antonio!"

"It is," Kate agreed. "It's been quite an adventure."

Emmaline returned to the room with a tea tray after a few moments. It bore three cups of tea and a selection of cookies. The three women ate and drank as Kate shared the story of their dramatic arrival in Copper Mill at the very moment their new church was burning to the ground.

Both sisters were horrified. Emmaline said, "Why haven't I heard this story before?"

Kate shrugged. "We always had other things to talk about."

Emmaline's gaze slid away from Kate's as she said, "Yes, I suppose you're right." To her sister, she said, "Kate's an artist too. She works in stained glass."

"How interesting!" Francie smiled. "I don't have an artistic bone in my body. I've always envied Em's talent."

For several minutes, the talk turned to art, and Kate began to relax. Kate thought of her conversation with Old Man Parsons. It was clear that Emmaline was the elder by some years. Possibly a decade. Was there any way to tactfully find out exactly how many years? Kate knew she was clever at figuring things out, but even she couldn't find an appropriate way to mention a woman's age!

Eventually, she said, "So, Francie, tell me about yourself. Are you also from Philadelphia?"

"I am," she said. "I'm a Creative Memories consultant, and my husband is a lawyer. He has his own practice."

"What a coincidence! My son is also a lawyer in Philadelphia. He practices real estate law. Perhaps they know each other."

"Perhaps." Did Kate imagine it, or did Francie's jaw tighten just the slightest bit? Emmaline, oddly, almost seemed to shrink in her chair.

Kate said, "And Emmaline mentioned that you have children?" That led to a discussion of Francie's three teenage children, Emmaline's nephew and nieces.

Since Kate also had a boy and two girls, she and Francie found quite a bit of common ground there, and before Kate knew it, the tea tray held nothing but crumbs.

Just as Kate was about to say she must go, an electronic melody began to play.

"Oops, that's my phone. Excuse me," said Francie. "I promised my children I would answer if they called." She stood and headed for the stairs, pulling her phone out of her pocket as she went.

Emmaline stood also. "I just need to visit the restroom, Kate. I'll be back in a moment." She, too, went in the direction of the stairs.

Well, thought Kate, *do I smell?* She grinned to herself, deciding that she might as well begin clearing away the tea tray. It wasn't as if she was a stranger to Emmaline's kitchen.

Picking up the tray, she backed through the door that led to the kitchen and set it on the counter beside the sink. As she turned on the water, put some soap in the dishpan, and began washing the dishes, she heard footsteps coming down the stairs.

The footsteps approached, and Kate heard a voice. It was Francie, apparently still on the phone. Then the footsteps halted just outside the kitchen door. Kate turned the water on more forcefully, so there was less opportunity for the conversation to be overheard. But Francie's voice carried, and Kate still could hear every word. She began to say something so that Francie would realize she wasn't alone, but then Francie's one-sided conversation became clear, and Kate closed her mouth.

"No, she hasn't told anyone here, I'm almost positive . . . I don't know if I should warn them or not. What do you think?"

So did Francie know that Emmaline's television wasn't tuned in to the same channel as most of the rest of the world's? Was she referring to warning folks about Emmaline's sudden illnesses, or was the warning about something else? It helped, somehow, to know that someone else recognized that Emmaline had problems.

"No, it's very nice. She could live here permanently if you don't want her to come back to live with us. But I don't know where else she'd go. And she doesn't want to stay here in Copper Mill . . . I know, honey. I'm not trying to push the decision off on you. But after all, you're the one who was hurt most by what she did . . . Well, of course it impacted my life too . . ."

Kate nearly dropped the teacup she had just picked up. It sounded very much as if Emmaline's sister, Francie, had a deciding role in whether Emmaline would return to Philadelphia. What could Emmaline possibly have done to make her own sister consider banishing her?

Kate plunged her hands into the dishwater just as the kitchen door swung open. Francie came into the kitchen.

"Oh my goodness," she exclaimed. "Here you're a guest, and we put you to work."

"Not a problem." Kate smiled as Francie picked up a dishtowel and began to dry plates. Kate debated with herself for a moment, then realized she might never have a better chance to get the answer to her question.

"Would it be rude of me to ask you how far apart you and your sister are in age?" Kate asked.

Francie chuckled. "Only if you ask Em. I'm the younger by thirteen years."

"Wow," Kate said. "So she was a teenager when you were born."

Francie nodded, her expression softening. "She was like my second mother. At least, she wanted to be. Our mother was very protective, and it seemed as if she spent a lot of time scolding Em for touching me or picking me up. By the time I was in school, Em had moved out, and we really didn't have a lot of contact until after Mom passed away when I was fifteen. Then Em stepped back into my life." She smiled. "For a while, we even lived next door to each other. Those were good days," she added as her smile faded.

Francie's sad expression nearly mirrored Emmaline's, Kate realized. Although Kate didn't sense the deep-seated loneliness that Emmaline seemed to wear like a second skin.

Just then, the door opened again.

"Oh, you shouldn't have!" Emmaline cried, rushing forward to take the dishcloth out of Kate's hands. "Here you are again, working. That just won't do, Kate." Emmaline babbled on and on in an animated tone about how happy she was to have two of her favorite people in one room.

It was too much for Kate. After the way Emmaline had behaved with Livvy and Paul, she was distinctly uncomfortable with being one of Emmaline's favorite people. She backed away and began to dry her hands.

"Em, I haven't had a chance to ask you how you've been feeling," Francie said, turning to her sister.

"I've been fine," Emmaline said abruptly. "And you don't have to worry. I'm perfectly well." She didn't look at Kate as she said this.

Kate stayed silent. What was going on here? Emmaline had *not* been perfectly well by any means. It was becoming clear that, as Kate had suspected earlier, Emmaline was indeed lying, either to her sister or to Kate. Kate suspected both. She intended to figure out exactly what the lie was, but the bigger question was *why* Emmaline was lying.

Was it simply embarrassment or shame? Kate could almost understand if this were the reason. But she strongly suspected something altogether different was going on.

Chapter Thirteen

At ten thirty on Saturday morning, Kate changed into a pair of silky olive pants and a warm beige twinset. She was meeting Livvy for lunch after doing some Internet research at the library, and she enjoyed the chance to put on a pretty outfit even though she and Livvy weren't going anyplace that required a particularly nice dress code.

After fastening on a beaded necklace, Kate slipped into a pair of comfortable beige pumps and transferred the contents of her handbag into one that matched the pumps. Then she headed for the library.

Livvy was busy. Kate slipped by her with a wink and a wave and went straight upstairs to the computers.

Quickly, she slid into one of the few empty seats and opened an Internet browser. Although she had done a search on "Emmaline Ashford" at home last week, she wanted to try it again on the faster, more powerful computers in case a link showed up that she hadn't seen before. And this time, she was going to try more specific sites.

First, she brought up the home page of the *Philadelphia Inquirer*. With Livvy's library code, she was able to gain access to the entire paper. She typed "Emmaline Ashford" into the search box and hit Enter.

A moment later, she saw she had gotten no results.

There were a few other options. She also searched on the *Daily News* and the *Philadelphia Inquirer*, both of which featured local news. But she found no news about one Emmaline Ashford. On a hunch, Kate ran a search for "Emmaline Ash," but she came up with the same results.

She sighed. She'd have to try being less specific. This time, she just searched for "Ashford" on the *Inquirer* site. If Emmaline's husband had indeed passed away, perhaps his obituary would be listed. Or perhaps she would get lucky, and something would have been posted recently about one of Emmaline's articles.

A few minutes later, she came up empty yet again. It was as if Emmaline didn't exist. Not a single mention at all, even for just "Ashford." It was hard to believe there were no Ashfords in Philadelphia. Perhaps they were all quiet and unnewsworthy people.

Sighing again, she gave up. It was time to meet Livvy for lunch, anyway.

Kate was just closing the Internet connection when she heard her name called. She turned to see Livvy walking toward her. Her sedate navy suit and accessories made her look every inch the librarian, particularly when one noticed the glasses pushed haphazardly atop her head and the pencil she'd obviously forgotten she'd tucked behind one ear.

Kate greeted her, then reached out and gently removed the pencil. "Here."

Livvy rolled her eyes, accepting the writing instrument and stashing it in her handbag. "Sheesh. You can't take me anywhere, can you?"

Kate laughed. "Ready to eat?"

"Famished!" Livvy tugged open the door and motioned to Kate to precede her.

They walked the short distance to the diner. Kate shared her excitement over the impending visit from Andrew and his family the very next day.

Moments later, the friends were seated at one of the blue vinyl booths along the wall.

"Afternoon, ladies," drawled LuAnne Matthews. The waitress was wearing a polyester dress and a white apron tied around her sturdy waist. Horn-rimmed glasses dangled from a jeweled chain around her neck until she snatched them up and perched them on her nose. "What can I get y'all today? Special's chicken-noodle soup and tuna salad on our tasty ol' homemade bread." She paused, her pencil hovering expectantly over the order pad in her hand.

"The special sounds good to me," Kate said. "And could I have hot tea?"

"Sure thing, honey," said LuAnne with a grin.

"Coffee for me," Livvy offered. "And the special works for me too, LuAnne."

LuAnne scribbled on her pad and then ripped the top sheet off with a flourish. "I'll be back faster'n a possum crossin' the road on a hot day!" She winked and then whisked away.

Kate and Livvy looked at each other and burst out laughing. "Now there's an image I won't forget," Livvy said. "So. Tell me what's going on with your new friend's drama."

"That's an excellent word for it." Then Kate said, "So let me tell you all the things she's told me—and some she hasn't."

She went on to enumerate the finding of the wig, the discovery of the sneakers, finding the hospital bracelets and the prescription medication bottle, and the existence of Emmaline's sister, Francie. She told Livvy about Emmaline's plea for silence when she arrived to visit the previous afternoon. Then she repeated the odd conversation she overheard between Francie and her husband. She sat back and crossed her arms when she had finished.

Livvy said, "Gracious! I agree, it does sound as if she's deliberately hiding something, doesn't it?"

"At this point, I'm positive that she is," Kate said. "Did I ever tell you what Dr. McLaughlin said to me?" She repeated her conversation with the physician in which he had insisted that she not worry about Emmaline. "He actually has a background in cardiac care," Kate said. "Since he told me not to worry, I'm fairly confident she isn't having significant heart trouble."

"He definitely implied that," Livvy said, putting her finger to her chin. "Plus, even if he's not an oncologist, would he have been so emphatic about you not worrying if she had cancer or any other life-threatening illness?"

"I don't think so," Kate said. Livvy had a great way of putting things into perspective. "So it's likely, in my opinion, that Emmaline doesn't have cancer or a serious heart condition."

"I agree," Livvy said. "The question is, what is *really* ailing this lady?"

Kate held up a finger. "For a while, I suspected she is having problems with anxiety, which could lead to panic attacks. But her symptoms don't closely resemble the ones most people with panic disorder suffer."

"Panic attacks." Livvy leaned back, nodding thoughtfully. "That could fit, though, couldn't it?"

"Especially if she's got hang-ups about anyone finding out. You know, thinking she's crazy."

Livvy was still nodding. "Could it be that simple?"

Kate snorted. "Somehow, I doubt it."

LuAnne came back with their hot drinks as well as glasses of ice water and utensils, and the talk turned to community and family concerns.

Later, after the two friends departed, Livvy turned to Kate on the sidewalk in front of the diner. "So, what are you going to investigate next on Emmaline? Every time I talk to you, something has changed. First it sounds like she has heart trouble, then you wonder if she could have cancer. Dr. McLaughlin acts decidedly odd. Now you suspect she might have an anxiety disorder. And it's possible the medication she takes for that could be causing the chest pain and shortness of breath. And the sister... What was that all about? What reason could she possibly have for refusing to let Emmaline come back to Philadelphia?"

"All great questions that I've been mulling over too," Kate said. "It sounded to me as if having Emmaline was causing problems for Francie and her husband in Pennsylvania." Kate thought back over the meal she and Paul had unwillingly shared with Emmaline at the Bristol. "And they would be justified not to want her living with them. I suspect she can be quite the agitator, although from what I heard, there may be something specific she did to cause significant harm."

"You think she's dangerous?" Livvy sounded worried.

"Not physically," Kate said. "But I wonder what kind of trouble she is capable of stirring up."

"Yikes! That's unsettling. So back to my question," Livvy said. "What next?"

Kate thought over her options. "I suppose the first thing I am going to have to do is confront her directly. I've been too polite. Every time we've talked about illness, I've allowed her to slip out of the conversation without giving me the truth. Next time, no evasions."

"No evasions." Livvy nodded her head once, short and sharp, for emphasis. "Good luck. And be careful, Kate. Emmaline Ashford doesn't sound like the most stable domino in the design."

To work off her lunch, Kate decided to take a walk.

She had an idea regarding her stained glass, and she wanted time to think it through before she closed herself into her studio again. Besides, she needed to work off a few pounds, and what better way was there than walking? She couldn't even imagine having the discipline to run like Paul.

As she walked along Smoky Mountain Road toward town, a car came over the hill in front of her and closed the gap. As it drew closer, the vehicle slowed. Kate stopped.

It was a midsize SUV that Kate instantly recognized as the vehicle parked in Emmaline's driveway during Francie's visit.

As the SUV halted, the window on the passenger side where she stood rolled down with a barely audible whir.

"Hello, Kate!" called Emmaline.

"Hi, Kate." Francie put on the flashers and waved from behind the wheel.

"Good afternoon," Kate said. "You picked a beautiful day for a drive."

"We've been exploring," Emmaline said. "When we were little, we used to come down here and stay with Grandma for two weeks every summer. It's interesting to see what's changed and what hasn't."

"Have you found it very different?"

Emmaline hesitated. "Yes and no. There's not as much development as we had feared, but stores have gone out of business. Old homes are gone, and new ones have been built on the same spots."

"How about you, Francie? Has Copper Mill changed very much from the town you used to visit when you were a child?" Kate leaned down a bit so she could see the driver.

"No." Francie made a face. "It's little," and they all laughed.

"You can say that again," Kate said.

"I'll be thankful when I can go back to Philadelphia," Emmaline said. "I don't think I'm cut out for small-town life."

Just then, Kate saw Francie lean across the seat and tug at Emmaline's sleeve. She said something in an undertone, but Kate still caught the comment.

"You have several more months here, you know."

Kate acted as if she was unaware of the tension between the sisters, although she was saddened to see Emmaline deflate as thoroughly as a Thanksgiving balloon after the Macy's Parade. What on earth could the cryptic comment mean?

"Well," said Francie, leaning toward Emmaline's side once again. "I had better say good-bye now. I'm leaving as soon as we get back to the house to drive back to the airport."

"It was nice meeting you," Kate said. "Have a safe trip home, and please come and visit Copper Mill again."

"Will do. Good-bye!"

"Good-bye." To Emmaline, Kate said, "Don't forget our spa date. I'll pick you up in a little while, all right?"

"All right. I'll see you then." It was nearly a whisper.

Emmaline gave Kate a wave as they drove off, but Kate noticed her friend had barely said a word since her sister had admonished her.

She wondered if Emmaline was disappointed that Francie wasn't staying longer. But even more, she wondered what was going on that necessitated Emmaline staying away from Philadelphia when she obviously longed to return to the city she called home.

AFTER SPENDING about an hour working in her studio, Kate decided to arrive a little early at Emmaline's house for the spa appointment. She figured she needed the element of surprise to keep Emmaline off balance, to get her to answer her questions honestly without having time to formulate answers. She'd witnessed Emmaline lying to Francie about her health, and she strongly suspected that Emmaline had also been lying to her, although separating truth from lies had been difficult because Emmaline shared so little information. She intended to correct that.

Kate pulled into Emmaline's driveway about thirty minutes before they needed to leave for the spa. She hoped that

would be long enough to get them started on their discussion
if Emmaline would answer Kate's questions without any evasions or diversionary tactics.

She was surprised to see another car in the driveway, so she
pulled her Honda alongside the curb. Who might Emmaline
know in the area who drove a dark green Mercedes?

The moment she stepped out of her car, she found the
answer: Dr. McLaughlin came striding down Emmaline's
walk directly toward her.

He wore casual clothes—khaki pants with a white shirt,
a brown suede bomber-style jacket, and shiny loafers. He
stopped short when he saw her, clearly dismayed.

"Hello, Dr. McLaughlin," Kate said, completely shocked to
see him at Emmaline's house. Still, she stood squarely in the
middle of the sidewalk. She had made up her mind to have
this chat with Emmaline today, and he could just answer her
questions too. She was in no mood for evasion. From anyone.

"Hello, Kate. Beautiful day, isn't it?"

"It certainly is." Kate relaxed her shoulders and tossed in
a little extra Southern belle attitude for good measure. "What
are you doing in these parts, Dr. McLaughlin?"

"I stopped to visit Ms. Ashford." He squared his shoulders
when Kate only stared at him with raised eyebrows. "You
know I can't discuss more than that with you."

"Oh, so it wasn't a social call." If he was worried about
doctor-patient privilege, then he must have been there in an
official capacity.

"Uh, no. No, it wasn't."

"So, you were here as her physician."

It wasn't a question, and he looked chagrined, realizing he had just been outmaneuvered. "I'm not her primary physician, no."

"Listen, doctor. I've been very concerned about Emmaline," Kate told him. "She seems to have more potential illnesses than an entire wing of the Pine Ridge Hospital. And she doesn't seem happy with her medical care."

The doctor stared at her. Finally, he said, "Perception is often different from reality."

Kate stared at him. "Meaning?"

"Nothing. I can't tell you anything, Kate. I'm not saying another word." The physician clamped his lips shut, making an emphatic gesture.

"All right . . . okay," Kate said, abandoning her plans to not let him pass. She stood back and let him stride past her to his car.

So much for Mrs. Tough Girl. She hoped she could better maintain her stance with Emmaline.

The doctor reached the car and opened the driver's side door. Then, with one leg already in the car, he paused. "Kate? Be careful, okay?"

She was taken aback. "Careful about what?"

Her first instinct was to assume he was warning her about disease, as if perhaps Emmaline had something communicable. Then she stopped and thought about it. Could he be referring to Emmaline's unpredictable personality? The idea gave Kate a little chill.

"Just be careful," he repeated. At that, he slid the rest of the way into his car and slammed the door.

Chapter Fourteen

Kate stood watching as Dr. McLaughlin backed out of Emmaline's driveway. He gave her one brief wave as he drove away. Thoughtfully, she turned and started up the walk again.

A motion at one window caught her eye. Had the curtain twitched? She wondered if Emmaline had been standing there watching her speak with the doctor. She mentally braced herself. Only one way to find out.

Stepping onto the small porch stoop, Kate pressed the doorbell firmly.

After a moment, the door opened. Emmaline stood there, an icy expression on her face.

Kate's heart sank. So she'd been right; Emmaline had seen them. Taking a deep breath, she said, "Good afternoon! I'm a little early. Are you ready for our big treat?"

Emmaline frowned, and Kate read anger in her gaze. "You are indeed a little early. I saw you chatting with that man. What did he tell you?"

"Nothing personal," Kate assured her. "Dr. McLaughlin is very discreet about his patients."

"Ha!" Emmaline burst out. "If he was discreet, he wouldn't be coming here unannounced and uninvited, would he? If he was discreet, you never would have seen him, would you? He's harassing me, that's what he's doing! I told him he's not my doctor, and my life is none of his business. He had no reason to come here!"

The tirade had a vitriolic edge that shocked Kate. The doctor's words echoed in her head. *Be careful, okay?*

"Are you sure he's not just concerned about you?" she asked.

"He has no right!" Emmaline nearly yelled the words. "No right at all. He's *not* my doctor."

"All right." Kate put out a hand as if she might calm the distressed woman that way.

"I'll sue him," Emmaline said, her voice rising. "That's what I'll do. I'll take him for every penny he's worth. He'll never spread lies about a patient again."

"Emmaline!" Kate put a sharp edge into her tone as she raised her volume significantly. "Please stop!"

There was a shocked silence. Emmaline's hands flew to her mouth; she stared at Kate with tears welling in her eyes.

Kate slipped an arm about Emmaline's waist and turned her into the house. "Let's take a deep breath," she advised. "I'll call and cancel the spa appointment and we can talk—"

"No." Emmaline sounded pleading. "Please don't cancel. I was so looking forward to it. I'm sorry, Kate. I don't know what got into me."

"Are you sure?" Kate was doubtful.

"Positive." Emmaline took a deep breath, plastering a shaky smile on her lips. "Let's just go and have a good time."

Kate didn't want to go and have a good time. But after that alarming display of near hysteria, the last thing she wanted to do was trigger another tantrum. "All right," she said reluctantly.

"Good." Emmaline seemed much calmer. "Just let me get my purse."

Kate waited while the other woman retrieved her handbag and locked the door. They walked to Kate's car together. They were going to be a little early at the spa, but that didn't matter.

As Emmaline rounded the car to get to the passenger side, she exclaimed, "This is going to be so much fun!"

Kate said nothing. She felt as if she was accompanied by Dr. Jekyll and Mr. Hyde. At the moment, Dr. Jekyll was calmly seating herself beside Kate. But not long ago, the crazed Mr. Hyde had clearly been in control.

Again, she thought of Dr. McLaughlin's oblique warning. What had he meant? Kate knew that she had to be careful in terms of becoming too close a friend to Emmaline, but surely the doctor had no knowledge of the jealous behaviors that had cropped up at times.

And could she even trust him? Wasn't it unorthodox for a doctor to make an unannounced house call? And what did Emmaline mean that the doctor was "spreading lies"?

Uneasily, Kate decided again that she had better not say or do anything to upset Emmaline's precarious good humor. It seemed that her determination to get some answers was going to have to wait a bit, and she would have to figure out another time and possibly another way to confront Emmaline with her suspicions. Kate let out a long breath, realizing that sometimes even the best-laid plans had to be rearranged.

WHEN PAUL BEGAN HIS SERMON the following morning, he glanced at Kate immediately, hoping to catch her reaction. Often, when he started his sermon preparation at the beginning of the week, Paul bounced his ideas off Kate. Not only did it help him clarify his ideas, but Kate frequently contributed something meaningful that changed or cemented the direction of his thoughts.

But this week, Paul hadn't talked to her at all about the topic of his sermon: "Do You Keep Your Faith in Shape?" It was the second in "The Five G's of Discipleship" series that he had begun the previous Sunday. The first sermon had been about grace; this week's sermon was about growth—purposeful Christian growth.

"As many of you know," Paul began, "Eli Weston talked me into training to run a 10K marathon to benefit the American Heart Association. I wasn't sure I could do it. I'm a lightweight runner. My regimen is usually no more than three miles, tops. A 10K is more than six miles, easily double what I believe I can do.

"And that's exactly how I approached my training. I wasn't sure I could do it. So when I began to train, my attitude was more of the 'I'll try this and quit if it's too tough' variety than the 'I intend to work up to this until I can do it' kind."

He caught Kate's eye as he surveyed the congregation. She winked, warming him inside.

"Race running, when it comes right down to it, is a pretty

good comparison to our training efforts toward achieving our eternal reward in heaven," Paul said.

From there, he segued into a reflection on how his training for the race approximated the ongoing growth of his own faith. He couldn't skip training sessions if he wished to be a success with his running. He likened that to being a Christian and the practice of prayer, Bible study, and service in God's name. If one skips the "training," one gets "out of shape," and it becomes more difficult to begin again. He went on to explain how exploring a relationship with God has its ups and downs just like any training routine.

Paul wrapped up the sermon by reminding the congregation that everyone is a work in progress, and to not forget the first G of discipleship when training for the race: grace.

After the service, he received a great many compliments and observations on his words. The accolades were pleasant, but what he really prayed was that he had moved people to speak and think and reflect. What more could a pastor wish for than to motivate his congregants to seek God's will actively?

KATE BAKED ALL AFTERNOON. She had tons of nervous energy jumping around inside her, and she expected it would keep jumping until Andrew pulled the family's rental car into the driveway.

Her counters were laden with four loaves of cinnamon-raisin bread and two more each of her pumpkin and apple pies. With these apple pies, she took special care, cutting decorative teardrop-shaped holes in the top of each crust to release the steam.

Just as she took the pumpkin pies out, there was a knock

at the door. Paul was out on bereavement call, so she quickly set the pies on raised racks and hurried to the door.

To her surprise, Emmaline stood there.

"Well, hello," Kate said. Her heart sank. Sunday was supposed to be a day of rest, and dealing with Emmaline had ceased to be restful some time ago. "I didn't expect to see you today."

Emmaline shrugged. "You drop in on me. I didn't realize it would be a problem."

"It's not," Kate hastened to assure her, wondering if her expression had given away her thoughts. "Please come into the kitchen. I've been baking. Would you like a slice of pumpkin pie and a cup of tea?"

"I'd love some," Emmaline said. As they rounded the corner into the kitchen, she said, "Goodness! You've been busy. Who is all this for?"

"Most of it's for the Faith Freezer program," Kate told her. "And a little for family."

"Goodness," Emmaline said again. She held up a sketch pad. "Remember the iris sketch I started after seeing your iris panel?"

Kate nodded as she took down a mug from the cupboard.

"Well, I had a brainstorm." She crossed the room to the kitchen table and flipped the pages of the sketch pad. "I thought it would be nice to do a seasonal set. Irises in spring, maybe a sunflower for the summer one, for autumn maybe a chrysanthemum or an aster, and for the winter, either poinsettia or holly. Wouldn't that be striking?"

Kate nodded. "It sounds lovely. What colors would you use?"

The two women began to discuss the pieces in earnest as Emmaline's fingers flew, adding detail to the sketches and jotting down notes for color. Kate started working on dinner while she talked.

Then Emmaline said, "I'd like to commission you to do these in stained glass, Kate. The iris panel should be easy, since you've already done your own, which wouldn't be too dissimilar. What do you think?"

Kate stared at her friend, nonplussed. "I-I don't know, Emmaline. I'd have to think about it."

"I'm certain you could do it," Emmaline said urgently. "Please, Kate? It would mean a lot to me. I'd pay you well."

Kate wondered at this statement. How could the woman afford to make such an extravagant offer when clearly her medical bills were piling up?

Just then, she heard a car door slam. Paul was home, she thought with a surge of relief.

"Excuse me," she said to Emmaline as she went to meet him at the door. "It's Paul."

"I smell pie," Paul said, inhaling an exaggerated breath as he walked in through the front door. As Kate approached, he slid an arm around her waist for a kiss. "*Mmm-mmm.* Smells delicious, Katie."

"I have a guest in the kitchen," Kate whispered, smiling up at him. Louder, she said, "Thank you. But you still can't have any pie." Then she stepped away from him.

As she turned to lead him into the kitchen, she stopped abruptly. Emmaline was standing not ten feet away in the large living room.

"Paul, you know Emmaline. She dropped by to visit for a few minutes."

"Hello, Emmaline," Paul said. "It's nice to see you again."

"You too." But Emmaline's voice was tight. Why did she always behave so curtly with Kate's husband?

Paul pulled off his suit jacket. "Ah, what a long day."

"How was the visit with the Davies?" Kate asked. To Emmaline, she said, "Paul was with a family who lost their dad and granddad today."

The old man who had passed away, Harold Davies, had gone suddenly in his sleep during the night on Saturday, and the family had called Paul right after church. It had been something of a shock for the Davies family, since Harold had been in good health, even at eighty-three years of age.

"The family is doing all right," Paul responded. "Grieving, of course, but the general feeling is that he had a good life, and this is how he would have wanted it."

"Well, it's surely a blessing that he passed so peacefully. But let's focus on some happy thoughts now," Kate said. "It's only a few hours until Andrew and his family arrive."

"I know." Paul grinned. "I bet the kids have grown a foot." He headed for the bedroom. "I'm going to change my clothes."

Kate turned to glance at Emmaline, who had been silent but now was breathing heavily. The woman put her hand on her heart.

"Emmaline, are you okay?" To Kate's dismay, Emmaline had tears in her eyes.

Emmaline abruptly returned to the kitchen and gathered her sketch pad, her handbag, and her jacket. "I'm fine. I have to go."

"But . . . you look upset," Kate persisted.

"I'm fine." Her voice was brusque. She started for the door. "I have to go." Halfway across the room, she stopped.

Without turning around, she said, "I really want you to do those panels, Kate."

Kate frowned. That had sounded more like an order. "I can't make any promises. I'll let you know in a few days."

"Why not tomorrow?" There was a belligerence in Emmaline's tone that, unfortunately, Kate was coming to know all too well.

"My son, Andrew, and his family are arriving in a little while," Kate reminded her. "I'll be too busy to think about much of anything until they leave on Wednesday."

"Oh, all right." With poor grace, Emmaline grabbed the door handle and pulled the door wide. "I'll talk to you soon, I guess."

"I . . . All right." Kate didn't want to offend Emmaline, but it appeared the only thing that made Emmaline happy was Kate's undivided attention. "I'll call you in a couple of days."

Emmaline closed the door with what Kate thought was unnecessary force as she left.

A moment later, Paul returned. "Did Emmaline leave?"

"Yes," said Kate in a tone that didn't disguise her relief.

"Is she being difficult?" Paul asked.

Kate snorted. "Difficult, no. Impossible, definitely yes."

Paul sighed. "That bad, huh?"

"Well . . ." Kate felt bad about her exasperation. "She just seems so unhappy."

"This friendship has turned into something of a burden for you," Paul said regretfully.

"In some ways." Kate didn't know what else to say, so she just replied, "Why don't you set the table? Dinner's nearly ready."

She had prepared a grilled fish fillet, lightly breaded

zucchini slices, and some of her homemade applesauce. Even though Paul was the one who had requested additional fish dishes after Eli suggested a special prerace diet, he made a joking complaint about the lack of cholesterol. But Kate noticed he appeared to savor every bite.

After eating, they cleaned up the kitchen, and then Kate took one last tour through the house to be sure everything was neat and clean. Not that it would stay that way for long with four extra people living there for several days.

She smiled wistfully. She wouldn't mind cleaning every day if only the kids could stay longer. Sometimes it was difficult living so far from their family, although Tennessee was quite a bit closer than San Antonio had been. And Atlanta, where their middle child, Melissa, her husband, John, and their daughter, Mia, lived, wasn't even five hours away. An easy drive compared to visiting Andrew in Philadelphia or Rebecca up in New York City.

She prayed a long, silent prayer, thanking God for her precious children and for the upcoming visit with her son and his family.

As if on cue, she heard the sound of tires crunching on the driveway.

"They're here!" Kate and Paul both rushed for the door.

Andrew, his wife, Rachel, and their children, Ethan and Hannah, spilled out of the van, stretching. The children rushed toward Paul and Kate, and chaos ensued, everyone talking and hugging at once.

Andrew went around to the trunk of the rental vehicle and pulled out their suitcases, which he and Paul took into the house with the children's exuberant assistance. Kate and

Rachel followed, arm in arm. Oh, they had so much to catch up on!

"SO, MOM," Andrew said sometime later, after the children had been put to bed on air mattresses on the floor next to the sofa bed in Paul's study, "what kind of mystery are you embroiled in now?"

After moving to Copper Mill, Kate had helped figure out so many mysterious goings-on that people now came to her on purpose when they had a problem or mystery to solve. Paul sometimes said she was rather like a free private-detective service.

Kate filled in the details about Emmaline's unexpected collapse in the Bristol and her own subsequent unsuccessful quest to learn the truth about the woman.

After Kate finished the long story, Rachel's eyes looked troubled. Hesitantly, she said, "But if she doesn't want anyone to know what's wrong, shouldn't you respect that? I'm just trying to see things through her eyes," she added hastily.

"I understand," Kate said. And she did. Her daughter-in-law was an exceptionally sensitive and thoughtful girl. Kate paused. How could she articulate the feeling she had about Emmaline? "I'm not just pursuing this because I want to know what's wrong with her. I sense that she is very troubled emotionally and spiritually by something other than an illness. When I say spiritually, I don't mean in terms of a relationship with God because, unfortunately, she doesn't appear to have one. But she is very troubled, and I sense something in her reaching out for help, even though she can't say it and may not even acknowledge it."

Chapter Fifteen

K ate arose at her usual early time in the morning. As the days grew shorter and winter approached, it was quite dark until well after six, and she had the quiet house to herself while she began her day with prayer and Bible reading.

Just as she finished, Paul and Andrew staggered blearily out into the living room. Paul was completely dressed.

Andrew had his sneakers in his hand. While Paul waited, Andrew sat down on the floor and put them on. "Ready?" he asked his father.

Paul nodded. "Anytime."

"All right." Andrew yawned hugely as he got to his feet. He came to Kate's side and bent, kissing her cheek. "Morning, Mom."

"Good morning," Kate said softly. What a delight it was to see her son first thing in the morning.

Andrew said, "I want it on the record that I made this sacrifice for my father, despite the fact that I am on vacation. I could be snuggled happily in my warm bed for another hour, but no, I play the part of a dutiful son and accompany my father on a training run. I was really looking forward to skipping my runs for a couple of mornings."

"Slacker," Paul said, grinning.

"Slave driver." Andrew punched him in the shoulder as the two men went out the door, leaving Kate smiling after them.

THE MEN WERE BACK shortly before eight. Paul rushed off to get a shower, and then came to the kitchen still knotting his tie. Kate made silver-dollar pancakes and heated maple syrup for breakfast. Andrew joined Paul at the table. Rachel was sleeping in, Andrew explained, and Ethan and Hannah wouldn't be up before nine unless they were awakened.

Kate hadn't eaten earlier, and her stomach let her know that it was *not* okay to wait for a meal more than two hours after rising.

She sat down at the table with Paul and Andrew after pouring juice and coffee. The three of them clasped hands, and Paul offered a heartfelt prayer, thanking God for the safe arrival of his son and family, whom he'd missed very much. Kate and Andrew echoed "Amen," and then they picked up their forks.

"Thanks, Dad," Andrew said, and Kate was surprised to see the faintest glimmer of tears in his eyes. "It's good to be here."

Paul nodded, gazing into his son's eyes. "It's good to have you here," he responded.

The talk at the table was family-oriented. Kate caught Andrew up on his sisters' lives, and then Andrew shared stories about his children's recent doings. Ethan was playing soccer; his team was the only undefeated team in its league, and Andrew had several stories about the matches they had won. Hannah wanted a dog, Kate knew from their telephone conversations, but Andrew explained that it had to be a black dog with a white spot on its chest. And its name was going to be Banksie.

Kate and Paul said, "Banksie?" in unison, and Andrew laughed.

"That's exactly what Rachel and I said. I have no idea why. When we ask her about it, she just says she likes the name."

Soon afterward, Paul rose from the table and carried his dishes to the sink. "Thanks for running with me today," he said to his son. "You're welcome to join Eli and me tomorrow."

"I don't know, Dad," Andrew replied. "You made me look bad today."

Paul chuckled. "That is highly debatable." He came around the table and bent down to kiss Kate on the cheek. "See you this afternoon," he told them both.

"Have a good day," Kate replied as he headed out the door. The moment the door closed behind her husband, Kate turned to Andrew. "So, tell me, how is he *really* doing with the running?"

Andrew hesitated. "It seems to me he's doing pretty well. I mean, he didn't have any trouble keeping up with Eli, and he did everything Eli suggested or asked him to try. But I'm no marathon runner, Mom, so I couldn't say for sure. Why?"

"Just checking," Kate told her son. "Until recently, he was concerned that he's not going to make it . . . that he's not in good enough shape."

Andrew's eyebrows rose. "I don't think there's any danger. He's in amazing shape and he's running really well."

Kate nodded in satisfaction. "Good."

"If anything," Andrew went on, "I got the sense there was a bit of competition involved. Not from Eli as much as Dad."

"Competition!" Kate's mouth fell open. "He's supposed to be doing this for charity, not as a way to proclaim his youth and fitness."

Andrew began to laugh. "Can I listen when you tell him that?"

LATER IN THE MORNING, the telephone rang as Kate was playing a game of Parcheesi with her grandchildren, who turned out to be a pair of übercompetitors themselves. They came by it honestly, she thought.

"Hold on a sec," she said to the kids. "Nobody rolls until I get off that telephone." She reached for the receiver as the children giggled. "Hello?"

"Katie, I think we have a problem."

Kate's heart nearly stopped. "Paul, what's wrong?"

There was a silence on the other end of the phone. "I think you'd better come over to the church when you get a chance." His voice was very serious.

"Now? Are you all right?" Her heartbeat picked up as concern rose.

"I'm fine," Paul said. "Honest. But I do need you to come over here. It won't take long."

When Kate hung up the telephone, her grandchildren were regarding her expectantly. "Come on, Grandma, it's your turn!" called Hannah. "Ethan just sent you home again."

Kate groaned. "It'll take me forever to roll another two or five."

"Sorry, Grandma." But Ethan didn't sound sorry at all, and he was grinning.

Kate laughed. Then she said, "I'm going to have to find a substitute. Your grandfather needs me at the church."

"Right now?" Ethan asked in disappointment.

Kate nodded. "Sorry, buddy. We can play again later if you like." She stuck her head into the living room, where Rachel was curled up in the big overstuffed chair with a book. "I hate to interrupt, but Paul needs me at the church. Could you take my place in the Parcheesi game?"

Rachel groaned. "Do you care who wins?"

Kate's eyebrows rose. "I take it the correct answer is no?"

Rachel smiled as she got to her feet. "I can't remember the last time I won a Parcheesi game when I played with those two." As she passed Kate on her way into the kitchen, she gave her mother-in-law a hug. "You are going to owe me so big."

Kate laughed as she grabbed her handbag and a jacket. "Shoe shopping, darling girl, next time I come up to your city. Just you and me. And that's a promise."

It only took her a couple of minutes to reach the church. She parked the Honda and went straight to the office.

"Hi, Millie," she said to the secretary. "Paul's in his office?"

"Yeah, and he's got a trustees' meeting in thirty-five minutes," Millie warned in her scratchy voice that sounded as if she'd been puffing on cigarettes for years.

"I won't be long," Kate said, hoping she wasn't fibbing. She went into Paul's office. It reminded her of a cozy den, with walls of bookshelves and toasty cocoa paint. It was perfect for Paul.

He was sitting behind his desk, and he looked up when she walked in. "Hey," he said.

"Hey. What's going on?" She hadn't seen him smile, hadn't noticed even a glimmer of amusement or humor in his warm blue eyes. "Are you all right?"

"Yes," he said slowly. "But there's something here you need to see." He got up and walked out from behind his desk, proffering a plain white envelope.

Kate took the envelope and sank into a chair opposite the desk as Paul leaned a hip against it. "What's this?" She opened the flap and pulled out a single sheet of paper. Quickly, she skimmed the printed message, reading out loud:

Reverend Hanlon,

> *If you love your wife, you must see how much potential she has as an artist. She needs time to pursue her passion. At the moment, her energies are far too focused on caring for your church and your congregation. That is your job, not hers, and you should not continue to monopolize her time with the inconsequential matters your position creates.*

"Paul," Kate said, outraged, "you know who wrote this, don't you?"

Paul nodded. "Just as well as you know."

Kate leaped to her feet. "I'm going over there right now and—"

"No," Paul said, grabbing her hand when she would have

flown out of the office. "I don't think that's a good idea, Katie."

Kate flopped back down in the chair she had just vacated as her husband's calm demeanor recalled her to her senses. "Oh, Paul, what am I going to do?"

"I could tell that Emmaline felt very entitled to your company," Paul said soberly. "But I didn't realize she felt quite so . . . obsessed with you. That's what it is, Kate." He flicked a finger against the envelope Kate had tossed onto a nearby table.

"Do you think she's dangerous?" Kate's insides had begun to quiver as the reality of the ugly letter sank in. Emmaline had sent that note to Kate's husband, the love of her life for almost thirty years. Was Emmaline mentally disturbed? The short answer: yes. Undoubtedly. Could she prove it? Probably not.

Paul regarded the letter. "I don't know if she's dangerous." He shrugged. "I hope not. I want to believe she's just sad, that's all. Maybe I'm naive."

"But I love you that way." Kate stood and came over, wrapping her arms around Paul's waist. He smoothed her hair, and they stood silently, drawing comfort from each other. After a time, she asked again, "What am I going to do?"

"What are *we* going to do?" Paul corrected. "We're a team. Never forget it."

Kate smiled as she leaned against his shoulder. "Thank you for reminding me."

"I think we should ignore it," Paul said.

She drew back and looked up at him. "Really? Because I was thinking of contacting the police."

Paul nodded seriously. "I understand your concern. But Kate, read the letter again. There's no threat voiced, no threat implied. It's a lecture. Delivered in rude, unkind language, it's true, but that's not illegal."

Kate fell silent again, looking away. Technically, he was correct, but it didn't make her feel any less angry and violated, any less protective of the wonderful, beautiful person with whom she was lucky enough to share her life.

It took a great effort for her to consciously begin to release the knot of emotion in her chest. Many . . . deep . . . breaths.

Finally, she looked up at Paul again. "Would you like to offer a prayer for Emmaline?"

"I think it's the very best thing we can do," he said.

Chapter Sixteen

Later Monday afternoon, Kate, Rachel, and the kids made cookies, which Ethan and Hannah had great fun decorating with icing and colored sugars. Paul took Andrew for a drive around the area to tour some of the historical sites and the beautiful geographic features that this mountainous part of Tennessee boasted.

By four o'clock, all the cookies were gaily decorated. The men had come back and were outside playing tag with the children while Kate and Rachel washed and dried all the kitchenware they had used in their baking efforts.

When they finished, Kate tugged on the last of her paper towels to wipe down the counter, table, and chairs. Then she grabbed a tube of hand lotion she kept near the sink and shared some with Rachel.

"Doing dishes always dries out my skin," she said.

"I mind it most in the winter." Rachel accepted the tube with thanks. She squeezed it several times, each squirt only producing small drops of lotion onto Rachel's hand. "Looks like we're cleaning you out of house and home, Mom. First the paper towels, then the lotion . . ."

"Oh, that's all right," Kate said. "I'd have you loot the entire house if it meant more time with you."

Rachel smiled wide and hugged her mother-in-law. "I love spending time with you too," she said. Then she reached back to put her hair in a ponytail, but before she was finished, her hair band snapped.

"It's not my day," Rachel said, laughing.

"It might be," Kate joked. "Maybe I'll run to the store—"

Just then, Andrew came in. "Water," he said, gasping for air. "I'm too old to play tag."

Kate laughed. "If you're worn out, I wonder how your dad feels."

"Oh, he's going strong," Andrew said. "That 10K training must be doing something for him, even if he doesn't feel like he's ready to run six miles."

Rachel and Kate laughed.

Rachel said, "I'll go out and replace you for a while."

"Thank you, my gorgeous, kindhearted wife," Andrew said. He picked up Rachel's hand and kissed it as she moved past him.

Rachel giggled. "Silly man. I expect diamonds for this, not just compliments."

Andrew snorted as Rachel went through the door. "Diamonds. Right."

"She'd probably settle for a new hair band," Kate told him. "I'm going to the Mercantile in a bit to get that and a few other things. Would you like to come along?"

"Sure." He fell silent.

When Kate glanced up, she saw that he had picked up the Philadelphia paper she had brought home from Old Man Parsons'.

"Rereading the news?" she asked with a smile.

Andrew looked up and grinned. "Yeah. Actually, I know one of the partners in the insurance firm that got scammed by this guy. It was a real shame."

"Insurance fraud?" Kate had insurance on the brain because of Emmaline's lack of it. "What did the guy do?"

"In this case, he overcharged the insurance company," Andrew explained.

"How did he do it?" Kate asked.

"He was engaged to a girl who worked in billing at the insurance company. He pretended to get sick and came into the ER. He was examined and released. Then his girlfriend changed the amounts due on the invoices, so the insurance company overpaid the hospital significantly for the guy's ER visit. So the hospital turned around and sent the extra to the guy, because—get this—he called the hospital billing office and told them he had paid the claim and needed to be reimbursed. I bet some heads rolled on *that* billing staff!"

OUTSIDE THE MERCANTILE, Andrew sauntered along at Kate's side. Tall like his father, he took far fewer steps than Kate did to get to the same destination. As they walked into the store, Kate waved at Sam Gorman, who looked busy stocking the candy bins.

Kate grabbed a basket and gave it to Andrew to carry. In

short order, she filled it with paper towels, milk, more eggs, some brown sugar for a new batch of cookies she planned, and string cheese for the grandchildren. Then she went to the health-and-beauty-products section to get hand cream and hair bands.

"Whoa, Mom," Andrew complained, smiling. "Didn't realize I was a pack mule."

Kate grinned. She was about to reply when a familiar figure passed the end of the aisle in front of them from left to right, then vanished.

Kate felt her hackles rise. That was Emmaline, she was certain. Thinking of Emmaline's supposed illness and her ill temper, and the kindnesses Kate had showered on her, had Kate fighting to conquer her anger. Funny, but she would have found a slight or hurt directed at her easier to forgive than one directed at Paul. She sent up a fervent prayer, asking God for the grace to work on forgiving Emmaline and the mercy to treat her kindly.

"Mom? You okay?" Andrew's voice held concern. "You look like you could chew nails."

"Sorry," she said, "just thinking of something unpleasant."

She forced herself to continue shopping at her normal pace. Sooner or later, she knew, they would run into Emmaline.

It was sooner.

In the very next aisle, Kate heard her name called with delight.

"Kate! Hello, hello, how are you?"

Be as kind as you can. She took a deep breath and smiled. "It's been wonderful having my son and his family with us."

She laid a hand on Andrew's arm. "Emmaline, this is my son, Andrew. Andrew, Emmaline Ashford."

"It's nice to meet you," Andrew said, extending his hand and shaking Emmaline's.

"It's nice to meet you also," Emmaline responded conventionally. "How much longer will you be staying? I know Kate told me, but I've forgotten."

"We leave on Wednesday," Andrew said. "The kids have to be back in school on Thursday."

"You two have something in common," said Kate. She was having trouble looking Emmaline in the eye, but she forced herself to smile. *Let go of the anger,* she reminded herself. *You only hurt yourself when you nurse a grudge.*

"What's that?" Emmaline asked.

"You're both from Philadelphia."

The effect this had on Emmaline was fascinating. She turned white, then red. "How interesting," she said faintly.

"I thought so. Andrew, Emmaline just moved here a few months ago. She still has a sister living in Philly."

"Oh, really? Where did you live?"

"Chestnut Hill." Emmaline's voice sounded strained to Kate.

"Really? That's where we live! Where—"

"The house I live in now belonged to my grandmother," Emmaline broke in with the usual absence of social grace. "She passed away early this year, and we decided to keep the house for a while. I moved down here, and I can't tell you how delightful this little town is, although I would love to go home," she said, her voice tapering to a near whisper. Then she perked up again. "Your mother has been so kind."

Andrew put an arm around Kate's shoulders and squeezed gently. "She's always been good at the welcoming thing. It's part of being a pastor's wife."

"And did you inherit that trait?" Emmaline appeared to be regaining her composure.

Andrew laughed. "I suppose I must have, since my wife always has to drag me away from every conversation."

They spoke generally about Copper Mill for a few moments, then Kate said, "We must be going. The children are waiting to trounce Grandma at Parcheesi again." She thanked God for the touch of civility she was able to pull off.

Emmaline smiled. "Sounds like fun."

There was an awkward silence. Kate realized that Emmaline was hoping for an invitation. She said nothing.

Finally, Emmaline said, "I must be going too. Kate, would you like to get together this week? I've done another fleshed-out sketch in my flower series that I'd like to show you."

"No thank you." Kate didn't sugarcoat it or make excuses. She wanted Emmaline to understand that she knew exactly who had left that horrid note for Paul.

Emmaline's eyes widened just the slightest bit. Kate saw realization dawn. Turning on her heel, Kate said, "Good-bye," and Andrew followed after her.

A FEW MINUTES after leaving the Mercantile, they were on their way back to the little ranch house on Smoky Mountain Road when Andrew said, "Mom, I get the impression that Emmaline rubs you the wrong way. You're not usually that abrupt with folks."

Kate nodded. "That's true, I'm not. And yes, she has gotten under my skin a little."

"How?"

Kate shrugged. "It's too much to get into. She's just been frustrating."

"I think she looked familiar."

"What?" Kate turned to look at him as she considered that for a moment. "Well," she finally said, "she lived in your neighborhood, didn't she? Maybe you saw her there."

Andrew chuckled. "Mom, Chestnut Hill isn't a neighborhood; it's a small city. Nearly twenty thousand people live there."

"Oh." Kate had known Andrew's address was Chestnut Hill, Pennsylvania. She realized she should have known it wasn't just a small community of a few blocks. But since moving to Copper Mill, she had begun to find small towns just the right size. "She looks familiar, huh? In what way?"

Andrew said, "It's not coming to me how I know her, but maybe I'll remember later."

ON TUESDAY, Paul suggested a "field trip." None of Andrew's family had ever been to the Tennessee Aquarium down in Chattanooga. The children immediately were excited.

The aquarium was a huge hit. They spent long periods of time watching the penguins and the river otters. Both creatures had unique, extremely funny behaviors that entranced the children. Ethan especially liked the sharks; he stared at them so long that his face slowly morphed into an imitation of a shark's snarl.

The children loved the sea horses, with their odd motions and long prehensile tails that often appeared to have minds of their own. The interactive "Finding Nemo" activity also kept the children entertained as they moved through the aquarium.

Paul, Andrew, and Ethan were fascinated by the wall of sinuous moray eels lurking in caves and holes. Predictably, the women wanted to move past it, fast.

"Those things are scary," Hannah said.

"They creep me out too, honey," said her mother.

"You know, this reminds me," Andrew said, turning to Kate as though a lightbulb had switched on. "I'm certain I've seen your friend Emmaline, or at least her identical twin, before. I think it might have been in the newspaper, but I can't remember when."

Rachel looked taken aback. "Moray eels made you think of Kate's friend? I'd like to meet her."

Andrew laughed. "I was looking at the eels," he said defensively, "and I thought of an article I read about them in the paper. And then I thought of your friend, Mom, and I'm pretty sure it's because I associate her with someone I saw in the news."

Rachel rolled her eyes. "He's always seeing familiar faces he can't quite place in the newspaper. If I had a nickel for every time he says he recognizes a face, we'd be lounging on the Riviera."

Kate laughed. "Emmaline did tell me she used to belong to the local studio club."

"Ah." Andrew nodded. "Maybe that's it. Sometimes they publish the award winners' pictures in the paper."

Kate had gotten up early on Wednesday morning and made chicken-salad sandwiches from the recipe she had used ever since Andrew was a child. She packed the sandwiches along with apples and slices of pumpkin pie for the family's trip home, then she prepared a hearty breakfast for them. She wanted Andrew and his family to have full stomachs before heading back to Philadelphia.

While Andrew loaded the van and Rachel supervised the children's final tooth-brushing effort, Kate filled a large ziplock bag with homemade cookies.

Paul, observing her efforts, said, "You know, they aren't traveling to Africa."

"Very funny. I just wanted them to have enough to take in their school lunches tomorrow and Friday."

"I think you've succeeded," Paul said dryly. He laughed when Kate huffed at him, and he came over to wrap his arms around her from behind, rocking her gently from side to side. "I'm so proud of our son, Katie. He's a wonderful father."

"He is," she agreed, leaning back against Paul and resting her hands atop his at her waist. "Ethan and Hannah are delightful. And Rachel is like another daughter to me. We're very lucky."

Just then, Andrew came into the kitchen. He stopped dead when he saw his parents, then laughed and said, "You two. You were always hugging and cuddling when we were kids. Used to embarrass me to death. And you're still doing it!"

"Yes, and you should be too when you're our age," Kate said. She passed him the bag of cookies. "For the journey and lunches. Give them to Rachel. I don't quite trust you with a whole bag of cookies."

"Smart mom." Andrew held out his arms. "What a great visit. Thank you so much for making time for us. I know you two are busy."

"Never too busy for you," Kate said softly. To her chagrin, she felt motherly tears rising. "Oh, I wish we lived closer."

"I know," Andrew said ruefully. "But at least we're almost on the same coast now."

The family departed for the Chattanooga Airport after many hugs, promises of more visits, and tears from Hannah. As the van pulled away, Kate and Paul stood in the driveway, forlornly waving after them, and she felt his hand come down on her shoulder.

"God has blessed us," he said. "Let's go in and pray for their safe journey."

Chapter Seventeen

With Andrew's family leaving so early, Kate hadn't had time for her devotions, and Paul hadn't been able to join Eli for their run. The moment Andrew's van pulled away, Paul and Kate spent a few minutes in prayer for the family, then Paul went to the bedroom to change into running clothes for a solitary training session.

It felt odd to Kate that she had begun her day without her morning prayer and Bible study. She brewed herself a mug of coffee and then gathered her things and sank into the rocking chair. As she opened her Bible, Paul came back into the living room.

"Bye, Katie," he called. "I'll be back in a bit."

"Bye," she said. She chuckled, knowing it would be more than "a bit" before Paul completed his training run.

Despite the recent dampening effect that Emmaline's pettiness had on Kate's spirit, she was feeling refreshed and happy over the wonderful visit from her son and his family. Compared to her relationship with Emmaline—having to unravel clues and deal with Emmaline's erratic moods—the family's visit had seemed blessedly normal and relaxing. It seemed especially meaningful, then, that her Bible reading that afternoon was Psalm 150, the "praise psalm."

As she read and meditated, she gave praise and thanks for the visit. Reliving it in her mind, she recalled the many moments of sheer spiritual joy created by the presence of her beloved family members.

Andrew's words about Emmaline came to Kate. "I associate her with someone I saw in the news."

Perhaps the answer was right there before her eyes.

What was the Philadelphia paper called? She had glanced through the paper not too long ago . . . Oh, the *Inquirer*. The *Philadelphia Inquirer*.

She could search the online edition, using Francie Morlen's last name. Maybe that would yield results where the search of Emmaline's name had not.

Glancing down at the Bible lying in her lap, she smiled. Once again, God had shown her a direction to go in search of the solution to a problem. She would head for the library as soon as she was finished with her Bible study.

KATE DIDN'T KNOW WHEN she realized that it was taking Paul an exceedingly long time to complete his run.

She had finished her morning devotions, showered, and made the bed. Then she returned to the kitchen to start breakfast, which she often made while Paul was showering. Paul, however, wasn't back from his run yet. A glance at the clock told her he had been gone too long.

Alarm coursed through her. She hurried to the front door

and walked out to the road to see if she could see him coming from either direction.

No Paul.

Grabbing her handbag and a sweater, Kate rushed out to the garage and started the Honda. She backed out into the road facing toward town and then hesitated. Which way might Paul have chosen to run today?

A glance in her rearview mirror arrested her speculation. Far, far down the road, she detected movement. In an instant, the movement resolved itself into the figure of a man. He looked as if he were drunk, lurching along unsteadily.

Her heartbeat picked up as she reversed direction and zipped off away from town along Smoky Mountain Road. In moments, she was closing in on the figure, whom she had determined to be her husband.

Paul was limping badly, his face set in pain, as she screeched to a halt right in the middle of the road and leaped out.

"What happened?" she cried as she rushed to his side and wrapped an arm around his waist.

"I twisted my ankle," he reported grimly as he draped his arm across her shoulders and let her take some of his weight. "Stepped on a loose piece of asphalt along the edge of the road."

"How long ago?"

Paul shrugged. "I don't know. I think I'd been running for about half an hour."

"Heavens!" Distress colored Kate's tone. "And you had to walk all this way. Oh, Paul, you're never going running without the cell phone again."

"Next time I plan to run alone on an isolated road, I'll take it," he promised.

She got him into the passenger seat, then executed a three-point turn and headed back to the house. As soon as she had him safely lowered onto the couch, she raised his foot into her lap and untied the shoelaces. Slipping the running sneaker and sock from his ankle, she grimaced as they both leaned in to look at the ankle. It was already swollen and slightly purple.

"This doesn't look so good," Kate said. "I'd better call the doctor."

"It's just strained a little," Paul objected.

"Since when did you obtain your medical degree?"

After a tense silence, Paul said, "Oh, fine. Call the doctor. But would you at least get me an ice pack first?"

Kate did as he asked. But while she was placing the ice pack in a cover, a horrible thought struck her.

"Paul?" she called from the kitchen. "Was there anyone around when you hurt your ankle? Did anyone drive by?"

There was silence from the living room. Then Paul said, "Not that I recall. Why?" in a tone that meant he thought she might be losing her marbles.

Kate tried to chuckle, but the sound caught in her throat and she began to cry. As she returned and handed the ice pack to Paul, she said, "For a moment there, I had the ridiculous and slightly paranoid thought that Emmaline might have managed to cause your accident somehow."

Paul smiled a little. "You're really worried about her, aren't you?" He shook his head. "No, this was just plain ol' bad luck in action."

Relieved and embarrassed, Kate called their physician, who told her to bring him right in to the ER, since he'd probably need an X-ray anyway.

Twenty minutes later, the Hanlons were in an exam cubicle at the hospital in Pine Ridge. The doctor on call commended them for getting ice on the ankle as soon as possible. He gave Paul ibuprofen to help limit the swelling, then sent him off for X-rays.

Kate waited impatiently while Paul was taken to radiology. While she was sitting in the waiting room outside that department, she heard a little voice with a clipped Yankee inflection say, "Kate? What are you doing here?"

She turned her head to see Abby Pippins perching on the edge of the seat next to her. "Hello, Abby. Paul twisted his ankle, and he's getting X-rays."

"I see." But Abby's sharp eyes looked over every inch of Kate as if *she* were the one who needed treatment.

"I see you've got your goodies with you." Kate gestured to a small basket Abby carried. In it were two jars of some sort, adorned with pretty quilted covers. Abby made her own ceramics, and Kate suspected there were ceramic jars beneath the fabric.

Abby nodded. "Just a couple of visitations. You know how that is."

Kate chuckled. "Indeed I do."

Abby stood. "I'd best be moving along. If you need me, you call me. I'll be there."

As Abby headed for the next wing, a familiar figure in a white coat strode past. A second later, he backpedaled.

"Kate? Everything okay?" It was Dr. McLaughlin. He had

not been in the ER when Kate brought Paul in. Despite their recent frustrating interactions, Kate was glad to see him.

"Not exactly. Paul twisted his ankle. He's in getting X-rays now."

"Sorry to hear that."

"Me too," she said glumly. "He's been training to run in the American Heart Association 10K. This is going to put a crimp in his plans."

"Maybe not," the physician said. He came and sat down beside her, stretching out his long legs. "It just depends on what type of damage he did."

There was a silence between them for a moment.

Then Kate said, "I'm sorry if I put you on the spot before, trying to worm privileged information out of you."

Dr. McLaughlin grinned. "You wouldn't be the first." Then he sobered. "But seriously, Kate, please be careful."

She nodded, wondering what she should say to him. "I've seen some . . . behaviors that have concerned me," she said, careful not to use any identifying names. "I believe I understand what you're saying."

He gave her a long, intense look. "Good." After another moment, he sighed, got to his feet, and patted her shoulder. "I hope Paul is all right."

"Thanks." She smiled at him. "For everything."

He chuckled. "You mean for nothing."

"Right." She felt glad that her rapport with Dr. McLaughlin had returned to its typical cordial tone. More and more, Kate was confident that Emmaline's distaste for the doctor was unfounded, seeing how Emmaline had responded similarly to so many others. *Lucky me*, thought Kate sarcastically. *It would figure that I'd be the exception to that rule.*

AN HOUR LATER, they were back in the car driving home, with Paul's ankle wrapped and instructions to keep icing it and taking ibuprofen to reduce the swelling.

Paul snorted. "Might as well have diagnosed it myself," he grumbled. "A twenty-dollar co-pay and X-rays to tell me it's just sprained."

"At least this way you're sure it's nothing worse," Kate soothed. "A few days, and you should feel much better."

"A few days during which I won't be able to train," Paul said gloomily. "Eli's going to be disappointed."

"Eli will understand," Kate said. Privately, she hoped Paul's training days weren't over. But could he still run in a 10K in less than four weeks with this setback?

"Maybe, but if I can't run this race with him, I'll never be able to prove that an old guy can be just as fit as a young one."

Kate stifled a chuckle as she recalled her son's words about Paul's sense of competition. "You don't have to prove anything," she said. "Since when did this become about proving something? It's a charity event, remember?"

"I know, but I hate feeling like the ball and chain Eli has to drag while he runs."

"Paul! I can't imagine that Eli considers you a ball and chain. Andrew said you're holding your own, running just fine."

Paul snorted. "Andrew has to say nice things about me."

He lapsed into a grumpy silence until she turned into the

drive and parked in the garage. As she came around to help him into the house, he said, "I'm hungry. Can we have lunch?"

"Of course we can," Kate said. Breakfast had been many hours earlier. No wonder Paul seemed touchy.

She got him settled on the couch with an ice pack and then made a sandwich. She set up two tray tables so Paul didn't have to get up, and they sat together in the living room for their lunch.

After cleaning up the dishes, Kate called Millie to cancel Paul's appointments for the day.

The evening passed in much the same manner that the afternoon had. She felt as if all she did was fetch, carry, and feed the patient. She walked over to the church to pick up some paperwork Paul had requested so that he could work on it at home, then returned home and made dinner for the patient.

She handed the paperwork to Paul, and at his request, she sat with him and helped him organize everything. She brought him hot tea. She replaced the ice pack. She fetched his Bible, a yellow legal pad, and a pen from his study. It wasn't his "favorite" pen, so she went back to the study for the one he wanted. She brought him more pain medication.

She decided she was glad she hadn't taken up nursing as a career choice.

Andrew called shortly after that to tell her that his family had arrived home safely, and she told him what had happened. He talked briefly to Paul, whose mood seemed to have improved after eating and taking the pain medication.

Before she knew it, the day had ended. With chagrin, she realized she hadn't had a moment to go to the library and get on the computer to do any more digging into the mystery of who Emmaline Ashford was. It was starting to seem as if Emmaline had dropped into Copper Mill out of thin air, and if Kate hadn't met her sister, she'd probably believe that by now.

THE FOLLOWING MORNING, Paul stayed in bed while Kate got up and enjoyed a solitary half hour of time in the Word. When he came limping out of the bedroom a short while later, she was relieved to see his face arranged in its customary good-humored lines.

"Good morning. How does your ankle feel?" she asked.

"Not too bad," he said, sounding surprised. "I guess icing it faithfully all day yesterday really helped. Thank you." He smiled. "And thank you for putting up with me. I was a serious grouch, wasn't I?"

"You had your moments." She smiled back, crossing the room to hug him. "It was a sacrifice, but you're worth it."

As he followed her to the breakfast table, she pointed at the article Andrew had talked about the day before. "What do you know about insurance fraud?" she asked on a hunch.

Paul glanced at the headline. "I know you can go to jail for a very long time if you get caught. So I wouldn't plan on it to cover our retirement . . ."

Kate nudged him, and he got serious. "It's very, very difficult to pull off from what I understand," he said. "Insurance companies have already seen every trick in the book—dozens of times—and they know just what the signs are that point to someone trying to steal their money. Why?" he asked.

Kate wasn't exactly sure why. She remembered seeing the hospital invoice that indicated Emmaline had paid part of her bill with cash. Was it possible that she was perpetrating some sort of insurance fraud?

"Just grasping at straws, I guess," she said.

PAUL DROVE HIMSELF to the office later. He was lucky he injured his left ankle and was still able to drive. Kate was especially thankful. A Paul without independent transportation would have been a very grumpy Paul indeed.

Shortly after he left, the telephone rang. "Hello?" Kate said, after turning on the handset.

"Hello, hello." It was Emmaline.

Good grief, thought Kate. Of all the people who could be calling . . . "Hi, Emmaline. What can I help you with?" She deliberately used the slightly more formal query, hoping to subtly signal that she no longer viewed Emmaline as a close friend.

"I would like to invite you to come by this afternoon," Emmaline said. Was it Kate's imagination, or did her voice quiver the tiniest bit?

Kate pondered the invitation for a moment. Finally, she decided to accept. She had calmed down about the letter that Emmaline had sent Paul, and she felt she would be able to ask Emmaline why she had done it without getting too angry.

"All right," she said. "Did you have a time in mind?" Formal, she reminded herself. Keep some distance.

"Does two o'clock suit you?" Yes, Emmaline was definitely nervous.

"Two is fine. I'll see you then." Kate turned off the telephone without even a good-bye. She realized her hands were shaking a bit. Hmm. Maybe she wasn't as calm as she had thought.

Chapter Eighteen

At precisely 2:00 PM, Kate rang Emmaline's now-familiar doorbell. She smoothed down the ivory V-necked sweater she had worn over camel-colored wool slacks.

"Hello." Emmaline's low, quiet greeting was subdued; her normal effusive greeting usually included two chirpy hellos. "Please come in, Kate. May I get you a drink? A cup of hot tea?"

"Thank you." Kate took a seat on the sofa and let Emmaline treat her like company. All the way over, she had rehearsed different ways of introducing the nasty note into the conversation. She had yet to settle on one.

Emmaline rushed off to the kitchen for a few moments. Soon she returned with a tea tray. She took a seat in a wing-back chair and then turned her knees and body to face Kate.

Emmaline cleared her throat. "There's no easy way to say this, so I might as well just get it over with."

Kate didn't move a muscle, although inside, she was stunned.

"As I'm sure you're aware, I wrote Paul a letter at the beginning of the week. It was thoughtless and unkind, and I have regretted it every hour of the day since I dropped it in the church's mail slot."

She hesitated, as if waiting for Kate to speak, but Kate didn't move.

"I'm sorry, Kate," she said. "It was a rash, impulsive action. There is no excuse. I am"—her voice caught—"just so ashamed."

Kate inclined her head, much the way she often watched Renee do when she was at her most regal. "I appreciate your apology," she said. And she did. She hadn't expected an apology from Emmaline, and she felt herself softening just a little bit. "However, Paul is the one you wronged," she told the other woman. "He's the one who needs to hear what you have to say."

Emmaline drew a deep breath and let it shudder out. "I will," she promised, "I will." She raised a hand and absently patted her chest several times.

Kate forced herself not to react. Whatever Emmaline's health issues were, she was responsible for them. It wasn't up to Kate to fix Emmaline's problems. She reminded herself that Dr. McLaughlin had very pointedly told her not to worry about Emmaline's health and had warned her to be careful. She was determined to heed his advice.

Kate recalled her theory about panic attacks. She had set that theory aside on Monday when Paul had shown her the letter. Now she remembered wondering whether Emmaline was experiencing stress over her finances, which might lead to panic attacks. What better time to ask her than now?

"Emmaline," she said slowly, "the day I brought you home

from the hospital, I couldn't help but notice your hospital invoice lying on the table. You're facing an awfully large bill. Are you going to be able to pay it?" Perhaps more than one, if those hospital bracelets in the kitchen drawer were really Emmaline's rather than Francie's.

Emmaline dropped her gaze. "I don't have a choice," she murmured. "Do I?"

When she put it that way, Kate supposed she was correct. Still . . .

"If you're in financial difficulty," she said, "there are programs that can help. Money worries are a terrible thing. Financial fears can make a person too stressed to function, in worst-case situations. Anxiety disorders are not uncommon when finances are tight. Paul refers people to financial consultants as well as other types of counselors all the time."

"I'm not having panic attacks, if that's what you're asking," Emmaline said.

"Or heart trouble?"

"No, I am not having heart trouble."

"But you do take allergy medication that lists shortness of breath and chest pain among its side effects."

"It's just allergy medicine," Emmaline said defensively. "I've never noticed any side effects."

Kate sat back. "Those were the first straight answers you've given me when I've asked about your health."

Emmaline rolled her eyes. "I'm sorry, okay. I'm a very private person."

"I do have another question." Kate no longer cared so much about handling Emmaline with kid gloves, but she sensed she would get no further with more health-related questions. "How could you afford brunch at the Bristol if you're worrying about money?"

"Oh, that's easy." Emmaline's instant response carried the ring of truth. "Francie gave me a gift certificate there when I moved in." Then she leaned forward and smiled at Kate. "I'm so glad we're friends again."

SHORTLY BEFORE FIVE, Kate hurried home to start dinner, arriving just as Paul was making his way slowly into the house.

"Hello, Katie," he said. He had one hand behind his back and as he stopped, he drew out a pastel bouquet of mixed blooms with a flourish.

"Oh, Paul, thank you," she said as he handed her the surprise. Pink roses, carnations and beautifully scented pink stargazer lilies all vied for attention. "What's this for?"

He bent and kissed her softly. "For being such a saint," he said. "I know I was a bear yesterday." He looked away. "And I know it's ridiculous to be worrying about making a good showing in this race. Andrew told me he'd be proud of me whether I ran or walked, and that supporting the American Heart Association was the important thing."

Silently, Kate blessed her son.

"So, how is the ankle?" she asked. She was surprised that he didn't seem to be limping as badly as he had in the morning.

Paul shrugged. "Feeling better. It hasn't swollen nearly as much as I feared, either."

"Good," said Kate. "Why don't we ice it again? Tomorrow you can start using heat on it."

Over dinner, Kate shared with Paul the morning's surprise phone call and subsequent visit with Emmaline.

"She seemed sincere," she reported, "but if I were you, I wouldn't hold my breath waiting for her apology."

Paul chuckled. "Warning noted." He reached over and squeezed her hand. "I'm glad you and Emmaline have cleared up the letter incident. Although that doesn't exactly resolve any of the other issues, does it?"

"No, it doesn't. I appreciated Emmaline's apology, but our relationship is going to be different now."

"Oh?"

"I don't trust her. I forgive her, but I am not confident that she's reformed, and I don't intend to spend any more time developing a friendship with her."

PAUL HAD A MEETING with the church's finance committee after dinner. Kate needed to complete preparations for a Sunday-school lesson she had agreed to teach the coming Sunday. After Paul left, she was just settling down at the kitchen table with her materials when the doorbell rang. She crossed the living room and pulled open the door, a welcome ready on her lips.

Emmaline stood there.

"Hello," Kate said in surprise.

"Hello," said Emmaline. "I thought I would apologize to Paul. Have you eaten dinner yet? I brought zucchini muffins."

Kate noticed that Emmaline was holding out a covered container. She accepted it as Emmaline stepped inside.

"We're finished with dinner," Kate told Emmaline. "I'm sorry, but Paul's at a meeting. And I have work to do this evening."

"Oh. Okay," Emmaline said. "You just go ahead and do whatever you need to do. I brought my sketch pad."

Kate was taken aback by the audacity of the woman. "Sorry, Emmaline, that's not going to work," she said.

"Look." Emmaline pointed out the door that Kate had yet to shut. "Here comes the UPS truck. Are you expecting a delivery? Goodness, he's late."

Kate absently started out the door to meet the driver, something she often did to save the man the extra steps. Halfway down the front walk, she heard her telephone ring.

"Don't worry; I'll get it," Emmaline called.

Harried and increasingly annoyed at the way her evening had just been hijacked, Kate took the parcel from the delivery man with thanks and returned to the house. It looked like a delivery of books for Paul.

Through the window, she could see Emmaline setting down the receiver.

"Who was that?" Kate asked as she entered.

"Just a sales call," Emmaline said, waving a hand in dismissal. "I told him no thank you."

Kate nodded. Blowing out a determined breath, she said, "Emmaline, I appreciate the muffins, but this evening isn't a good time for me to have a guest. You'll have to excuse me. Perhaps we can get together another day."

Emmaline's eyebrows drew together; the resulting frown was intense. "But I wanted to spend time with you tonight," she said obstinately. "I'll be quiet. You won't even know I'm here."

"Yes," said Kate, "I will. This is not a good time," she repeated.

Emmaline's shoulders stiffened, and she drew herself up. "Well," she said in a huffy tone, "I'm trying to make amends, to be a good friend, and you're not cooperating *at all*."

She yanked open the front door on the last two words. Unfortunately, the latch must not have caught when Kate came back in from the UPS delivery, because it bounced back in Emmaline's hand and slammed against the wall.

Emmaline gave a small shriek of surprise. She twisted to one side, but the door hit her in the back, knocking her forward. Before Kate could even reach out, Emmaline fell onto her hands and knees on the entryway rug with an audible "Oof!"

She had been carrying a large handbag on one shoulder. The impact tossed it off her shoulder and it upended on the floor, spilling out its contents.

Emmaline began to scramble around, making a production out of picking up all the items from her handbag and putting them back inside. Kate automatically walked over to help. She picked up Emmaline's sketchbook, which had slid quite a distance. The book had flipped open, and a page near the middle was exposed.

Kate was surprised to see her own face looking back at her. Slowly, she reached out and picked up the sketchbook.

"Kate, that's private," Emmaline protested.

"Not when you're using me as your model," Kate said.

The sketch was astonishing in its detail. Kate was standing in the aisle at the Mercantile with Anna Miller on her hip. Both of them were laughing, and both were dressed exactly as they had been that day. The number one was circled in the bottom corner. What was number two, Kate wondered?

She flipped the page. Sure enough, there was number two: herself again, standing in Emmaline's kitchen holding the teakettle in one hand. Yet a third depicted Kate sitting with baby Alaina on her lap. Kate felt the back of her neck prickle, and a shiver ran down her spine. Hastily checking the pages, Kate saw five new sketches of herself in all. Every one was absolutely accurate, just as the first one Emmaline had given to Kate had been, right down to the jewelry Kate was wearing.

When she looked up, the silence was absolute. Emmaline appeared to be holding her breath.

"What," said Kate, "is the meaning of this?" She slapped her free hand on the sketchbook, dimly aware that she was shaking. Her voice sounded loud and shocked, even to her.

Emmaline spread her hands in appeal. "I only—"

"Never mind. I'm sorry to say that at this point, I don't care what the meaning is." Kate stood abruptly. "You never asked my permission, not the first time, and not now. You never even *mentioned* you were doing these. This is intrusive, Emmaline. Do you understand that?" Kate's voice rose further. "In fact, it's not just intrusive, it's creepy."

"Kate, let me apologize—"

"Not right now." She flung a hand toward the door, angrier and more unsettled than she could recall being in a long, long time. "You need to leave. Right now. Do not call me."

But Emmaline planted her feet. She took the sketchbook Kate held out and carefully replaced it in her bag.

Kate held her breath, not at all sure the other woman would leave.

Finally, Emmaline said, "Okay, fine." She cast Kate a hostile look, her eyes narrowed in a way Kate had never seen before. "You know, I heard a rumor about your husband at the diner today," she said.

"A rumor?" Kate was perplexed at the sudden change of topic. "About what?"

"I heard that he's been accused of embezzling from the church. I don't know if it's true, but mud sticks, you know. It might not matter whether he did it or not. The people of Faith Briar may just decide he's not the kind of pastor they want."

"Embezzling!" Kate was outraged. "Paul would never do that."

Emmaline widened her eyes in false surprise, a sly smile curling the corners of her lips. "No?"

A cold ball of fear settled in Kate's stomach as she suddenly realized what was happening. Emmaline was threatening her. She would start a vile rumor like that.

"Why would you do something like this?" Kate whispered. "I've been kind to you."

"You never have time for me," Emmaline said, with the sulky tone Kate had heard before. "I always feel as if I'm competing with a dozen other people for your time." She pivoted to the door. "Let me know when you aren't so busy with your family and friends," she said, slamming the front door behind her.

Chapter Nineteen

K ate groped for the back of a chair, thoroughly shaken by the confrontation. What on earth?

The telephone rang. Automatically, she went to answer it, still hardly believing what had just happened. As she picked up the handset, she realized her hands were shaking. "Hello?"

"Kate?" The voice was Livvy's, and she sounded odd. Cautious or wary. "Are you okay?"

"I'm not sure," Kate said. "Why do you ask?"

"I thought I'd call back one more time, just to be sure everything is okay."

"Call back?" A ball of anxiety knotted Kate's shoulders even more tightly.

"I called a little while ago, and a woman answered the phone. She didn't tell me who she was, even when I asked, but it sounded like Emmaline. She said you were busy and couldn't come to the phone, and then she hung up on me!"

"What?" Kate groped for words for a moment. "She . . . she . . ."

"It *was* Emmaline, wasn't it?"

"Yes," Kate confirmed grimly. "She came over here uninvited again and tried to force me into agreeing to let her stay even though I said I was busy. Then she got upset when I wouldn't let her stay. No, wait, upset isn't even the word for it." She considered for a moment. "Then she dropped her bag, and her sketchbook fell out."

Kate went on to detail the disturbing experience of finding herself documented in exact detail on page after page of Emmaline's sketchbook.

"She was hostile and mean and frightening, if you want the truth, Livvy. And she threatened to lie to people by suggesting that Paul is embezzling from the church."

"*What?*" Livvy drew in a shocked breath that Kate could hear through the telephone. "Why? What's going on, Kate?"

"Liv, I think she might have some kind of serious emotional problems," Kate said slowly. "She seems to resent the time I spend with you, with my family, even with my own husband. It's as if she wants to have my friendship all to herself."

"You can't let her harm Paul's reputation," Livvy said. "What are you going to do?"

"I'm not sure yet," Kate said. "But I'll figure out something, I promise you."

KATE FELT A LITTLE BETTER after talking to Livvy. But every time she blinked, she could see Emmaline's angry face and hear the threats she had uttered.

Briefly, she contemplated going straight to Paul at the church. But she hesitated to interrupt his meeting, even though Emmaline's threat certainly was serious enough. She took deep calming breaths. She would talk to him when he got home later that night.

SHE WAS SITTING in the rocking chair cuddling in an afghan when Paul walked in the door shortly after nine o'clock.

"Hi, honey. Did you get your Sunday-school stuff all organized?"

Kate made an inarticulate sound. She tried again. "Not exactly."

"What happened?" Blue eyes warm with concern, Paul walked over and took a seat on the couch.

Kate told him about the altercation with Emmaline, about the sketches, and about her own angry outburst that had followed. And then she told him about Emmaline's frightening, threatening behavior.

"I feel so"—she felt tears begin to sting her eyes—"so upset about what she could do to you."

"Oh, honey." Paul went to her, took her wrist, and tugged gently. "Come here."

Kate let him pull her out of her chair and snuggled up to him on the couch, taking comfort in the familiar warmth of his embrace and the gentle circles he rubbed on her back.

"We'll call Sheriff Roberts first thing tomorrow morning," he told her. "Just so that he's aware that she's made a threat. And I'll alert the church board."

"I wonder if I should call her sister Francie," Kate said. "She doesn't want Emmaline to move back to Philadelphia. It makes me wonder if she has had similar problems with

Emmaline. And maybe I should call Dr. McLaughlin. I have a feeling this would not surprise him in the least."

Paul pulled her closer. "You don't have to decide that tonight. We can talk about it more tomorrow."

WHEN THE TELEPHONE RANG shortly after breakfast on Friday morning, Kate looked at it as if it might be a snake. What if it was Emmaline?

Slowly, she walked over and picked up the phone.

"Hey, Kate." *Livvy.* "How are you this morning?"

"Nervous. Upset. Exhausted."

"I bet. I barely slept last night."

"Me either." Kate felt grateful for her friend's sympathy.

"So, what are you going to do now?"

Kate thought for a moment. "Remember when I overheard the conversation Emmaline's sister had with her husband about Emmaline doing something awful? I think it's time to find out more about that."

"How?"

"I'll show you. Give me fifteen minutes."

KATE WAS AT THE LIBRARY in under fifteen minutes, a fresh optimism flowing through her. Livvy was waiting for her, and together they went upstairs to the computers and pulled up two chairs.

"What are you looking for first?" Livvy asked.

"The name of Francie's husband," Kate told her.

It wasn't difficult. When she tried "Francie Morlen in Philadelphia," a list of nearly ten items came up. Most of the items were innocuous mentions of Francie's work for a local women's shelter. But in the third link, she was listed with "Jonathan Morlen" as a donor to the charity. The others were for "Jonathan Morlen," an attorney with a large law firm. Maybe he was a partner in the firm, although Francie had said he had his own practice, hadn't she?

The first link on Francie's husband was a newspaper article. Kate's heart sank as she read it. Morlen had been accused of some legal impropriety by a client who wasn't named. The charges had never been proved, but Morlen had been asked to resign from the law firm. It was the same firm she saw listed in the next few links.

Kate thought back to Francie's words to her husband: *You're the one who was hurt most by what she did.* A chill ran down Kate's spine.

"Look," she said to Livvy. "I'd bet my red cashmere scarf that the unnamed client was Emmaline. The circumstances are so similar."

Kate reread the article. "I'm going to make some calls and see if I can learn anything else. It's not likely, given confidentiality laws, as I've already learned. But I have to try. After that, we'll have to assess our position." She paused, then said resolutely, "I refuse to allow anyone to damage my husband's reputation."

Livvy hit the Print button, then handed Kate the piece of paper that zipped out of the printer. "Here. You might want to refer to this article if you get ahold of anyone."

Butterflies fluttered in Kate's stomach. She couldn't shake her concern for Paul or the shock she felt after reading

the article. Emmaline could seriously damage his relationship
with his flock at Faith Briar with just a few words if Kate
didn't get to the bottom of this fast.

She walked with Livvy downstairs to Livvy's office to call
the law firm. The library's telephone service had unlimited
long-distance calling. Surely this qualified as research, Kate
thought, trying to smile.

Consulting the article Livvy had printed out, Kate dialed her
son Andrew's office. Moments after his receptionist answered,
Andrew came on the line.

"Hi, Mom. How's everything down south?" He gave the
words an exaggerated Southern drawl.

Kate was not even able to summon a chuckle. "Andrew," she
said intensely, "do you recognize the name Jonathan Morlen?"

There was a moment of silence. "Are you all right?" Her
son's voice was filled with concern.

"Yes," she said immediately. The last thing she wanted to
do was upset her children, and she really was all right. "I'm
just in a time crunch. Does the name Jonathan Morlen ring
any bells?"

Andrew was silent for a moment. "He's a lawyer somewhere in this area," he said at last. "I recognize the name. But
I couldn't tell you who he works for or what type of law he
practices."

"Okay." Kate worked to keep the disappointment out of
her voice.

"Do you want me to check around?"

"No, that's all right. I have another resource," she told
him. "But while I have you on the phone, I need to ask if you

ever remembered where you saw Emmaline, the lady you met down here. You said she looked familiar," she prompted.

"I didn't," Andrew said regretfully. "Sorry, I'm no help at all today."

Kate chuckled. "It's a good thing I love you anyway."

Andrew laughed. "I love you too, Mom. Good luck with your pursuit of information."

Ending the conversation with her son, Kate immediately dialed the number of the law practice that listed Jonathan Morlen as one of its associates. Francie had said he had his own firm, so this might be outdated. But perhaps they could help her contact him.

When a perky feminine voice answered the phone, Kate asked to speak to Jonathan Morlen. As she had expected, she was informed that he no longer was employed there. Then she asked for the senior partner named in the article she had found.

When a pleasant masculine voice came on the line, Kate said, "Hello. My name is Kate Hanlon, and I have a situation with a woman related to Jonathan Morlen. May I ask you some questions about the circumstances under which he left?"

"I'm sorry, ma'am, but our employee information is confidential—"

"Jonathan's sister-in-law is threatening my husband just like she did Jonathan," Kate said bluntly.

There was a long silence at the other end. Finally, the man sighed. "All right."

A few minutes later, Kate hung up the phone. Livvy, who had stepped out of her office, popped her head back inside. "Well?"

Kate exhaled. "Jonathan Morlen's sister-in-law accused him of improper legal dealings. According to the senior partner I spoke to, there was no substance to the allegations, but the scandal reflected badly on both Morlen and the firm, adversely affecting their business. They were forced to request his resignation. The partner said that Jonathan is a fine attorney, and he has his own small practice now."

"Emmaline," Livvy said softly. "Why did she do it?"

"The senior partner said the woman had lost her husband not too long before that, and that the Morlens had taken her in because she was financially strapped. He said the woman had done some crazy things like insurance fraud. His theory is that the accusations she made against Jonathan were in retaliation because Jonathan asked her to move out after the fraud became public knowledge."

"So she committed insurance fraud and then compounded it by ruining her sister's family's life." Livvy's eyes were huge. "Kate, this woman really could harm Paul's reputation."

Kate nodded. "But get this: Jonathan Morlen is a very decent man. For the sake of his family, he asked that his accuser's name not be revealed. I asked if it was Jonathan's sister-in-law, and the partner did confirm that for me, although he wouldn't name her. He also said he heard it caused a big rift in the family. But, Livvy, here is the strangest thing: When I asked him if Morlen's sister-in-law was Emmaline Ashford, there was a long silence, and then he said no."

"No? So Emmaline wasn't the person who smeared Morlen's name?"

Kate shook her head grimly. "Technically, no. There is no Emmaline Ashford. I think our dear friend Emmaline has been masquerading under an assumed name." Then a thought struck her. "Livvy! When Emmaline showed me the painting she did that hangs in her grandmother's house, the artist's signature showed the initials E.N. She told me that was her maiden name. But what do you want to bet that E.N. are the initials of her real name?"

Livvy nodded. "Um, Kate? Forgive me for playing devil's advocate, but why is her real name important? We know she did it, regardless of what her name is."

"Maybe it's not important," Kate said. "But it might be. I won't know until I confirm it."

Kate's head was reeling. Leaving Livvy to her work, Kate headed home. She wanted to bake. Baking calmed her, helped her to focus, and heaven knew she needed calming and focusing at the moment.

She made four dozen coconut macaroons for the Faith Freezer Program. While she combined the shredded coconut, sweetened condensed milk, salt, vanilla extract, and almond extract, she reviewed the entire bizarre situation surrounding Emmaline Ashford, from the frightened woman who had collapsed into Kate's lap at the Bristol to the vindictive manipulator who ruined her own brother-in-law's career.

And now she was threatening Paul's reputation.

Kate had brought home the article Livvy had printed out, and she read it over and over again, as if the writing might change if she kept reading.

It wasn't until she had pulled the last of the macaroons from the oven that she saw it. At the very bottom of the article was a link to "Related Articles."

She debated for all of five seconds before grabbing her handbag and rushing back to the library. Her wheezing Internet connection at home would drive her mad if she had to wait until it cranked out each little piece of information. Livvy was out to lunch when Kate got there, so she went straight upstairs and got on one of the computers again. Pulling up the article about Jonathan Morlen's misfortune, she clicked the "Related Articles" link at the very bottom of the screen. She was counting on one of those articles being authored by someone who hadn't cared about protecting the privacy of Jonathan Morlen's sister-in-law.

Approximately ten seconds later, Kate sat back and said, "Well, hello there. It's nice to meet the real you."

"EMILY NASH," she said to Livvy when she went downstairs. Livvy was in her office, staring at her computer screen.

Livvy's eyes grew wide, and she put the sandwich down. "That's Emmaline's real name?"

Kate nodded. "Remember I couldn't find any articles written by Emmaline Ashford? Well, there are a whole bunch authored by Emily Nash. And I might not be an expert, but the writing style is similar enough to the way Emmaline speaks that I'm pretty sure she's the author."

"Emily Nash."

"Right. But that's not all. There was also an article in the *Philadelphia Inquirer* about her"—Kate handed it to Livvy—"which explains a lot."

As Livvy read it, her eyes grew wider. "Wow" was all she said.

"It gets even more interesting," Kate said. "With one of the Emily Nash articles, there was a link to a blog by an E. M. Nash. Here. Read this."

Livvy took the papers Kate had printed out. "E. M. Nash dot blogspot dot com," she read. "What's it say about the author? Oh, here you go: 'About Me.'" She perused the page on which the author had shared a few details about herself. "Just a Philly girl who loves the Eagles and her family. Right," she said, snorting.

"And listen to this," Kate said. "This blog is called 'If Only I Could Say I'm Sorry.' Livvy, I got chills when I read it. Emmaline—Emily—talks about how she suffered a huge loss, how alone she was. How she didn't feel her family was supportive enough, and anger and spite led her to make a huge mistake that harmed her family and destroyed her relationship with them. And how she's still making some of the same mistakes." Kate shook her head. "This blog was only written about two weeks ago. Emmaline isn't healed from whatever happened to cause the manipulative behavior and the vindictive acts. In fact, I think she's getting worse. She needs professional treatment. Until she can confront her pain and work through it, she's going to continue to suffer."

"She needs to get help. Any bright ideas on how to accomplish that?"

Kate considered the question. "I do have an idea. The thing is, it hinges on whether or not she is open to honestly facing her problems and getting psychological help. Here's what I'd like to do . . ."

Chapter Twenty

At home, Kate forced herself to eat a bite of lunch. She had to babysit for the Millers at two o'clock, a commitment she had made at church on Sunday when Frank mentioned his mother-in-law's schedule had changed. Before she left to go to the Millers', she laid the article she had found prominently on the kitchen counter where Paul couldn't miss it. Then she grabbed her handbag and dashed out the door.

Kate arrived at Frank and Stephanie Millers' home a few minutes before Frank left for work.

He answered the door when she rang the bell, looking even more harried than he had when Stephanie had been in the hospital, if that was possible. Baby Alaina was on his hip, screaming.

Automatically, Kate reached out and took the baby. "Goodness, gracious," she said, rocking back and forth with the distressed infant. "What's the matter here?" She realized she had assumed the same soothing voice she used to cajole and calm her own children and grandchildren through the years. Some skills never faded.

Alaina quieted almost immediately, laying her little head against Kate's shoulder as she heaved a huge sigh.

"She needs to sleep," Frank said, running one hand through his hair. "But she wants her mother. They all do. I can barely keep the other two out of Stephanie's room. Until her incision is healed, she isn't supposed to be doing any lifting at all. In fact, she probably should be napping all afternoon. I really appreciate you offering to take the children to your house this afternoon."

"It's no problem," Kate said. "May I borrow your portable crib? That way Alaina can nap, and I can spend time with the other two."

"Of course," Frank said. "I'll get the kids and their things together and just follow you back to your house. My mother-in-law can pick them up around five."

Kate handed Alaina back to her father. The baby protested, but she didn't start to scream again. Kate could tell that the tot was so sleepy, she'd be out the minute she got in her car seat.

Hurrying down the hall, Kate peeked into the master bedroom. Stephanie lay in the big bed, looking as if she was about to nap too.

"Hi, Kate," she said, clearly making an effort to appear alert. "Thank you so much for all your help. I don't know what we would have done without you."

"That's what friends are for," Kate said. "And church family. How are you feeling?"

"Sore," Stephanie said with a wry grin. "I sure wish I'd been able to have laparoscopic surgery. But when the appendix burst, they had to get in there quick and clean everything out. As a result, I have a huge, old-fashioned appendix scar."

"I'm glad it wasn't worse," Kate said gently.

"Me too. It's my own fault for ignoring it." Stephanie grinned. "The doctor couldn't believe I could stand that pain. I told him I barely had time to think about it with three little ones at home."

Kate laughed. "Well, you continue to rest. Your mother will bring the kids back home after work, so you have all afternoon to sleep." She genuinely wanted to help Stephanie, but she also had to admit that having the children's departure overlap Emmaline's arrival by a few minutes was crucial to her plan that afternoon.

"Thank you," Stephanie said, relief spreading across her face. She was practically asleep already when Kate stepped out of the room.

KATE DROVE BACK to her house, pulling into the garage before rushing out to the driveway to help Frank with the children.

"I'll leave the entire car seat," he told her as he lifted out a sleeping Alaina, still buckled into her seat. He handed the carrier to Kate and grabbed a Portacrib.

"You may not even need the crib, but I'll set it up anyway," Frank said. "She'll probably just sleep in her car seat for a couple of hours."

Kate hoped so. Not that she didn't adore the happy baby, but the older two kept her hopping. She honestly could understand why Stephanie had put off dealing with her appendix pain so long.

Frank set up the Portacrib, hugged the kids, and then left for work.

Kate was pleased that the two older children, Anna in particular, appeared to be content to be with Kate and barely acknowledged their father's departure. In her opinion, that indicated that they were happy and secure.

She put on a Disney movie that Frank had mentioned they liked. Kate didn't believe in using television as a babysitter, but it didn't bother her too much to use it as a sleep aid. They weren't five minutes into the film when Anna's little head began to loll against Kate's shoulder. As Anna nodded off, Kate simply laid her on the carpeted floor and covered her with an afghan. She was afraid to put the child on a bed, in case she should roll around during her nap.

Adam was happily watching the movie. It was a short one, less than an hour, so she let him finish it. While he was still engaged, she took the opportunity to call Paul and run her plan by him. Since it very well could involve his considerable counseling skills and he was also the one most at risk, she felt it was imperative to warn him.

Then she called Emmaline. If Kate's plan worked, it would be time for a heart-to-heart talk.

Emmaline answered the phone in a cheery voice. When she realized it was Kate, she was wary at first. But when she realized that Kate intended to be pleasant, she couldn't have been more responsive. If Kate hadn't seen her in action the night before, she would have found it hard to believe that this friendly woman could be so spiteful. At her invitation, Emmaline agreed to come for dinner.

When Adam's movie ended, Kate took the little boy into the kitchen, where his baby sister was still sleeping peacefully in her carrier. She moved the carrier into the living room and set it on the floor near the sleeping Anna. It would be easy to hear either of them if they awoke. Then she and Adam went back into the kitchen and made spritz cookies using a cookie press and several different decorative stencils. The press was hard for him to operate, but with Kate's help, they made several dozen cookies in various flower and leaf shapes. Then Kate got out her colored sugars, and the two of them decorated all the cookies.

While the cookies baked, Kate got out Play-Doh that Frank had brought along. She and Adam made Play-Doh animals and all sorts of things until all the trays of cookies had baked and were cooling on the counter.

The entire time, Kate was mentally rehearsing the plan she intended to carry out any minute now.

Chapter Twenty-One

The afternoon passed quickly. Alaina slept peacefully through most of the visit. When Anna awoke from her nap, she joined Adam in the kitchen. Both children stayed amazingly engaged with the Play-Doh for longer than Kate could believe. *Who needs the newest high-tech toys when a small amount of Play-Doh will do just the trick*, she thought.

Paul called as she tidied up, and she took the opportunity to explain her vision of the afternoon to him in more detail.

When she hung up the telephone, she sat down at the kitchen table for a fleeting moment and hastily offered a prayer.

Please use me to help your child, Emmaline . . . or Emily? Help her to come to terms with her behavior and turn to you for healing.

She turned to the task of cleaning little faces and little hands. Stephanie's mother would be arriving soon, and she wanted the children to be clean and neat when she saw them.

At ten minutes of five, Paul's truck pulled into the drive-way. He parked and sat in the driver's seat, waiting for his cue. Kate glanced at her watch. Four fifty-four. Emmaline should be here any minute.

It wasn't even a minute until Emmaline's car appeared, and she parked behind Paul's truck. She looked very nice today, casual in a light pink gingham blouse and a crisp pair of dark blue slacks. Over her arm she carried a pink jacket.

Paul got out of his truck and closed the door as if he had just arrived as well.

Showtime.

KATE WATCHED FROM INSIDE the house as Emmaline looked at Paul. Instantly the woman's face sobered. Paul took a step toward her, his expression filled with disappointment. Then she began to walk toward the house, clearly aware that Paul's gaze was still affixed on her.

She had taken only two steps when she clutched her chest and crumpled to the ground.

"Here we go," Kate said to herself.

Emmaline had crumpled very gracefully so that she appeared to simply be preparing to take a nap.

Kate was already holding Alaina, who had just awakened, and she snatched Anna up with the other arm, calling to Adam to follow her. She hated to alarm the children, but she couldn't leave them unattended.

Kate rushed out the door and hurried down the walk. Paul had hurried to Emmaline's side and was leaning over her. "Call 911!" he called to Kate.

But Kate just kept coming toward Emmaline, children in tow. "Emmaline? What's wrong?"

Behind her, Adam started to cry. "What's wong wif Miss Em?"

he cried out. Kate glanced around at Adam, noting the frightened, confused look on his face, and her heart clenched. While she had hoped to shame Emmaline into confronting and dealing with her behavior, it hadn't occurred to Kate that she would go back to her old routine of pretending to be ill, and she felt badly for upsetting the little boy.

Emmaline had continued to hold a tense hand to her chest but had opened her eyes when Paul shouted his order for Kate to call 911.

Kate saw the exact moment when Emmaline noticed the crying children behind Kate. Her eyes flared wide, and she quickly pushed herself to a sitting position.

"Wait," she gasped, flushing. "Please don't call an ambulance. It would frighten the children."

Kate knelt, not far from Emmaline, holding her gaze steadily as she called Adam to her and began to comfort him.

"I'm going to go ahead and call, Paul," she said, never looking away. To Emmaline, she added, "We couldn't possibly risk having you go into cardiac arrest, Emmaline."

Emmaline flushed even more deeply. "No. I . . . I'm okay," she said and settled into a more comfortable position on the ground. "It was just . . . a little chest pain." To Adam, she held out her hand and said, "It's okay, Adam. Come over here and sit in my lap."

Adam, clearly relieved, stopped crying. "Come see the cookies I made, Miss Em!" he said.

"I would love to, sweetheart." Emmaline climbed to her feet with Adam hanging on to one hand.

Kate also stood, lifting both little girls. She waited until her friend met her gaze. "Emmaline, you were never really sick at all, were you?"

A look of shock came over Emmaline's face. "Why, how dare you—"

"I saw the newspaper article, Emily," Kate said, interrupting her.

Tears filled Emmaline's eyes. She was silent for a long moment, then simply replied, "Oh no."

Just then, Stephanie's mother pulled into the driveway.

"Adam," Kate said, "look! Your grandma's here."

"Grandma!" she heard him shout.

A moment later, Kate helped her secure all the children in their car seats and then the car drove away.

EMMALINE WAS SITTING on the couch, her head down and her shoulders slumping. Kate placed a hand on one of those sad shoulders and gently squeezed.

"I'll get us some drinks," Kate said.

Paul picked up the afghan that had covered Anna and folded it while Kate filled three glasses with ice water. She also arranged some of the fresh-baked spritz cookies on a plate. Thinking ahead, she also pulled out a box of tissues and grabbed the article about Emily Nash that she had left out on the counter.

Paul carried some napkins into the living room behind Kate, and the two of them took seats on the comfortable overstuffed furniture around the coffee table with Emmaline between them.

Paul mouthed to Kate, "Take your time," and Kate nodded,

then held up the article from the *Inquirer* that she had printed at the library. She reviewed it again. There was a photograph of Emmaline coming out of a hospital entrance. She had a startled look on her face, as if she hadn't expected a photographer to be lying in wait for her.

The caption's single sentence encapsulated the contents of the article in one succinct blurb: "Emily Nash of Chestnut Hill is accused of defrauding Liberty National Insurance by falsely claiming illness."

Kate read out loud:

Emily Nash, 56, of Chestnut Hill, was arraigned before Judge William E. Vander on Thursday. Nash allegedly defrauded Liberty National Insurance Company by falsely claiming that she suffered heart attacks. The charges were later dropped when Nash agreed to reimburse Liberty National in full for claims remitted by the company to Albert Einstein Medical Center. Penalties were assessed on the reimbursements, and Nash was dropped from the company's insurance program.

Emmaline—Emily—began to sob.

Kate hated to be cynical, but given what she had learned about the woman's ability to manipulate people, she couldn't help but wonder how much of her distress was real and how much was put on for Paul and Kate's benefit. Kate felt anger rising, and she counseled herself to stay calm, to give Emmaline a chance to explain. She took her cue from Paul, and the Hanlons waited in silence until Emmaline began to wind down, finally sitting in defeated silence with a pile of soggy tissues crumpled in her hand.

"Will you tell us about it?" Kate prompted.

Emmaline nodded without looking at them. "I have never had a heart attack or a heart condition. Or any other serious illness."

"Why would you fake an illness?" Kate asked, not surprised by Emmaline's confession. She suspected she knew the answer, but she wanted Emmaline to admit it herself. "People in this community have assisted and befriended you. They extended hands of kindness while you were crying wolf. I don't understand why. It couldn't have been for profit. As far as I can see, the only ones to profit would have been the hospitals where you were treated."

Emmaline looked ashamed. "I am so sorry," she whispered. She cleared her throat and wiped her eyes. "It wasn't for money." She took a deep breath but remained silent.

Finally, Kate said, "What then, if not money? Help us to understand."

Emmaline still was silent.

"You lost your husband," Kate prompted gently.

Emmaline nodded. "Almost two years ago. He died after a long and ugly fight with prostate cancer. I nursed him at home. We had hospice care and support during the final weeks, but it was . . . an ordeal for him."

And for you, thought Kate sympathetically. "I'm so sorry for your loss," she said.

"Thank you." Emmaline's voice caught, but after a moment, she continued. "After he passed away, I couldn't

afford to keep our home. Everything had to be sold to pay for
his medical care. I went to live with Francie . . . my sister," she
said to Paul, who nodded. "She and her husband were kind
enough to offer me a home. They were sweet and thoughtful,
but it was difficult. I felt as if I was intruding. I was grieving
and so very lonely, and Francie had her own life to lead. She
has three teenagers, and she's very busy with them. One day,
I was alone in a store, and I had a panic attack. I went into a
dressing room to try to calm down, but I honestly thought I
was having a heart attack."

"Why didn't you ask for help?" Kate asked.

Emmaline shrugged. "I didn't want to be a bother or create a scene. And I really didn't care if I died."

"God would have cared," Paul said quietly.

Emmaline gave him a doubtful look. "Faith never has
been a part of my life. I guess I can't imagine why, if there is
a God, he would bother with me." She waved a hand. "But
that's beside the point."

Kate nearly interrupted to tell her that God's care for his
children was exactly the point, but she knew Emmaline had
more to say, and Kate suspected that the other woman wasn't
ready to accept God's presence in her life.

Instead, Kate asked, "So why, if it really was a panic
attack, did you fake a heart attack?"

"I didn't . . . at first. That first time it happened, eventually
someone came to the dressing room and found me. I was
taken to the emergency room and checked over. When they
didn't find anything, I went to my family physician the following week. Eventually, he diagnosed panic attacks. I had two
more, but I got medication, and they stopped."

"Medication other than the allergy medication I found the day Anna tossed things into the toilet?"

Emmaline gave her a startled look. "Yes. I think it was some generic form of Xanax. The allergy medication really is for allergies. In fact, I need to refill that." She heaved a sigh. "Anyway . . . I got a lot of attention when the one episode happened in the store and people thought it was a heart attack. I got a gift certificate from the store, and they sent me flowers. I stayed in touch with people who helped care for me, and some of them became good friends of mine, much like you. Or at least, like you were before I treated you so badly." Her gaze dropped. "It was so nice to have someone paying attention to me," she said wistfully. "So I faked two more heart attacks, even though I wasn't even having panic attacks anymore by then. I knew it was wrong to deceive people like that, but I couldn't seem to make myself stop. The attention was . . . seductive."

"How did you get caught?" Kate asked, also realizing that Emmaline's explanation confirmed that the hospital admission bracelets belonged to her, not her sister.

"My doctor ordered tests to be sure I really wasn't having some kind of heart trouble. He didn't find anything, of course, and he confronted me. He was very nice about it, told me he thought I might be faking, and he asked why.

"I denied it initially, of course, but when he started talking about ordering a psychiatric evaluation, I confessed. My doctor helped me understand that I couldn't continue doing it."

"But . . . ?" Kate prompted when Emmaline fell silent.

"But the insurance company got suspicious. I still don't

know what made them investigate. Perhaps it's routine. I
hadn't even considered that it was fraudulent or that I might
face legal consequences." Her face crumpled. "Investigators
from the police detective division came to my sister's house.
They made me feel like a thief. The only way I avoided being
prosecuted was because my doctor talked to them and
explained about my recent bereavement. I agreed to repay all
the money plus penalties, and that was because the insurance company was also understanding about it after they
heard about Geoffrey's death. Imagine, the insurance company was understanding!"

"You were very lucky," Kate said.

"It didn't turn out that way," Emmaline said. "Apparently,
reporters routinely look at the public police records, and my
name was in there. They started asking questions, and when
they found out what happened, that article was in the newspaper. Francie and her husband already were furious with
me, even when I explained I hadn't intended to cost anyone
money and that I was paying it back. So then when their
friends started calling and asking what on earth was going on,
they were terribly embarrassed. Francie suggested I find
another place to live." Her voice tightened again, and she had
to pause to fight for control.

"I was so angry. I can't even tell you how hurt and alone I
felt. I felt certain Jonathan was the one telling Francie I had
to leave. And one day it all just boiled over, and I accused
Jonathan—my own brother-in-law—of improper legal dealings. Of course it wasn't true, and nothing ever came of it, but
some of his clients heard about it, and eventually the law firm

suggested that he might be better off making a fresh start somewhere else."

She looked up, a devastated expression on her face. "I never meant for Jonathan to lose his job."

"And yet last night, you threatened to circulate lies about Paul that could have resulted in a very similar outcome," Kate said. "Do you understand how hard that is to forgive, Emmaline?"

Chapter Twenty-Two

I know. I'm a horrible person," Emmaline said, rubbing her temples. "Francie gave me two choices after Jonathan was forced to resign from his law firm: move away, or she would talk to a psychiatrist about getting me put into a psychiatric ward. But I'm not crazy!" she flared.

"Grief leads people to do things they would never do under normal circumstances," Paul said. "So you chose to move?"

"Yes. We had the house down here, so she agreed that me moving here for a while would be a good thing. I'd love to return home, but I'm bound by her rules at this point."

"So you begin faking heart trouble again because you wanted the attention," Kate theorized.

"Yes. It . . . I was so lonely," Emmaline said. "And unhappy. But I didn't plan it, I swear."

"You could have come to church or joined a social club to meet people," Kate said. "It probably would have been easier."

"I've never been much of a joiner," Emmaline said. "I'm very shy, and people don't really notice me. I've never been good at making friends."

There was an awkward silence.

Finally, Kate said, "If you didn't plan it, then what happened? That day in the restaurant, you did a similar thing to what you had done in Philadelphia, didn't you?"

"Not exactly," she said hesitantly, "I was sitting alone at my table, and you came along, smiling at everyone, asking how people were doing. And then I heard the two of you talking about art! And before I knew it, I was pretending to have a heart attack again."

"Dr. McLaughlin knew almost right away, didn't he?" Kate said, recalling her initial encounter with the ER doctor the day she first met Emmaline.

"Yes. He was quite angry. I told him I really did feel some kind of chest pain, and he asked me if I'd ever had panic attacks before. When I told him yes, he gave me the name of a psychiatrist, which didn't make me very happy. And then he even came to my house to urge me to get help."

Kate recalled another puzzling issue. "Why do you have a wig? I saw it on your dresser that day I vacuumed for you." Kate decided there was no need to mention the sneakers. Emmaline was obviously capable of engaging in vigorous exercise. "I thought you might have had cancer, Emmaline."

"It was a disguise I wore," Emmaline said sorrowfully, "after I was arrested. I used it not only to fool the media but to keep my former friends from recognizing me. I was afraid of what they might say."

Kate tried to put herself in Emmaline's shoes, but it was

difficult. She couldn't imagine losing Paul. The very thought softened the edges of her hurt and anger.

She took a deep breath and spoke as gently as possible. "Why did you threaten Paul last night?"

Emmaline began to cry again. "I hated myself the moment I did it," she said. "I just wanted you to be my friend."

"People can't be exclusive," Kate said.

"I know." Emmaline hesitated. "I think ... maybe Dr. McLaughlin is right. I need to talk to some kind of counselor." She took a deep breath. "It's hard to admit, but I need help."

Emmaline excused herself to visit the restroom. When she returned, it was clear she had splashed her face with water and worked to calm herself.

"Emmaline," Paul said when she sat down on the couch, "you seem to be carrying a heavy burden all alone. But there's good news. Even when we feel terribly lost and alone, God is there. All we have to do is ask him. He loves you so much and wants to give you the peace, hope, and comfort you're longing for through a personal relationship with him."

"I don't know," Emmaline said. "It's hard to believe that God cares about me after everything I've done."

"Sometimes it's hard to believe," Paul said. "We've all done things that seem unforgivable. But God is eager to forgive."

"I want to be forgiven," Emmaline said, swallowing. "Is there any chance you two can forgive me?"

"Of course we can," Kate said. "You might feel better, too, if you write your sister and brother-in-law a letter asking the same thing of them."

"Maybe." Hope gleamed for a moment in Emmaline's eyes, but in a mere moment, her expression returned to regret.

"Why don't we pray?" Paul suggested.

Emmaline nodded hesitantly. "I think that might be good," she said quietly.

Kate reached over and grasped her husband's and Emmaline's hands. At last, she felt that there was hope for her friend. Hope and healing.

LATER THAT EVENING, Kate and Paul were relaxing in their living room. It had gotten chilly enough for a fire, and the two were sitting on the love seat, drowsily enjoying the flames as they talked.

Paul said, "That was a stroke of genius, today, Katie. How did you think of using the children to call Emmaline's bluff? And what would have happened if she hadn't been shamed by little Adam's distress?"

Kate began to chuckle. "I had a hunch that when she saw you unexpectedly, it would be easy to make her believe that you were disappointed in her. And I suspected she would react in the way she almost always has when she's felt threatened or intimidated—she'd fake an episode." Kate was glad the scene was over but saddened that her suspicions turned out to be true. "And since I knew about her past, it would give me an opportunity to confront her point-blank."

"You've outdone yourself yet again, Katie girl." Paul beamed. "You knew that Emmaline cared more about soothing little Adam than she did about maintaining her deception. And that indicates a good heart. Which," he added, "is a necessary ingredient for change."

"Exactly right. I must remember to tell her that."

KATE FELL ASLEEP THAT NIGHT with a warm sense of accomplishment. She had solved the riddle of Emmaline's odd behavior.

As she drifted off, she decided that the next morning she would tell Livvy what had occurred. After all, her friend had also been fretting over the problem of Emmaline's health. At that, Kate shot a prayer of thanks for Livvy heavenward, then let sleep take over.

IT WAS ANOTHER gorgeous autumn Sunday in the Tennessee mountains.

Kate had loved San Antonio, but the ancient beauty of the forests that blanketed Copper Mill's rolling ridges and rounded peaks was more than compelling.

Paul took Kate's hand as they walked through the fallen leaves to Faith Briar Church, so unlike the massive urban congregation they had served before their move. Kate was glad to see that he was no longer limping. In a few more days, he should be able to begin running again.

"It feels great not to run today," Paul confessed. "I'll be glad when the race is over."

"So you'll go back to your couple-of-times-a-week jogging then?" The thought made Kate smile. She'd noticed Paul's new physique as he toned up during his training regimen, but she wouldn't mind at all getting back her former Paul—in good shape but not bulging with muscle.

"Yes, yes, yes!" He laughed at himself. Then he stopped in midchuckle. "Katie." His steps slowed, and his grip on her hand tightened. "Is that—"

"Emmaline." Kate couldn't believe her eyes. The woman was standing in front of Faith Briar Church. She wore a pretty green dress with a matching jacket, but she was shifting a bit awkwardly from foot to foot.

Emmaline caught sight of the Hanlons just then. A beaming smile lit up her face, though as Kate and Paul drew near, Kate saw nerves in her friend's eyes.

"Good morning," Kate said warmly.

"Good morning." Emmaline searched both their faces. "Would it be all right with you if I attended church this morning?"

Paul grinned, reaching out to gently squeeze Emmaline's elbow. "Of course, but more important, it's all right with God."

"Hello!" Another voice interrupted their exchange.

Kate took the time to whisper, "I'm so glad you're here," before they turned to see who was speaking.

It was another pleasant surprise. The Miller family was coming toward them. The *entire* Miller family. Stephanie's mother carried the baby, and Adam clung to her free hand. Frank had toddler Anna perched on one arm, and Kate was thrilled to see Stephanie holding on to Frank's other arm, moving slowly but steadily with a big smile on her face.

"Good morning," Kate called.

Adam shouted, "Yay!" and broke away from his grandmother, rushing up the sidewalk. To everyone's surprise, he threw his little arms around Emmaline's legs. "Can we go to the store again sometime? Going to the store with you is fun!"

Everyone laughed, and Emmaline knelt down to Adam's level. "I think that would be great fun too. We'll talk about it after church, all right?"

She rose then, and Kate introduced her to Stephanie.

"How are you feeling?" Kate asked the young woman, taking Anna from Frank when the little girl reached for her. "You look wonderful."

"I feel wonderful," Stephanie said. "Just getting out of the house and seeing fresh new faces is terrific. No insult intended," she said hastily to her husband and mother-in-law, both of whom chuckled. "As long as I move slowly and don't lift anything, I'll do just fine. And in another week or two, the doctor thinks I'll be able to resume all my normal activities." She beamed at Kate and Emmaline. "I can't tell you how much I appreciate the child-care assistance." She turned her attention toward Emmaline. "You must be really special to Adam. He doesn't warm up to just anyone."

Emmaline blushed a rosy shade of pink. Kate could see how tickled she was by the comment. "I'm Emma...Emily Nash. Adam is a doll. All your children are. I only spent time with them when Kate was keeping them, but I enjoyed every moment of it." She took a deep breath. "I'd be happy to come by and visit occasionally if you're in need of a break."

Stephanie put a hand to her chest as if overwhelmed. "Thank you so much, Emily. I may just take you up on that."

Paul went on into the church a moment later to prepare for the service, while Kate lingered outside, introducing "Emily" to everyone she saw. It was fortunate, she reflected, that her friend had chosen an alias that was so similar to her real name. It wasn't as difficult as she had anticipated it would be to call her by the less-familiar name.

Kate decided to go ahead and sing with the choir after Frank Miller returned and invited Emily to sit with his family during the service.

During the announcements that took place before the start of the worship experience, Paul shared the most recent information about his upcoming 10K race with the congregation. Explaining that the race would occur in just three more weeks, he talked briefly about the struggle his training had been, about how his twisted ankle had temporarily derailed his progress and how a positive attitude was his greatest strength. He invited the congregation to attend the race and cheer him on.

After the service, Kate joined Paul in greeting the members of the congregation as they left the sanctuary. When the Miller family came through, Anna squealed and lunged for Kate again, and they all laughed.

"I think she'd go home with you," Frank said.

"It would be nice to have them visit again one day soon," Kate told him. And she meant it. She was going to miss seeing the lively children on a regular basis.

Just then, the children saw Emily, who already had passed and was waiting for them in the sunshine just outside the door. Adam made a mad scramble for her, and Frank said, "Whoa! I'll talk to you later, Pastor, Mrs. Hanlon," as he hurried after the child.

Renee Lambert was one of the last to come through the line, her Chihuahua Kisses under her arm. She greeted Paul and then turned to Kate. "Are you aware that there is a rumor going around about you, Kate?" Renee said.

Kate was dumbfounded. "A rumor? About what?"

"A rumor that you're ill," Renee said.

"I feel fine." Kate looked at her in confusion.

"Well. I'm not naming names," Renee said. "But you were caught talking to the oncology specialist."

"Caught talking to . . ." Kate was mystified. "I never saw an oncology specialist."

"At the hospital," Renee said, her heavily made-up eyes narrow and suspicious.

And then the lightbulb came on, bright and shining. Kate began to laugh as she remembered the conversation she'd had with Dr. Sue Velden.

"I did talk to an oncologist!" she said. "But it wasn't about my health. She purchased one of my stained-glass pieces, and she wanted to commission a companion piece."

Memories from the past few weeks began to roll through Kate's head. As she recalled the offers of help she'd mistakenly assumed were for the Millers, she began to laugh harder, tears coming to her eyes.

Then she realized that Renee wore a hurt look on her face.

"Oh, Renee," she said, taking the woman's hand. "I appreciate your concern." She dropped Renee's hand and reached for her, hugging her friend tightly.

After a few more moments of conversation, Renee said good-bye and moved away. Paul laughed as he held out Kate's light jacket. "This little town is never without its drama, is it?"

"No, but I wouldn't change a bit of it."

As she slipped her arms into the sleeves, he tugged her hair from beneath the collar in a sweetly familiar gesture.

"You're right," he said. "It's absolutely perfect."

They saw the Miller family leave, then Emily stuck her head in through the front door. "Kate? Paul?"

"Yes?" Paul escorted Kate to the door, and they moved outside with Emily. "Did you need us for something?"

"I am still struggling with forgiving myself," Emily said. "My behavior was inexcusable, and the embarrassment and upset I caused my sister and her family is a hard memory to overcome."

"It will take time," Paul told her, "but with God's help, the best thing you can do for yourself is forgive, no matter how hard the task. A lack of self-acceptance can be one of the biggest stumbling blocks in a person's faith journey. We can learn to accept ourselves by remembering that God loves and accepts us as we are, and we can forgive ourselves because he's forgiven us in Christ."

"I suppose it could be considered arrogance," Emily said thoughtfully, "to assume I know better than God how I should be treated. If he's willing to forgive me, I need to forgive myself."

"Exactly!" Paul beamed. "I'm glad you joined us for worship today, Emily. Please consider Faith Briar as your church home while you're living in our community."

"Thank you. Thank you for everything." She included them both and then turned to Kate. "I'm going to see Livvy and then Renee. I'm going to ask them to forgive my deception too."

Knowing her friends as she did, Kate was certain Emily's efforts would meet with success, even if Renee put her through an inquisition beforehand.

"I think that's a fine idea," she said.

THE FOLLOWING SATURDAY, Kate was about to enter Betty's Beauty Parlor for an appointment to trim her hair when she heard someone calling her name. She turned.

Coming down the street from the direction of the Mercantile was Emily Nash.

"Hello, Emily," Kate said. "How are you?"

"Terrific." Emily beamed as she drew close. "I've spoken with both Livvy and Renee. They were very gracious." She shook her head in wonder. "People in Copper Mill seem different from the rest of the world, Kate. It's easier to believe in second chances here."

"Are you planning to stay?"

Emily shook her head. "Oh, I forgot to tell you. I wrote a letter to Jonathan and Francie asking for their forgiveness, and we spoke on the phone yesterday. They were very kind," she said.

"Oh, Emily, that's wonderful." Kate was so happy for her friend.

I'm going back to Chestnut Hill in two months. We'll sell Grandmother's home here, and I'm going to find a place of my own," Emily said.

"Your sister loves you," Kate said gently. "She'll be so glad to have you close again."

"Yes." Emily nodded. "More than I realized."

Kate smiled and then glanced at her watch. "I have to go now. I'll be late for my hair appointment if I don't get moving."

"I'll go in with you," Emily said, and Kate instinctively tensed. Emily noticed and said, "No, it's okay. I just have to ask you something."

Kate noticed that Emily's tone seemed happier and more confident than it had since Kate had met her, so she pushed her residual discomfort aside. "Oh?"

As the two women started into the shop, the bell over the door jangled merrily. Kate watched Emily's face, hoping to catch her reaction to the salmon, white, and aqua color scheme and the vintage decor. She wasn't disappointed.

"Oh my," Emily said in a faint voice.

Kate chuckled. "It's a bit dated, I know—"

"A bit!"

"But all three of the stylists do a great job keeping up with modern trends and color techniques."

"That's good to know. Very good." Emily exchanged a glance with Kate, and they both chuckled.

"Good morning, Kate," sang out Betty Anderson, the owner of the shop. "I'm running a little behind. Just have a seat on the bench, and I'll be ready soon." She turned her smile on Emily. "Can I help you, honey?" With an expert eye, Betty assessed Emily's short brown hair which had a significant amount of silver threaded through it. "Oh, you do need help, don't you? I can cover up that gray for you in a jiffy. Just let me finish here and trim Kate."

"Thank you, but I'm not here to have my hair done," Emily said with a smile.

"Oh." Disappointment was clear in Betty's tone. Kate knew it wasn't about the money; Betty just couldn't resist the chance to get her hands on a new head of hair.

Kate settled on the bench inside the door and patted the space beside her. "So, you wanted to ask me something?"

Emily nodded as she sat. "I've been thinking about how to atone for my behavior when we met."

"Oh, Emily, God has already—"

"Just hear me out. I think I would feel better about settling into the community if I felt that I had given something back."

The explanation made sense, and Emily's tone rang with sincerity.

Kate's eyes sparkled as a new thought came to her. "Well, if you're serious, I have one idea . . ."

"Good! Let's hear it." Emily leaned closer as Kate began to speak.

Chapter Twenty-Three

Three weeks later, on a chilly Saturday morning, the American Heart Association 10K Appalachian Ramble was about to begin.

Paul lowered himself to the ground and wrapped the ankle he had twisted. Then he began to stretch.

Kate watched him proudly. Paul had raised several hundred dollars with the help of the congregation.

"Are you nervous for him?" Livvy spoke in her ear. Kate's friend had come along to cheer on Paul and Eli.

"No." Kate shook her head. "He's prepared, I believe, and the ankle is fine, according to the doctor. Wrapping it before he runs and icing it afterward has helped."

The two women watched as all the participants lined up in a large unruly pack at the starting line. Moments later, the starter's pistol cracked, and the runners surged forward. Some, like Paul and Eli, were serious runners, and they quickly outdistanced the bulk of the crowd, who were walking.

Kate and Livvy clapped and cheered until Paul was out of sight.

"Now what?" Livvy asked. "Shall we wait?"

Kate shook her head. "We can walk to the first checkpoint and see them come through if you like. The route is a big loop, so we can cut across without going nearly as far as the 'ramblers.'"

"Makes me think of a car my family had when I was a little girl. A pretty copper-colored Rambler. Daddy bought it new, and we all thought it was the greatest car in the world." Livvy grinned. "Of course, a dozen years later when I was starting to drive, I wasn't nearly so pleased to be seen around town in that old car."

Kate chuckled.

The two women walked to each of the checkpoints along the route, waving and cheering as Paul and Eli came through. Kate was pleased to see that Paul looked fit and comfortable, running strongly. She had supervised the wrapping of his ankle earlier and felt confident that the joint was supported as much as it needed to be. He grinned and blew her a kiss as he saw her at one of the spots.

Kate and Livvy linked arms and then strolled to the area where the finish line was located. They found a place near the tape, and Kate got out her camera. Just then, she heard her name called. She turned and waved at the couple walking toward her.

"Who's that?" Livvy asked.

Kate smiled mysteriously, arching her eyebrows. "I'll introduce you."

Livvy eyed her friend. "Why do I get the feeling that I'm about to be surprised?"

The couple reached them, and Kate hugged the woman. "Hello, Francie, it's good to see you again."

"You too." Francie turned. "Kate, this is my husband Jonathan. This is Em's friend Kate," she said to the tall man at her side.

"And this is my friend Livvy Jenner." As the newcomers shook Livvy's hand, Kate said to Livvy, "This is Emily Nash's sister."

"It's a pleasure to meet you," Livvy told the couple, shaking hands with each of them.

"Emily told us she'll be returning to Philadelphia soon," Kate added. "We're going to miss her when she moves back to your area."

"I can't wait," Francie said. She had tears in her eyes, and Kate reached out and gave her a hug.

"She's doing well," Kate said softly. "She has joined a widows' support group, and she's been attending our church. She also helps out a young mother in the congregation once a week. The three children in the family adore her."

"I'm so thankful," Francie said, her voice trembling. "You can't imagine how worried we were. The past couple of years have been an absolute nightmare."

"And we hope the nightmare has ended," Kate said.

"Kate, heads-up!" Livvy said. "Here come Paul and Eli."

Kate lifted her camera and snapped pictures, pausing to blow a kiss to Paul as he approached the finish line. She got a marvelous shot of him as he crossed it. She couldn't wait to send it to the kids.

Livvy, Francie and Jonathan were clapping.

"Way to go, Paul!" Livvy called.

He flashed them all a grin before he went on to cool down. They watched more runners cross the line.

"Well, that was fun," Livvy said.

"We can't leave yet," Kate told her.

"Huh? Why not?"

"Patience," Kate counseled. "Let's just watch the rest of the folks come in."

Livvy sighed. "All right." She turned to Francie. "So you're visiting Emily? How long are you staying?" A funny look crossed her face. "And where is Emily, anyhow?"

"Hello, there." The Miller family, Frank, Stephanie and the two little girls, joined them. Adam was the only one missing.

Kate beamed as Anna came readily into her arms. "Hello, Frank. Hi, Stephanie. And how are these girls today?" She introduced the Millers to Emily's family.

"How are you doing?" Kate asked Stephanie.

"I'm great," came the reply. "Almost back to normal."

Paul and Eli joined them a moment later, and more introductions were made. They were quite a bunch by now, which suited Kate just fine. Unobtrusively, she kept an eye on the incoming group. The person she sought appeared in the distance, and she began to smile.

She nudged Francie. "There," she murmured.

Francie slipped to the front of the group and peered down the street. "Oh, I see her!" She began to wave her hand wildly in the air. "Em! Em, here we are!"

Livvy and Paul both looked at Kate. "Em?" they said in unison.

Kate began to laugh. "Surprise," she said. "Look."

Everyone turned their attention to the incoming race participants.

Emily was right in the midst of a group coming at a fast walk, pushing a lightweight stroller in which Adam Miller sat.

"Adam! Hey, buddy," his father called. "Great job!"

The two crossed the finish line and then came over to join the assembled company.

"I runned a *lot*, Daddy," Adam said in his childish treble.

Everyone laughed, and Emily nodded. "He really did." She leaned over and held out her hand for a high five, which Adam provided gleefully.

Paul was beaming. "This is a surprise," he said.

"A *big* surprise," Livvy added. "Kate, you're a devious, devious person."

Emily grinned. "Kate would have told you, but I thought you might enjoy the surprise." She hugged her sister and Jonathan, as well as the Millers, to whom she said, "Thank you for letting me borrow your son."

"It was our pleasure," Stephanie said. "He has been so excited! This was all he talked about for a week before the race." She smiled at Francie. "Adam adores your sister."

"The feeling is mutual," Emily said.

Just then, the announcer spoke over the sound system. "Ladies and gentlemen, if I could have your attention, please. All the race participants have come in, and we are delighted to announce that we have raised a grand total of seven thousand, three hundred dollars for the American Heart Association."

Everyone whistled, clapped and cheered.

"That's a huge amount for a community of this size," Livvy noted.

The announcer continued. "Now it is time to announce the top fund-raisers among the racers." The third and second place fund-raisers were called, and then the announcer said, "And in first place, we have . . . Paul Hanlon!"

Their little group shouted and whistled as Paul, grinning and bowing, returned to the finish line to receive a certificate of recognition.

Then Emily came to Kate's side, reaching out for an enthusiastic hug. "If it wasn't for you, who knows where I might be now."

Kate returned the hug. "The only ones responsible for the changes in your life are you and our Creator," she told her friend. "Welcoming him into your life has opened up a whole new world of possibilities for you, Emily."

Emily smiled. "Just the same, thank you. He might be responsible, but there is no denying that you're a formidable instrument of his will."

Kate laughed. And silently, she thanked God for Emily's transformation.

About the Author

A BEST-SELLING AUTHOR with multiple awards to her credit, Anne Marie Rodgers has more than three dozen novels of inspirational and romance fiction in print. She has been honored by Washington Romance Writers with the chapter's highest volunteer award for outstanding chapter service. Anne Marie enjoys needlework, singing with her church choir and Nittany Lions' sporting events at her home in State College, Pennsylvania. She and her family have raised guide dog puppies, and she has worked in animal rescue for many years. After Hurricane Katrina, she volunteered at the Humane Society of Louisiana. Anne Marie currently volunteers at a wildlife rehabilitation center.

A Note from the Editors

THIS ORIGINAL BOOK was created by the Books and Inspirational Media Division of Guideposts, the world's leading inspirational publisher. Founded in 1945 by Dr. Norman Vincent Peale and Ruth Stafford Peale, Guideposts helps people from all walks of life achieve their maximum personal and spiritual potential. Guideposts is committed to communicating positive, faith-filled principles for people everywhere to use in successful daily living.

Our publications include award-winning magazines such as *Guideposts* and *Angels on Earth*, best-selling books, and outreach services that demonstrate what can happen when faith and positive thinking are applied in day-to-day life.

For more information, visit us at Guideposts.com, call (800) 932-2145 or write Guideposts, PO Box 5815, Harlan, Iowa 51593.